Other Books by the author:

Unlocked Secrets

Just before midnight

Payback

Shattered

Desley Polmear

Copyright © 2019 by Desley Polmear.
The cover design – Artwork - Wood block printing by Desley Polmear
Australian hut photo was supplied by **Catherine Picton**

Library of Congress Control Number:		2019901653
ISBN:	Hardcover	978-1-7960-0083-2
	Softcover	978-1-7960-0084-9
	eBook	978-1-7960-0085-6

All rights reserved. No part of this book may be reproduced or transmitted in any form or by any means, electronic or mechanical, including photocopying, recording, or by any information storage and retrieval system, without permission in writing from the copyright owner.

This is a work of fiction. Names, characters, places and incidents either are the product of the author's imagination or are used fictitiously, and any resemblance to any actual persons, living or dead, events, or locales is entirely coincidental.

Any people depicted in stock imagery provided by Getty Images are models, and such images are being used for illustrative purposes only.
Certain stock imagery © Getty Images.

Print information available on the last page.

Rev. date: 03/07/2019

To order additional copies of this book, contact:
Xlibris
1-800-455-039
www.Xlibris.com.au
Orders@Xlibris.com.au
790401

Granny Maud and Pa's home

CHAPTER 1

The Lawson family

It happened on a Friday, 8th August 2008. The Chinese believe that this day was the luckiest day of the century. Good fortune or prosperity: the eighth day of the eighth month of the eighth year of the millennium. The Chinese timed the opening ceremony of the Olympic Games for this day because of its lucky connotations. For the Lawson family, those lucky numbers couldn't be further from the truth.

Ten years later, when thirty year old Gracie Lawson closed her eyes she couldn't get the vision from her mind. The sight of her father, Harold Jack Lawson, shoulders slumped, as he walked out the front door leaving his family to fend for themselves.

Her tears flowed of course, but it was the heartache he caused the family that confused the love she had for him. How complicated and painful life was for her and her twin brother, Jack.

CHAPTER 2

2018

Gracie Lawson held the secateurs in one hand and a glass of water in the other. She sipped the water, the sound of birds in the gum trees music to her ears. She remembered when her Granny Maud planted the wisteria and now it covered the broken down shed. The soaker hose was set to a timer for the beds of roses. She'd planted varieties of winter roses but they bloomed sparingly. She had hired a gardener to prune them and now his son, Nick, did the job for Gracie. He tended the hybrid teas, floribundas, grandifloras and the climbers that were protected from the harsh winter. Nick's father taught him everything about the proper care of all varieties of roses. Gracie had roses in vases everywhere in the house just like her granny used to.

She gazed into the cloudless blue sky thinking about her mother, Megan, who now lived in the UK. She wouldn't see a sky like this in England. After her divorce from her husband, Harold Lawson she met with an old friend. They married and moved to his home country, England.

Her thoughts were interrupted by the sound of her mobile ringing. She raced inside, flicked it open.

'Hello.'

'Hi, it's…Lara.' She'd just come back from a run and her words came in short breaths. 'Would you bring along a list of places of interest you'd want to see when we meet up on Friday night?'

'Sure. Are we still sticking with France and Italy?'

'Yes, just the two countries…I think the majority of us want to stay away from the tourist areas though, but it's not to say we can't do *some* places of interest.'

'Okay. I'll give it some thought and create a list. Is that all?'

'Yes. I've got to rush now. I've just been for a long run and need a shower before I head out the door to a BBQ.' She laughed. 'I'm not what you call in the mood, but I guess once I get dressed I'll enjoy it. So I'll see you Friday night at the hotel.'

'See you then.' Gracie liked Lara she was considerate and kind. Not like the newcomer to the group, Jayde Carlson. She seemed to take over, compassion not a strong point. She'd moved up from Sydney a few months back. Her dress code would get any man gawking.

In her early twenties, after Gracie finished her studies at the conservatorium of music she joined the Sydney symphony orchestra. Then, years later, Granny Maud passed away and left her the little cottage west of Cloverdale, about forty five minutes by car from the coastal town of Port Macquarie, NSW. It was on a level block below the original homestead where her and her brother Jack spent their childhood, the house of secrets. Secrets were a heavy burden and Gracie found out that carrying them was a lonely business.

Gracie always had a yearning for the arts, perhaps following in her mother's footsteps. As a child, she loved listening to her mother play the piano at Granny Maud's house. Her father had kept her mother away from her love of music and his promise of buying a grand piano for her never eventuated. Granny Maud purchased one for her daughter-in-law and had it delivered to *"Rose Cottage"* so Megan could sneak down the hill playing her beloved music while her husband was busy travelling to Sydney and back.

It was a big decision for Gracie to move back to the small country town but something told her it was time, especially since her beloved granny had left her the cottage in her will. She'd landed a job teaching music at the local Catholic school.

In the music room in the cottage the sheet music sat on top of the grand piano where Granny Maud had left it. Gracie didn't want to disturb it. She loved this room as it brought back so many happy memories from her childhood. In the spring, the buds on the rose bushes would greet her. She would see the variety of shades from the music room which often gave her inspiration to compose her next piece.

Her granny's words rang in her ears. "My sweet darling Gracie, if you have flowers in your garden, books on the shelf, music in the background and selected pieces of art on the walls, you have everything you'll ever need."

Granny Maud had six children, four sons and two daughters. Their first born, Harold Jack Lawson, Gracie's father, was born in nineteen fifty five and was sent to Brisbane Boys Grammar middle school as a boarder staying in Harlin House full-time when he was ten years of age. He excelled through the years and when he left, he left with honours.

His father insisted he see the world so sent him off by ship to the UK to attend Birkbeck University in London. From a young age studying at boy's grammar he knew he wanted to study law. His father paid for a studio in Grosvenor house near Victoria Station, close enough to the Department of criminology, Malet Street building.

Gracie Lawson closed the curtains permanently on the western side of the cottage. The less she saw of "Grasstree" her father's house, the better.

CHAPTER 3

The girls

2018

Jayde Carlson looked towards the bar, her eyes locking with the tall elegant dark haired gentleman. He took her breath away as he stood leisurely talking to an older man. He gave her a wide smile before gesturing to the barmaid. Jayde grabbed the money purse, sauntered across the room and ordered another round waiting patiently while the barman mixed the drinks. She felt the guy's eyes boring into her and turned to face him. He raised his glass, a wink. Her heart fluttered, her face reddening. She smiled back, a small smile. He had olive skin, blue eyes bright under dark bushy eyebrows.

'Thanks' she said to the barman. She lifted the tray carried it to the table where the girls waited, Lara, Abby and Gracie. She leant into Abby, whispering. 'Do you happen to know the guy at the bar in the dark suit talking to the older man?' Abby was born and lived in Cloverdale all her life and knew most people in the small town.

Abby craned her neck towards the bar, jerked her shoulders.

'Never set eyes on him. Don't think he's a local. We come here every Friday night and I've never seen either of them before. He's probably here on business, a blow in. Who knows?' Abby was here to discuss their up and coming overseas trip and paying attention to the opposite sex was the last thing on her mind. She'd never had a good track record with men since her husband passed away from cancer at the age of twenty eight. She seemed to choose the wrong types. They love her to death in the beginning then within a few months try to control her, others taper off. Perhaps things might be different today though, she'd learnt a lot since then about herself but she didn't hold high hopes of finding a nice man in Cloverdale because the desirables moved on to Sydney or Brisbane to attend university and stayed. She made a clear decision to focus on her family, no more dating.

Jayde leant into Abby. 'Something about him…' Her whole body shuddered. 'Oh! He sends shivers down my spine.' She let out a giggle, like a teenager. Jayde needed love as much as she needed food. She wanted a partner for life, a soulmate. Someone to share her bed with, someone whose thoughts were consumed with sex and Jayde Carlson.

Abby glared at her. 'Oh, for goodness sake Jayde we didn't come here to go all googly-eyed over a guy in a suit who's probably happily married. Let's get back to this holiday planning.' Jayde turned back to the group and let out a long sigh. She met Abby about two months ago at a friend's BBQ and from then on, she made up the group of four. It's when the idea arose about perhaps travelling overseas together. Most of the arrangements were done at the hotel every Friday evening over dinner and a few drinks.

Gracie, open-faced, looked towards the bar meeting his eyes. He smiled then went back to converse with the older gentleman. Her stomach fluttered. God, he *was* a handsome devil.

'What month are you all thinking of going?' asked Abby. 'I have to put in for my holidays soon, otherwise my boss, cranky pants Emeline, will put a stop to them if I don't apply two months beforehand. They're the rules she kept hammering into all of us nurses.'

'I'd like to go after their holiday season. That would be around September. The weather would still be nice in Europe then' said Gracie. 'I will need to work in with our school term holidays though.'

'It suits me.' Having organised her friend to look after her fashion boutique at the drop of a hat, the elated Lara could relax now. She could barely wait to head off on her dreamed overseas holiday. She used to stare at her passport, the first one she'd ever had. The one she's yet to use. Brad, her husband, wasn't the little bit interested in travelling overseas. Give him a trip out west camping in a tent and he'd be happy.

'Okay then' said Abby. 'Get the dates Gracie and we'll work around them. Flick an email to me tomorrow.' Abby put her hand up to stop the chatter. 'Does everyone agree with the itinerary? If so, how about checking online Lara and once Gracie gets back with the dates, we'll go ahead and book.' She took a sip of her wine and leant back in the chair. 'How exciting is this trip going to be?' she let out a long sigh as if her part of the organising was over. 'As soon as we're all happy with the itinerary and the dates it's all go. So once it's booked, we'll all need to get the money into Lara's account straight away.'

'Sure. I'll get onto everything once I get Gracie's email. This is going to be one holiday I won't forget. I've dreamt of going to Paris and Rome since I was a child.' Lara flicked her long auburn hair back and grinned. 'A trip of a lifetime…now the fun begins sorting out the clothes to take and keeping things calm in the household. Brad is *not* happy.' She raised her glass, her laugh filling the room.

'Which brings me to the next point, I think we need to talk about the luggage' said Jayde. 'If we can all travel with cabin luggage it will be much easier. We don't want to be lugging around those massive suit cases when we're rushing to get onto public transport. We want to all enjoy this holiday so the easiest way to get around is to take as little as possible.' Her eyes were focused on Princess Gracie. A nick-name she secretly created for the model face.

Shit! What did Jayde just say about luggage? She heard, but she still said, 'What?'

'You heard.' She glared at Gracie, her perfectly groomed long blonde hair falling down her back. Her long fingers adorned with gold, precious stones and diamonds that went with money, her nails painted red like her stylish jacket.

'How will I ever do that with all the makeup and clothes, not to mention my shoes' said Gracie, voice raised. Panic took over, her chest heaving. Her fingers fiddled with the knee of her skirt under the table.

'Calm down Gracie' said Lara. 'It's only a discussion. Anyway, let's get the booking done then we can sort all that out later.'

'I remember Mum and Dad saying the first time they travelled overseas the worst thing was carting their luggage' said Jayde. 'They took far too much. Now they just take a cabin bag each. They travel with as little as possible. Mum said you only need two pair of shoes, a couple of pairs of pants and a few different tops. Most places we'll be staying at will have facilities to wash our clothes.' She stared at Gracie, straight face. 'Cut down on the makeup because that all weighs a ton.' Jayde had seen her type before. They got what they went after every time.

Gracie was 172 centimetres tall, long blonde hair, model-perfect face with huge green eyes, long dark lashes and full voluptuous natural pink lips. She wondered why Jayde always picked on her. *Try not* to *take it on board it's her problem, not yours.* Easier said than done, she thought. She stood, arms folded and walked across to the window looking out onto the busy street. She'd already bought new clothes and shoes for this trip. Staring at car headlights, she was determined she'd not shove all her belongings into a cabin bag. She linked her hands in front of her tummy, curling her fingers then uncurling them. Who does Jayde Carlson think she is anyway, bossing everyone around? She's a bloody control freak, that's what she is.

Silence filled the air back at the table.

'Gracie for God's sake, come back over here? This is a discussion between all of us. It's something to think about, that's all. Let's forget about it for now.' Lara always took the role of peacemaker. 'C'mon Gracie, come sit down?'

Gracie took a deep breath, then another, her nostrils flaring. She approached the table, sat, lifted her wine glass and drank the contents in one gulp. She almost started to cry but her face became contorted and her eyes remained dry. 'I've invested my hard-earned money and time for this trip as I'm sure you all have. We've been organising this vacation for some time and ideally it would be great if the arrangements can be made without all this stress.' Every word she spoke was fully enunciated. She was called on often to speak on stage at school, and many a time was chosen to be the main character in plays because of her clear diction, so did her brother Jack.

'What!' Jayde yelled.

'I wish...' Gracie broke off at a sharp look from Jayde. 'I wish we could discuss this without all the stress.' Her lips trembled, hands balled into fists under the table.

'I don't feel any stress, do you, girls?' said Jayde tapping her wine glass with her fingernails, thin lip smile.

'Look, stop all this' said Lara. 'We're all adults so let's stop acting like children.'

'She's the one carrying on. I'll get us all another round. Who's got kitty.' Abby handed over the money purse. Jayde headed towards the bar. When she looked his way, he gave a huge smile, she gave one back. 'The same all round Samantha.' Her face burned, like she'd been in the sun all day. She hated the waiting knowing he could be staring. 'There ya go luv' said Samantha. She walked back to the girls the tray shaking. She wondered if he was married. Someone that handsome wouldn't be living alone she reckoned.

Gracie forced herself to stop twisting her fingers together under the table. A habit when she was nervous or upset. She has never been one to speak up, never coped well with confrontation. Although, when she was on stage she became someone else. At school she stayed away from arguments, preferring to take herself off to the library. She crept away to the study with her book or diary when the arguments started with her father and her twin brother, Jack. Her body shuddered. She didn't want to think about those terrible days all those years ago back at "Grasstree."

In the past ten years, she had lived with searing hurt, grief, resentment and guilt. Pain she couldn't avoid but it hadn't killed her. The psychiatrist told her, "Tough times don't last, but tough people do." She'd had help over the years but sometimes she didn't think it had helped her at all. The doctor told her to leave the past behind. How could she? The numbers 08.08.08 would fill her mind forever.

After finishing off the next round of drinks, a bit of gossip, laughter and making further plans about their trip it was time to head on home. 'Before we go' Gracie said, almost in a whisper. 'What about discussing the luggage situation? It's important to me.'

'We'll talk about it next Friday night. Give it some serious thought over the week' said Jayde, eyes plastered on Gracie. She noticed that Gracie had hardly joined in after her short outburst earlier. People like her need to get a backbone. She reckoned she wouldn't be the type to pick up a guy in a bar for a bit of fun.

'Ok girls' said Lara. 'All give some thought about the luggage. We'll meet up here next Friday night. If I have anything to discuss with you I'll text or flick an email. Otherwise I'll bring what I have to the table next Friday night.' She smiled at Gracie before putting her folder into her briefcase alongside the paperwork from her fashion boutique that she hoped to get to over the weekend. She hired a casual to work Saturdays as she wanted to be around to take the children to their sports. She certainly couldn't rely on Brad. Even when he was home from working in the mines, he took no interest. Too tired, he'd said.

Jayde stood, looked back towards the bar but the handsome man was chatting to the barmaid. She hoped she'd see him next Friday night. They all headed for the exit. Jayde stopped, turned to Gracie. 'Start giving some serious thoughts about what clothes you will have to leave behind?' She smirked before following the others out into the street.

Gracie gripped the strap of her handbag like she wanted to strangle Jayde's neck. She waited for them to leave then proceeded to the rest room. Once there, she made a pillow with her arms and rested her head on the porcelain basin, her heart racing. She took a look in the mirror. Her fiery eyes shocked her. She grabbed her makeup case, touched up her nose, eyes and covered her full lips with gloss. She closed her eyes aiming to relax the lids. *Breathe slowly through the nose and out through the mouth.* Some people count to ten but Gracie prefers to focus on her breath. It's something her psychiatrist taught her.

After spraying her favourite perfume behind her ears, she headed for the bar. The barmaid caught her eye. 'Be there in a tic luv.' Gracie checked her mobile phone for something to do. She tilted her head slightly, gave the handsome one a smile. He picked up his glass and came towards her, broad smile.

You might take the lead when it comes to taking small luggage Jayde Carlson, but I'll take the lead tonight. Go fuck yourself.

CHAPTER 4

Gracie & Booker

2018

'Well hello' he said, deep voice. He moved in closer. 'Obviously a girl's night out.'

'The four of us are planning an overseas trip and we meet here every Friday night for dinner and a few drinks.' She parted her lips slightly.

'Good luck with that.' He raised his glass, his eyebrows, slight chuckle.

She shrugged. 'It's not easy I must admit.' The barmaid approached. 'Yes Darlin'.'

'A Chardonnay please.'

'Let me get your drink?' he said.

'No thanks, I'm okay.' She didn't want to owe him anything, besides she'd only said two words to the guy. Up close, his profile was something like she'd seen in the movies, perhaps someone like the British actor, Henry Cavill. Clean cut, olive skin, clean shaven, strong jaw line. She noticed his beautifully shaped lips as he turned towards her with those piercing sky-blue eyes.

'My name's Booker.' He held out his hand.

'Gracie' she said. He had a strong handshake, smooth-skin. The barmaid sat her wine on the coaster before tending to a loud-mouthed youth giving orders from the other end of the bar.

'Cheers Gracie.' They clicked glasses before taking a sip. 'How about we find a table' he said. 'It'll be a bit more comfortable. Besides, standing beside a bar is not a place for a lady.'

'Sure' she said. He led her across the room.

'Are you a newcomer to town?' she asked.

'No. I moved to Cloverdale a while back now.' He found a table in the back of the room, quiet.

'Are you a regular on Friday nights?'

He reached into his pocket and pulled out a small packet of Peter Stuyvesant cigarettes. He rested them on the table with his lighter. 'No, my father is in town for a few weeks so I decided to meet him here Fridays. He has known the publican since his school days.'

'What about you are you a local?' On her long pale neck sat a lapis lazuli on a silver chain. It reminded him of his mother. In her day she wore a Citrine pendant around her neck. She reckoned it brought positivity, joy and prosperity.

'Yes, I was born here and went to primary school here, but like most students I left Cloverdale to go to finishing school in Sydney. After that, I studied at the conservatorium of music in Sydney.'

'Wow. That's hard to top. Tell me more?'

'Oh gosh where do I start? In year seven my father drove me to Abbotsleigh independent girl's boarding school in

Sydney. I excelled in the arts and music but only thanks to my teacher, Mrs Ryan. She said to me one day, "What do you ache for?"

'I said music. So I'm forever grateful for Mrs Ryan's help and inspiration. With a lot of study and dedication I graduated senior college then went to the Sydney Conservatorium of Music where I studied piano and composition and at the end of it all, became a doctor of music.'

'Wow, that's impressive.'

She smiles, takes a couple of sips of her drink. 'At the same time, my twin brother, Jack, was sent to board at Brisbane boy's grammar, like our father had done years before. Jack found it difficult to settle away from home. A country town was different to the big City. Most of all, he missed his family.' She blew her nose. 'So, up until recently I played with the Sydney symphony orchestra. Then six months ago I decided to move back.' She took another sip staring at his unblemished olive skin and the most even white teeth she had ever seen.

A flash of her father appeared and how he took a keen interest in her concerts, appearing at most of them in Sydney. She knew how proud he was waiting after to introduce his friends to his daughter. Because he represented his clients in Sydney, he had rented an apartment close to the courts. Once she told him she wanted to stay overnight with him but he fobbed her off saying there wasn't room for two.

'So I applied for a job at the Catholic school and got it.'

'You obviously like it.'

'Oh yes, I do.'

'What about your family, have they lived here most of their lives?'

'Oh yes. My Granny Maud, along with my father, told me all the stories about my ancestors.'

'Do tell.' He leant back, waiting.

'Are you sure?'

'I'm all ears.'

'I'll tell it as I remember it.' She settled back in the chair, drink in hand. 'Okay…' She breathed in. 'My ancestors, Isaac and Marion Lawson started a dairy farm west of Cloverdale. I believe it was the first in the area. They moved there in the late 1800s building a log cabin to house the newlyweds, added rooms when the kids arrived. Later, they built a homestead on top of the hill, which housed nine, two adults and seven children.' She took another sip. 'After settling into the big house they realised the potential in selling timber off the land. So they did. Granny said they tried to grow crops, sometimes successful, but other times the frost hit them and wiped them out overnight. She told me lots of stories from way back then. Even as I grew I still loved listening to them.'

'I enjoy you telling them too. I'd love to hear more. These old timers deserve to be kept alive. What a hard life it was back then. If only they could see life today' said Booker.

'I know, but back then they had nothing to compare with did they?'

'True. Are you going to continue?'

'Perhaps another time, I think I've talked enough for one night.' She leant in, locking her eyes with his. 'I don't know about you, but as I get older, the years seem to fly.' She chuckled, her hair falling about.

'My father always said, the older you get the quicker the years pass by. I'm not so sure about that because they seem to fly by quick for me even at this age.' He raised his eyebrows, took a sip.

She stared into her wine glass. 'The only reason I came back was because Granny Maud passed away, and in her will, she left me her little cottage. It had sat idle for quite a while but the gardener looked after the grounds.'

'It's an interesting life you've had. Is the little cottage in Cloverdale?'

'No, it's about a thirty minute drive out of Cloverdale, west. It's on the family property. As the family grew so did the houses. I think there are about six homes now. Most of the men work on the property. Some of us gather for kid's birthdays, Christmas, that sort of thing. I stick to myself mostly. I like it that way, especially with family.' She raised her eyebrows.

'Do you like being that far out of town?'

'I love it, it's quiet. I play the piano morning and night, no neighbours to worry about. The bush, the birds, animals, they all give me inspiration to write. The cottage is called *Rose Cottage* mainly because of the various beds of roses Granny planted. What about you. What do you do?'

'I'm the Principal at Rockland high school.'

She screwed up her face. 'I didn't have you pegged as a Principal. I thought more like a banker.' She let out a small giggle.

'Is that so? One cannot tell by looks alone can they?'

'True.' She fiddled with the drink coaster. 'How long have you been teaching?'

'Well that will give my age away won't it?' He had a twinkle in his eye.

'Does that really matter?' She leant in ready to listen.

He looked down, played with the moisture on his glass. 'I'll come clean. I finished at teachers college about thirteen years ago but I've only been Principal here for the last two. Before that I did a variety of stints at different schools around NSW.'

'A little bit ahead of me.' She grinned. 'I taught private students in Sydney outside of work and when the job was advertised here I jumped at the chance. Something about your home town, I think it's set in your DNA.' She crossed her legs. 'At this school there is a great emphasis on music and the arts. I absolutely love it.'

'I did hear that. The school's got a good name.'

'You certainly have your days though don't you? Especially dealing with some little brats, and I think at times it's the parents who want the children to be budding musicians. But really, I lived to be a teacher of sorts. Ever since I was a small child it was my dream.' As she looked into his eyes, her cheeks flushed her stomach churned.

He leant in, whispering. 'I was going to be a pilot.'

'Seriously!'

'A child's dream, that's all.'

'Oh, the other thing I dreamt about was being an actress.'

'An actress eh!' he raised his eyebrows.

'I suppose I act everyday with my students.' They both laughed.

'Well, at the end of the day I can sit back with a drink in my hand knowing I've done the best job on the day. No day is the same but that is what I like. I dislike mundane.' He picked up his lighter and played with it in his hand before looking at her. 'Have you travelled much Gracie?'

'A little…but I hope to do a lot more.' She rummaged through her handbag. 'And you' she asked, not looking at him. She didn't know what the hell she was looking for. She pulled out her phone and looked at the screen. 'Sorry' she said, 'I thought I heard the phone ringing.' Why did she do that? She hadn't heard her phone ringing at all. Just another of her nervous habits she guessed. He was gorgeous and if she were standing, her knees would have buckled beneath her by now.

He put his hand on hers. 'You don't have to be sorry. Yes, about the travel, I've travelled far and wide. I went overseas when I was about eighteen the first time. I headed off for three months before I started university. I went on the cheap but met some great people. So I got the bug and every year during the school holidays I head off somewhere different.' He touched her arm. 'Do you mind if I light up' he said, pointing to the cigarette packet.

She felt a tingle go up her spine at his touch. 'No, that's okay. I remember years ago with my Aunt Jess. She used to light up a smoke and drink Marsala and coke. She gave me a taste once but it was too sickly sweet. Yuk!'

'Gee I think that's what my Mum used to drink. Wow that brings back memories from my childhood. Drinking nights, Friday and Saturday…friends dropped in, sometimes strangers. The music blared, lifeless bodies the next morning.'

She stared at her red fingernails. 'That didn't happen at our house. Our family wasn't the kind of family that even gathered for Sunday lunch.' She went quiet for a moment, remembering.

'Excuse me Gracie, but I think I'll have to find a table outside in the smoker's area.'

'Okay. I'll come with you.' They picked up their drinks and found a small table in the corner protected from the crisp night air. She put her arms through her red coat and did up the front buttons.

'I'll be quick. It's a bit cold to be out here for too long.'

'I think you're right. We're the only ones out here. People would call us mad, and all for a cigarette.' They both laughed at the silliness of it. She didn't like the smell but she didn't say.

He liked her smile, her easy going nature. He lit his cigarette and drew in. 'I'll blow it the other way.' He waved the smoke away with his hands not wanting it to land in her face.

'Thanks' she said. The traffic had died down, less noise. 'How long have you been smoking?'

'I think too long.'

'I don't know of anyone in my family who smokes.'

'Well, my mother and father smoked so I guess it was there in front of me all my life.' He shrugged his shoulders.

'Suppose so.'

'All finished.' He popped a mint offering her one. She declined. He stood, taking her hand. He put his arm around her. 'I'll keep you warm.' They went back to the little table inside and began where they left off.

'Have you got sisters or brothers?' Gracie asked.

'One sister and two brothers but we actually have nothing in common, except the same parents and our childhood history.' Conversation flowed easily for the two of them. After another wine, Gracie looked at her phone and realised it was 10.35pm. 'I have an early start in the morning, so I'd better get going.' Nothing interfered with her workout at the gym on Saturdays. He moved in close and brushed past her lips and kissed her on the cheek, whispering. 'Could I take you out for dinner Saturday night?'

He smelled of peppermint over tobacco. She pulled away. 'Like, tomorrow?' she said, confused look.

'Yes, like tomorrow.' He grinned, forgetting that the following day was Saturday. 'No time like the present.'

Gracie thought for a moment before speaking, cocked her head. 'Are you married?'

He laughed out loud. 'No, no. But I do have a son. Sylvia and I were together as teens and when I was twenty one she told me she was pregnant. Neither of us thought of marriage but we were both keen to go ahead and have the child. We lived together for the first five years of his life but it wasn't working, so we split. Now we have James week about. This is my non week. I pick him up Sunday evening.' He held back from saying anymore wondering what she was thinking.

She looked at him. 'That's great. How old is he now?'

'That's one way to find out my age.' He laughed, took a sip of his wine. 'He's twelve. And his name is James Robert Harrington. We both agreed he take my name.'

She ran her finger around the rim of the wine glass before lifting her head, meeting his eyes. 'Thank you for telling me about James. I'd love to go to dinner with you. Have you got any ideas? It's fairly limited here as you know.'

'I'll surprise you.' He took hold of her hands and squeezed

them, smiling. He leant in and they brushed cheeks before he met her lips. She pulled away first then swallowed the last of her wine. She fumbled in her handbag again. She always kept her house and car keys on a yellow ribbon in the inside pocket of her handbag. Her mother did the same. She grabbed them and stood.

He stood to join her, looked down into her eyes. 'How about I pick you up no later than 4.30 pm and I'll take you out of town. I know a great place for dinner. It is a little west of Cloverdale. By the time we arrive, the sun will be ready to set.' He took hold of her hands. 'And wear something warm. July's a cold month.' She let go and scribbled her phone number and address on a piece of paper.

'Grasstree, 88 Gumtree drive' he said, before placing the scrap of paper in his top pocket.

'Once again, my ancestors named the property back in the late 1800s, mainly because of all the timber and tall clumps of grass I believe. My cottage is close to the entrance. The family homestead is on the hill, so don't get them mixed up.' She poked him in the stomach jokingly.

'I'll look forward to seeing you then. Can I walk you to your car?'

'No, I'm good.' She stood on tiptoes, kissed him on the cheek. 'Thanks for the company, it's been lovely.'

'It's my pleasure.' He watched her walk towards the exit. His heart pounded in his chest. It had been a long time since he'd taken an interest in dating. Of course he'd been with other women but that was for his own satisfaction. Women wanted closeness, men wanted sex and until he found the right girl he's not prepared to change his ways.

CHAPTER 5

Jack Arthur Fairchild Lawson

2008

In the school term holidays at "Grasstree" Jack Lawson lived with fear and withdrew from the family, spending many hours in his bedroom. At times his father forced him to come home for the school holidays, but when Jack arrived, there was nothing but arguments and abuse. He would cower in the corner of his bedroom while his father beat him, voice raised to high heaven. 'Do you think because you have the looks and charm it'll get you everywhere and everything? If you follow in my footsteps you're on your way to success. Do you think covering a canvas with paints will bring you wealth? Use your brains that God gave you instead of running a brush over a piece of canvas. Start focusing?'

Jack put his hands over his ears and stared at the knot in the timber of his work desk his father made for him from the Eucalyptus trees on the property.

'You're nothing but a good for nothing' he yelled. 'Who do you think is paying these exorbitant prices at your boarding school? Do you think I sit on my fucking arse all day plucking money out of the air so you can sit day after day dreaming? You are an embarrassment to the good Lawson name.' He pushed Jack hard against the wardrobe door and grabbed hold of his shirt. 'Are you listening to me?'

Jack dropped his head his father quickly lifted it with his fist. 'You're just a bloody good for nothing…why don't you get in the kitchen and help your mother prepare the dinner, like a girl. That's about all you're good for, a mummy's kitchen hand.' Jack felt his face burning up. 'Just looking at you makes me sick. Why can't you get your head down and study like your sister? All your school results say the same. "Jack could do better. Jack's not putting in the effort."

Jack wiped his eyes with his shirt sleeve, head down. His father grabbed him by the shirt front and lifted him fully off the ground shoving his head hard against the wall, back and forth. With force, his father flung him across the room before slamming the door behind him.

***

Listening to the verbal abuse and beatings, Gracie clutched her book and ran to the study locking the door behind her waiting for it all to be over. She sat on the hard wooden floor, her head between her legs. She found it hard to make sense of the treatment her brother received. Not everyone can cope at high school and Jack happened to be one of them. She'd spoken quietly to her mother a few times urging her to let him go to the local high school in Cloverdale.

At Gracie's girl's school, she sat listening to a lecturer speaking about neuroscience. It's where she learnt about the legacy of her father's upbringing and how people like him find others to dump their bad feelings onto. It made some sense into his behaviour, not that she condoned it.

When silence filled the house later in the day, Gracie looked for her mother. She found her in the sitting room, sewing on her lap, eyes closed. As she sat down in the chair opposite, it made a squeaky noise which woke her Mother.

'Can I speak with you Mummy?'

'Of course darling' she said, sitting up straight.

'Look, Jack and Daddy's relationship is toxic. This abuse is making Jack sick. Can't you see?'

Megan Lawson stared at her knitting on her lap. 'Your father wants him to stay at that school. It is where he finished with honours before heading overseas.' She looked at Gracie, wet-eyed. 'He expects his son to do the same. I can't change your father's thinking darling.'

'Mummy, he's not happy. Why would you want your own son to suffer like this? Aren't parents supposed to protect their children?'

'I have tried talking to your father but I don't get anywhere. He has such high expectations for his son. Jack is not smart like him but he doesn't see that. He has paid the fees in advance and has given a healthy donation so he insists that Jack persevere.'

'He told me he's got no friends there. It makes me sad.' She grabbed a tissue from the box, dabbed at her falling tears.

'Dad is so against Jack being involved in the arts. He's such a good artist and you've seen him on stage, he's a born actor. It's not for anyone of us to tell him what career to follow. He's seventeen, for God's sake. I knew what I wanted to do when I was thirteen. I've followed my love of music and it's been a successful career. Dad doesn't seem to mind if I follow *my* creativity. Mummy, Jack needs to follow his love so he can be free. His Soul is tortured.'

'Hush Gracie…let's leave it?' She patted her daughter's hand before heading off to the bedroom. Megan's headaches were becoming more frequent these days and it affected her vision. She needed to lie down.

Gracie often wondered how happy her mother really was. She seemed to be always walking on egg shells avoiding the next explosion. Gracie had heard the fights and beatings he gave her. Many a night growing up she heard her mother's sniffling of a night in the dark. Whatever her father's wishes were, she met them. Picked up after him, cooked his meals. No matter what time he got home from an evening with the boys at the club she'd get up and hover in the kitchen preparing his meal. She'd even witnessed her father throwing a plate of hot food at her mother at dinner one evening when it wasn't up to his expectation.

Gracie had seen too much of her mother's meek behaviour and she'd never allow herself to be a doormat. She'd find a man who was happy in his own skin and to be equal in a relationship.

CHAPTER 6

Jack

Jack could never understand the cycle of his father's violence against him and his mother. It was never his sister, Gracie, he never touched her. Nor should he! If he touched her, there would be hell to play. He struggled living each day with shame and failure and couldn't even look to his mother for help. Gracie listened but he wondered if she truly understood. Suicide thoughts were more common of late. His only relief was his dope.

In Jack's teen years, he had difficulty coping with insomnia, anxiety. At school, to opt out from it all, he began to drink alcohol, next marijuana with his mate, Brian Day. By the time he turned seventeen he was obsessed with drugs. His grip on life was taking a downward spiral. He struggled with his school work at the Brisbane boarding school. He found most subjects difficult and he had warnings of expulsion more than once. Being bullied at school left him isolated so he closed off from other students. Sometimes, his unhappiness caused him to go into a rage. Jack hung onto two secrets. He held down a casual job modelling, and at around the same time, he realised he was gay.

On graduation day at Brisbane Boys Grammar, he looked into the audience searching for his parents. His father sat tall, his mother small beside him. Jack got through the drug-filled day his parent's none the wiser.

He left the City of Brisbane behind him wanting to be closer to Gracie. The use of Heroin came once he started university in Sydney. He met another damaged person, a girl, Sophie. She became his loyal friend and regular user. The house he rented with his father's money became a drop-in place. He began writing poetry and concentrating on his art. He sold pieces as quick as he produced them, sold them for pittance. However much he received, it was still money for his next hit. Before long he'd clocked up huge debts with his dealer. He asked his father for a loan to purchase a car but straight away rushed to pay the dealer. He and Sophie left the rented premises and became street junkies living off the money his father sent for the rent. They were high most days. It was his leisure he told himself. He continued his studies off and on and the two users hung out wherever they could find a room, keen to have their next hit.

At the end of his second year of study, Jack planned on spending Christmas with the family at "Grasstree." If he were honest, the only reason he stepped inside the family home was to spend time with his sister Gracie and his abandoned mother. He jumped for joy when he found out that she had joined a group of women who played Bridge one day a week and scrabble another. She enjoyed playing tennis one afternoon a week in Port Macquarie with a mixed group. Sometimes the tennis girls went off to the movies. If she waited for Harold to take her anywhere, she'd be a skeleton.

At the dinner table, Jack's first night home, his father asked about his career intentions. Jack glared at his father with steel eyes and raised his shoulders. To begin with, he didn't want to say but then he thought he may as well just come out with it. 'I'm thinking of dropping out of uni and setting up a studio to concentrate on my art.'

His father stood, his face burning up. 'You're what?' he screamed. His mother fled the room. Gracie grabbed hold of her brother's arm, tugging it. Jack pushed her arm away, leapt from his chair, his body ridged. He lowered his voice staring into his father's eyes. 'I need to earn money and my art will do that.' He pushed out his chin. 'I'll tell you why. You see father, I'm in a lot of debt with my dealer and he's threatened to kill me, and then find my family.' He pulled his sleeve up far enough for his father to see then he turned away, slumped shoulders and hung his head like a small child. He felt the bile rise in his throat and ran to the bathroom. Gracie followed him.

His father was left speechless but like a fool he paid the debt only to find out, that later, his son went straight back into using. To feed his habit, Jack began stealing from friends. He stole anything that was worth selling. He sold his art at the weekly markets to bring in extra money.

Jack met a man, Jason Perry, another art student who became his lover and the two of them moved in together. They became weekend junkies. During the week they were both high-functioning addicts.

His mother knew what dreadful things these drugs did

and how it was destroying her son's life. She suggested to him that he go to detox but he refused. She knew she was losing her boy and she had no way of helping him if he didn't want to help himself.

His father had many sleepless nights terrified a late-night phone call was going to be bad news. In his position the last thing he'd want would be a knock on his front door from the police. He held his head up high in Cloverdale and in his business in Port Macquarie too. The Lawson name was well respected in the area. The vial taste in his mouth reminded him of the days of his own childhood when his father beat him senseless. The only relief Harold had was when he went off to boarding school and over time, with good grades, the beatings declined.

Harold Lawson worked with criminals and agonised over murder cases. Defending clients he knew were guilty. He heard about the shocking treatment his clients had done to other humans. The photographs of mutilated bodies were proof enough. He sat in his study of a night going over the cases, sometimes his head in his hands the whiskey bottle close by.

His mind was in overload working out ways to get his clients off like he'd promised. He touched the secret compartment behind the drawer in his desk which held a good supply of cash thrown into his briefcase by the desperate. A couple of cops were in like Flynn on certain deals, but right now on his current case one of them seemed to get cold feet, right when Harold was counting on him. The groomed prosecutor could produce flimsy evidence that could weaken the case, send his client out the front door, set him free. Without his backing

Harold had little hope of winning. It'd happened before at the last minute sending his client off to prison instead of walking the streets, leaving the client's family to threaten Mr big shot lawyer causing him to look over his shoulder in fear for his life.

CHAPTER 7

Megan Lawson

2008

As a mother, Megan Lawson wanted to help her son, Jack. He attended university in Sydney but his behaviour was getting worse. After discussing at length with him about getting help, he broke down and cried. 'I do Mum, I do want help.' She got off the phone and called Gracie. If Jack were to be assessed he'd need backing and Gracie would help her twin brother wherever she could. 'This is between us. Don't mention a thing to your father' she said to her. 'Can you imagine what he'd say and do?'

Between Megan's doctor, Doctor Hand, in Port Macquarie and Jack's doctor in Sydney, Doctor Lambert, they came up with a plan. Doctor Hand comforted Megan. He told her that anyone can become mentally ill. 'Rich people, poor people. Any type of person can have this problem. Now you've heard often about his suicidal thoughts.' He looked at the screen on the computer. 'He was diagnosed with bipolar when he was in year eight and over those years you've clearly seen a lot of his mood swings. The medication won't help a darn if he continues taking drugs.' The doctor had repeated the same story over and over again to many patients.

Megan felt lighter after visiting doctor Hand and she now had a plan. If all went well with Jack's assessment, he would be admitted to Liverpool mental health unit in Sydney, close to Gracie.

With the news of being accepted as an inpatient at Liverpool hospital, Jack knew he would have the right help there especially with controlling his addiction. And he'd be well cared for. He needed to feel safe somewhere, anywhere. He also knew he'd have support and help in there at any time he needed it. The first time he entered the mental hospital, he stayed for twenty one days. He was put on the drug, Epilim. When he went back home to Jason, he ended the relationship quick smart.

CHAPTER 8

Gracie Rose Lawson

2018

Gracie was on cloud nine when she walked from the carport to the front of her tiny cottage. She swung around then stood staring at the stars. What a magical night she whispered to her surroundings. She pulled her overcoat tight around her then sat on the deck in the cool night air drinking from her water bottle, thinking. If she hadn't taken the initiative she would never have met him. She could still feel Booker's lips on hers and a tingle went down her spine. She smiled to the man in the moon.

She opened the drawer of her Grannies dresser in the music room and took out her colourful journal and silver biro. Most nights over the last ten years she had written down her feelings and what she'd achieved throughout the day. It had been suggested by her psychiatrist and now it was a habit, like brushing her teeth.

"*Today I met the most gorgeous man. His name is Booker Harrington and he has invited me on a date.*"

She held her journal to her chest and closed her eyes. 'I feel so happy, the happiest I've been for a long time' she called out to her Granny, as if she was sitting in the green velvet chair.

She swallowed her medication, stripped, throwing her clothes onto the single arm chair. Despite the chilly evening she omitted to throw on her winter nightwear, instead, she flopped on the bed, closed her eyes and smiled. Her heart was happy. It took a while tossing and turning and when she woke to the alarm she wanted to roll over and sleep some more. Not today, she had a workout at seven, a Saturday ritual. Her mind went straight to Booker. What had she done? She hardly knew the guy and she accepted a date. What if he'd just come out of prison. Maybe he *was* married and his wife was away and he could be out on the lookout. Geez, what the hell had she done?

CHAPTER 9

Gracie

2018

Gracie reached the ocean ready to catch the sunrise. The sky was the colour of her Lapis Lazuli pendent her granny had given her. "Wear this and you will have the ability to bring about insight and spiritual transformation" she'd told her as she put it around her neck on her 18th birthday. She'd worn it ever since on a silver chain.

She stood, waiting for the touch of red-orange to appear and there it was like magic. Could anyone not be in awe of a beautiful sunrise? Blink and you'd miss it though. The colour branched from violet, red-orange to orange then deep yellow and faded to the colour of the lemons in her bowl on the kitchen table. She looked at the people running along the sand. Did they stop to watch the sunrise? She doubted it. She loved it. It was one of her favourite things. When the sun completely rose, she sat for a while taking it all in then unlocked her car and travelled to the gym a few blocks away satisfied with her wonderful start to the day.

After her workout, Gracie ran through suburbs where

leafless trees grew in front yards. She revelled in the crisp morning air. In front of her she met the ocean, the blue sky. The rough ocean, just the way she liked it. She wondered if that's how she felt at times. Rough and blue, how interesting! She ran down the embankment reaching the white sands. People were walking the beach, some running, like her. She loved the early mornings, the sunrise, the gym, and a long run after. At least one day over the weekend she drove the long distance to the beach. She knew how good it was for her Soul. She had a Gym membership in Cloverdale and went at least three mornings a week before beginning her day.

She drove home, sat on the front steps. She tried to avoid the rickety step as it was rotting away and soon she'd have to get a handyman to fix it. Looking around, she noticed the paint on the window frames flaking too. So many jobs she's not interested in doing. She glanced around the rose garden and thought about doing some weeding, perhaps later. Nick, her gardener had gone on a month's holiday. Her Granny would turn over in her grave if she could see the state of her garden now. She'd named the cottage, *"Rose Cottage"* because it looked a picture all year round, filled with beds of roses, with such an array of colours for all to see. Camelia's when in flower put a smile on Gracie's face too. People had often stopped at the gate and taken photographs. As children, she and Jack would go as far as the gate and chat to admirers.

Mopping her brow, Gracie sat thinking about the lush green grass this time last year, flourishing crops and plenty of feed for the stock. The scene this year at "Grasstree" was hard, crusty, ochre-coloured soil. It's been over five stressful months without rain on the Lawson property and surrounds.

Gracie realised others had it worse. "Ride it out, it's all one can do" her Pa used to say.

She began to think of the stories her Granny Maud told her, and there were many. She recalls her saying that the biggest nightmare on the property was the droughts and the lack of water in the dams because water was needed for the crops to flourish, to keep the animals alive. At times, her Grannies father became tired of the fight, heart broken, body sore. One day, she said he didn't know how to go on so he knelt down in the dried-up dam and prayed to God for rain. Another day it broke him up to see his youngest daughter overcome with grief walking towards him, clutching her lifeless pet lamb. He heard her screams in his head for years, he told Granny Maud. She'd always remembered it too because it was her baby sister, Kelly and her mother consoled her for days.

The sun cracked through the clouds. She closed her eyes listening to the sounds: geese cackling, birds chirping, and Cindy, her Labrador, sleeping by her side. She looked up into the sky and reminisced about her childhood here with her granny.

She mopped her face with her hand towel and went inside to shower leaving the thought of chores behind her. She looked at the time on her mobile phone. She'd better get a move on she had her first music student at 10 am in Cloverdale.

CHAPTER 10

Lara Saunders

2018

Today, it was the 3rd July and Lara Saunders turned thirty three years of age. Did Brad, her husband remember? No. After he left for work that morning, Josh and Primrose, her two children presented her with a gift. Something she loved, a bottle of her favourite perfume by Katy Perry.

'We used our own money that we saved, Mummy' said ten year old Primrose. Lara pulled them both in and gave a group hug. 'Oh my darlings you remembered. Thank you.'

After the children went off to school, she printed the itinerary and in about ten weeks the four girls would be covering a lot of ground in Italy and France. It was something all the girls had discussed, the desire to visit these two countries. She knew that Brad, her husband, wasn't too pleased about her plans but hey, he wasn't interested in travelling overseas at all so why not live her dream. Yes, she was going whether he liked it or not. He spat abuse at her about her recent plans but he could say all he liked, she was going and that was that. He hadn't spoken to her since then but she shrugged her shoulders and began planning her trip. She was shitty that he'd forgotten her birthday but pleased the children had remembered. *Two beautiful Souls.*

Mid July, Brad insisted that Lara attend his mid-year work dinner, something she'd always avoided previously. It was always full of speeches and awards to workers she'd never even heard about. Brad was excited to catch up with his old mate, Alex Simpson. The two were inseparable in high school and now they both worked for the same company in the mining industry. Brad worked more than an hour's flight from Port Macquarie and Alex a two hour flight west of Sydney. He lived in a suburb somewhere on the outskirts of Sydney with his wife and children. Alex joined the company two years ago and this was their first catch up in a number of years. In two night's time they'd be heading off to Surfers Paradise, QLD, for the dinner all expenses paid. The children were happy to be going to their grandparents to stay.

Alex Simpson sat next to Lara Saunders, bodies touching. A shiver ran down her spine the minute his body met hers. Brad sat across from his wife making a big issue about her up and coming overseas trip and how he was forced to take his holidays to take care of the kids. She scowled, raised her glass. *'Happy life darling.'*

With flour coloured skin, he glared, drew in a quiet breath before changing the subject.

Before Lara married Brad, she and Alex had a thing for each other but that was when they were teenagers.

After dark, mingling with others in the garden that led down to the ocean, she brushed past Alex, their hands touching. His aftershave hung in the wake. She walked away and stood under the leafless frangipani tree, glancing up at the stars mesmerised by the millions and marvelled about the wonderful planet. She folded her arms and gave thought to her grandparents who died within two months of each other over a year ago. It gave her peace as she took it all in knowing that their spirits were out there somewhere.

'Can you see the saucepan?' said Alex, as he came closer in the dark.

'I wasn't looking for anything really, just looking in wonder and thinking about my grandparents.'

'It's just what I was doing at dinner. Looking in wonder at you…such beautiful green eyes, the same long auburn hair…I think you are outstandingly beautiful Lara, but I've always told you that.' He stood close, her scent drifting up his nostrils.

She froze. It was like a setting in a movie. Here she was standing in the dark near the leafless frangipani tree next to a tall handsome man who a long time ago had sex with her nearly every weekend. He was within touching range. She turned to him and smiled. 'I'm not used to such complements of late, but thank you.' He had always said nice things about her looks, her clothes when they were younger. She gazed back at the sky not knowing how to react.

He rubbed her arm and sparks ignited once more.

'Don't' she whispered. 'I am married to your friend and this is not acceptable, so back off Alex?' As she turned to leave, he grabbed her and pulled her in close.

She jerked back. 'Let me go' she said, his hand running up and down her spine.

'Lara, I needed to hold you. It's been too long.'

Her body went limp and within seconds, she let her head rest on his chest. He clung to her tight.

He led her away from a couple passing by. 'Please, may I kiss you' he whispered. 'Just once.'

She squared her shoulders. 'Of course not!' She leant in, letting the smile drop from her face. 'I'm now a married woman and my answer is no. Read my lips Alex?'

He laughed. 'It's too dark to read your lips. Please Lara, I just want one kiss.'

She folded her arms, her skin prickled. 'What the hell are you thinking?'

But without warning his mouth found hers. His kiss was anything but light, it left her limp. 'Alex' she whispered. 'This is wrong.' She wanted more but her mind went to Brad. How could she do this to him?

'I have been wishing to do that all night. You have such sensual moist lips. Nothing's changed with you after all these years. Oh Lara!'

She didn't know what to say. This was a shock, a wonderful shock. She'd never been kissed like that with Brad and over the years Alex had learnt a lot since those awkward teenage years. She pulled away. The moon shone on his face, his eyes sparkling. He found her lips once more, this time, kissing her hard and long. When she pulled away he nestled into her breasts.

'Please Alex, don't go any further. This is all wrong. Brad might fly around the corner at any minute.'

He pulled away like an obedient child. 'I know, you are right but how can I help it. Your skin is so soft and your breasts so full and firm. You are irresistible to me, and always have been.' Her body had always turned him on. 'Since the moment I knew you were coming tonight the days dragged by. I wondered how I would feel seeing you but nothing has changed. You are still gorgeous and I still want you.'

She got caught up in the moment: his words, his wants, touch. Why did she allow this to happen when she had a good husband? Because this was exciting, a no-go zone and she loved living on the edge, always did. Besides, a little petting wouldn't hurt. Right now it was perhaps what she wanted, a little attention. Brad hadn't spoken to her civilly for days, less alone showing her any affection.

'Can I see you alone away from prying eyes? There are people wandering around and I can't relax and it's true, I don't quite know where Brad is.' He didn't wait for her answer pulling her away to a bench seat under the ancient Norfolk pine. He leant in kissing her firm breasts, one at a time, hard, teasing with his tongue. On the seat, her head fell back the moon lightening her auburn hair, falling like a waterfall. Her breathing quickened, her moans indicating her wants. She touched his hardness.

'I want you?' he said. 'I want you now?'

'This is not right. It's not fair on Brad. Besides, I'm not a teenager anymore, and I feel cheap petting on this bench seat.'

'Right now, I'm not thinking of anyone but you. Please Lara, touch me again?'

A week later, Alex was still infatuated with Lara. What began as a conquest, turned into an obsession, he couldn't stop thinking about her and wanted to find time away from his wife. Sometimes of an evening in bed, he had fantasies about making love to Lara in such ridiculous places, like they used to.

CHAPTER 11

Gracie & Jack

2008

Jack checked himself into the mental unit for the third time. He ran into some weird inpatients this time, clearly upsetting him. He stayed another ten days.

Gracie and Jack would often go into Port Macquarie to watch a movie when they came home for the term holidays. Jack told Gracie he needed to get out of the house as he hated being anywhere near his abusive father. 'I need to escape from him.'

'Please don't hate. It's not a good word, maybe dislike is a better word' she said to him.

'I mean it. I hate the site of him. My stomach tightens the closer I get to home. I hate coming back. Most of the time all I think about is running away.' He blinked hard as tears threatened. 'I only come home to see you and Mum.'

'Stop thinking about running away and where the hell would you go? Remember Jack, you need money to survive.

You don't think *he'd* give you any do you?' she raised her eyebrows, straight face.

'I'd find a way. Actually someone else approached me about doing modelling stints with them. Can you imagine if I told him that? Phew, that'd really send him into a spin.' He laughed, flinging his arms. 'If he knew I'd been modelling for the last twelve months, he'd really give it to me.'

'Really, why don't you look for more work in that field? You're tall, have a great look, and you've got a good physique. Jack, if you're not happy you need to find a way of earning money so you can piss off away from him. Do you know how much it hurts me when I hear him abusing you and beating you? He's got a short fuse and he seems to let off his anger on you. Jack I'm sorry he treats you like that.' She patted his shoulder. 'You need to stand up to him. He's a born bully.'

He looked at Gracie. 'I hate how he treats Mum too and that's what starts some of our arguments. Like the other night when he came home drunk and got stuck into her. She ended up with a split lip and a swollen eye. Have you seen how she cowers in the corner, like me? When I went to step between them, I copped it too. All I've ever wanted is to feel safe in the family home.' He wiped his eyes with the bottom of his shirt. 'You're right, he's a bully…that's just what he is. He told me on Friday night that I'm a good for nothing and a disgrace to the family. Gracie, I'm not clever like you. I can't grasp the subjects like you. Besides, how can I focus? All I think about is the way he treats me. Even mum has changed towards me.' He turned away as the tears trickled down his cheeks once more.

Gracie took hold of his hand. 'Mummy is scared to get involved. You know what happens to her if she speaks out.'

He wiped his cheeks. 'I know, but why the hell does she stay?' His voice cracked.

'We can't answer that. All the years since they've been married, Mummy has never been out there in the world. He has kept her here. When has he taken her out anywhere nice? I'm pleased she's joined a few things in the area. A person can go crazy without an interest.'

'I know. She is like a prisoner in her own home. She does everything for him and what thanks does she get.'

'Getting back to what Dad said to you. In what way are you a disgrace? Because you haven't achieved like him! Stand up to him and tell him what you think. And while you're at it, tell him again you want to study art. You told me that it is your dream, to paint. We are both creative Jack. There's nothing wrong with that. We are not all intellects like him.'

His shoulders shuddered. 'I can't stand up to him, I just can't. Why does a person have to be so nasty? I get knots in my stomach when he starts on me. And when is he ever home? He spends more time in Sydney than at "Grasstree." He never cares about Mum and the isolation she has to deal with.' He grabbed his handkerchief from his trouser pocket and blew his nose. 'He shows no love at all Gracie, just abuse. I've put up with this since I was in primary school.' He stood up and looked out the window towards the hills gazing out to a cloudless blue sky. 'Our father has no shame. The big lawyer, the popular one everyone looks up to. Behind closed doors he lives a different life. He's a Dr Jekyll and Mr Hyde.' He turned to Gracie. 'Why did he insist on me going to boarding school? I hate it...I hate it and I hate the site of him.'

She pulled him in and hugged him tight. 'Why don't we get lunch into us then we'll go and have a good laugh at the movies. That'll at least cheer you up for the afternoon.'

'Great, let's go?'

She drove to Port Macquarie and when she locked the car, she hooked her arm through his and they walked into "Harries" the famous bakery. Within no time they were giggling and teasing each other, searching their phones to see what was on at the movies.

'Hey, how about Mamma Mia' she said.

'Yeah, that'll be a bit of fun. I could do with some comedy, a good laugh.'

'That's it then. It starts in twenty minutes. We both need a laugh.' Drinking her milkshake, Gracie remembered her father's big hands and the day he knocked her brother from one side of the room to the other. Twice Jack was taken to hospital with lacerations to his head and face and a fractured arm. Jack told Gracie he heard the bone crack, but in the emergency section of the hospital his father told another story. How all the family lied to protect the Lawson name.

Many a time Gracie remembers Jack crying, his father grabbing him by the throat and yelling out to him to grow up and be a man. "Get some balls and become a Lawson man."

After the blows kept coming, Megan would lock the bedroom door and disappear for the entire day struggling to muffle her screams. She too suffered the horrendous abuse, headaches, nosebleeds, and swollen face. Megan hated the dance, like a hard blow to the cheek one minute and talking about new plans for the property the next as if nothing had happened and he was his exuberant self. A slow dance, one step forward and two steps back.

Later, Gracie would put her eye up to the keyhole and all she saw was her mother's still body curled into the foetal position. She pulled a kitchen chair and sat it outside the door and held her diary to her chest. *Please Mummy, don't die? I need you.* It was twenty four hours before her mother appeared: lifeless body. Purple bruises the colour of the passionfruit that clung on the vines. These are the times she despised her father. She tensed her muscles, tightened her fists.

Talking to Jack later, his mother suggested he return to the mental health unit for a lengthy visit, he waved his hands in the air. 'I'm not going back there, it's a loony bin.' His mother knew that wasn't true. He got clean in there and went home a better person.

CHAPTER 12

Gracie

2018

Coloured rose petals scattered the ground after the wild winds the night before but still the smell of roses drifted through to her music room. She sat, closed her eyes, hands poised and began to play her favourite piece that she played for her Granny every time she came back home. Granny loved the piano sonata written by Ludwig van Beethoven and asked Gracie to play it often. She could picture her granny's beautiful face, sitting on the regal green velvet chair in the corner, her shoulder length grey hair hanging loose, her hands clasped on her lap, eyes closed.

Out of all the family, Granny filled her mind a lot. In the corner of the lounge room sat her record player. Gracie had kept all of her records, 78's, 45's and albums stacked neatly in the rack. Sometimes she played her favourites from her childhood days but more often than not she sat teary thinking of the times they listened together.

"This, darling Gracie, is where Pa and I live now. This is the old log cabin, still standing." She remembered her saying that. Also Granny's face beamed when telling Gracie all the stories about her ancestors.

Gracie looked around the walls trying to picture what it was like without the extensions and how hard it must have been for the Lawson family to begin way back in 1891. Clearing the land and cutting down the gum and cedar trees to build the cabin would have been hard on them and then later as the children grew they built the homestead high on the hill, "Grasstree." She thought about her life now with all the mod cons, i Pads, phones and all the rest of it, everything that opened and shut. She shook her head in amazement. How did they do it?

When Granny Maud went crazy as the family termed it, she was diagnosed with Dementia and was put into the nursing home in Cloverdale. She knew some of the close relatives for a short while, then, within no time at all that part of her memory had disappeared. Gracie and Jack visited her each time they came home and after, rushed away with tear-filled eyes. Their own mother, Megan, stopped her regular visits telling the family it was a waste of time. All her mother did was look at the four walls, no recognition of her daughter or surroundings. Five years later, one after the other they died, granny first and grandpa followed seven months later after he slid onto the kitchen floor as if his legs had gently given away. He was hospitalised, but never came home. Gracie believed he gave up. His life force had died with his wife of close to sixty years. Granny would say fifty nine years too long married to the man with a short fuse.

For Gracie, the last ten years had been full of grief, pain, and agony after her father left on the 8th August 2008. Block it from your mind, she said to herself. *After all Gracie Lawson, you are an expert at it.*

Gracie arrived home at 1pm after her music students but the time seemed to drag waiting for her date that afternoon. She kept thinking about the way Jayde treated her about the stupid luggage thing. She is such a control freak and deep down, Gracie knew that she would not get to take her large luggage bag but she may get to keep the man at the bar, Jayde's dream. Her gut feeling was telling her not to go with the girls, but it was her long-time dream. She wasn't the type of person to head off on her own she knew that for sure. Jayde had only been on the scene for five minutes and she is ruling everything and everyone. Worst part is the others are silly enough to follow.

She brushed the thoughts of Jayde away thinking only of Booker. How could she be so lucky to be asked out by the mysterious man at the bar, the one Jayde was after, the gorgeous one she went all gooey over. She smiled. *The universe works in mysterious ways Jayde Carlson and I believe I'm being looked after right now.*

CHAPTER 13

Jayde Carlson

2018

Jayde went to the local pub like she did every afternoon after work. The men crowded around her, laughing, drinking. She knew she'd go home with someone tonight: but who? She cottoned on to a newcomer to town, a diesel mechanic. 'Call me Hunter, because that's what I do' he said. She laughed, her boobs jumping up and down. He laughed too. 'I reckon there's more than a mouthful there.'

'You'll have to find out won't you?' He sat his beer bottle in her cleavage, leant in and kissed her on the lips, hard. Pulling away, he found the mouth of the bottle and glugged away, leaving her panting.

She worked in the office of a local car yard. She got the job the minute she hit town. At times to boost the sales, Mr Clifford, the owner, would get her to wear her tight shorts, sexy top, high heels. Out she went to the car lot and began washing the cars. It worked. She got extra in her pay packet for that playful job. There had been a few accidents on the road, perverts craning their necks.

Mr Clifford married his childhood sweetheart years ago and the children had grown into adults and she no longer wanted him in the bedroom. He'd tried to come on to Jayde but she kept teasing him, bending over showing her breasts. He loved her voluptuous body, a man's dream. He'd wait.

CHAPTER 14

Gracie & Jack
2008

Gracie and Jack took time off from University to attend their cousin Carmel's wedding which was being held on Saturday the 2nd August 2008 at a farmhouse over an hour's drive north-west of "Grasstree." Gracie was one of the bride's witnesses. Adrian, Carmel's fiancé, had been given seven days compassionate leave from the army to marry his sweetheart. After that, he would return to Afghanistan.

Jack had straightened out somewhat and had another year to go to finish his arts degree. He'd been sought after for many main roles in amateur theatre in Sydney and surrounds. Gracie sat proudly in the audience to see all his plays but their father made it clear that it was a waste of his valuable time. She'd asked her mother to come down to Sydney to watch Jack, but she said it was best to stay home and keep the peace. Besides, her husband told her his studio apartment in Sydney didn't have room for two.

The day before the wedding, Jack had been cooking, creating a feast. A few family members from Adelaide were coming to stay after the reception. Megan had tried to instil culinary skills in Gracie, but she'd used her creativity in her music spending as little time as possible in the kitchen. Jack had slow-roasted beef and lamb and would carve it the following day. He'd prepared a lemon merengue pie, a bowl of fruit salad and home-made ice cream. On the morning of the wedding he would make up fresh salads from the garden. His mother had a great indoor garden set out on the enclosed verandah facing the sun. She spent many hours tending to the variety of pots. She could pull the plastic blinds up or down to cater for the weather.

To make the house cosy, Jack lit the open-fire ready for his father after a long day flying in from Sydney. He served up lunch for Gracie and his mother.

'Wow! Why don't you open your own restaurant' said Gracie. 'You cook the best food, so creative.'

'You're a jack of all trades son' his mother said. 'You've made the beds for all the guests, prepared all the food. I didn't expect you to do all that but you have and I'm so grateful. You're a good son Jack.' She walked over and hugged him. 'You'll make someone a wonderful wife one day.' They all laughed.

'You're all being too kind. I must admit it is one of my set jobs in the house when visitors stay over in Sydney. I don't mind really, I quite like it. Sometimes some of the boys light the BBQ and help out.' Jack's body stiffened as he heard his father's car drive up the hill. 'Well, I'll leave you two to clean up while I head off to have a shower. I've done my bit.' He skedaddled down the hallway his stomach muscles tight.

CHAPTER 15

Jack

2008

While having an early afternoon tea, Jack's father wanted to talk to him about university, how he was going, his latest results. It wasn't long before arguments arose. Jack's mother called for them to stop but like always, her urging went on deaf ears. One swoop by Harold and she found herself up against the wall. She escaped running to her bedroom, Gracie fleeing downstairs to the study carrying her diary and her latest crime novel she got from the library.

Jack held his hands over his ears while his father tore strips off him. 'Get to your room? The sight of you makes me sick.' Jack fled as if he was being chased by a killer. He sat on his chair controlling his breaths. In out, in out, breathing deep from his diaphragm, struggling at first until his breathing finally settled. He wished he had something to take to calm him down but he was off that shit now. He stared out the window looking at the cows grazing. So contented he thought, I wish I could say the same for myself. His father coming home changed the whole dynamics in the household within thirty minutes. Jack had been so happy cooking today, and tomorrow he'd do the rest, carve the meats, prepare the salads.

He jumped when he heard the door swing open. His father's big frame filled the doorway, red-faced, fists tightening.

'Get up? What sort of future are you ever going to have? Where are your fucking brains? I paid your fees to one of the best schools and now I'm supporting you 100% at university in Sydney. You are wasting your time *and* my money.' He grabbed his son's shirt, pulled both sleeves up and as expected, his arms revealed extensive marks. 'What the hell is this' he said, pulling the sleeve of his right arm up higher. 'So you're right into it again. Your lies keep coming…'

Jack lifted his chin. 'I'm off the drugs now. But what do you care about my future.'

His father's eyes widened his face red as a beetroot. Jack knew he shouldn't have spoken up, provoked him. He'd been down the road of destruction before, but now he was clean, but how could he prove that to his big fat lawyer father.

Harold felt the sweat build on his forehead, his face burning up. He moved closer, just inches from his son's face. 'You'll not get another cent from me. You're on your own.' His son's future flashed before his eyes and it was not good. He took hold of Jack's shirt, lifted him up and hit him hard in the face with his right fist over and over again.

'I'm off the fucking drugs. Did you hear me? Dad, please. Listen to me?'

'Pull the other leg. You're mixing with scum and you've become scum.' With the next hard blow, Jack lost his balance and his head struck the corner of his work desk before hitting the floor like a rag doll.

'As I've always said, you are a good for nothing and these marks I can see prove it 100%.' He left the bedroom slamming the door behind him ignoring the flow of blood oozing from his son's head.

***

Gracie had heard the chaos and rushed towards her brother's room passing her frantic mother on the way. She screamed at her father as he ran down the hallway. 'When are you going to stop treating him this way? You're nothing but a bully.' Gracie's body shook on seeing her father's face. He walked towards her and lashed out hitting her across the cheek for the first time in his life. 'It's none of your fucking business. Stay right out of it?' Spit flung from his mouth, rage filling his beetroot coloured face. He turned towards his wife but Megan ducked.

He stumbled back. Why did he do that to Gracie who wouldn't hurt a fly? He stormed down the hallway, back stairs, and ran into the backyard heading for the stables pulling his cardigan tight around him. He sat on the stool, steam pouring from his mouth thinking about his son's future, his heart racing. 'Bloody lying cow, off the drugs, do you think I came down in the last fuckin shower?'

'Moo' said the cow looking over the fence. 'Moo.'

'I wasn't talking to you.'

Any dreams he had for his son had gone down the drain. And why did he hit his Gracie? He held his head in his bulky hands and without any warning he blubbered like a kid. The roar came from deep within. The outpouring of grief, shame, and hate engulfed him. He'd always promised himself not to follow in his father's footsteps but he had a short fuse and it came out of nowhere, within seconds. He knew if he wasn't provoked he wouldn't lose his cool. They should watch their mouth.

The son of the well-known lawyer involved in heavy drugs. He'll be the talk of Cloverdale and word will reach his office in Port Macquarie before it was on the news. He rubbed his eyes with the ball of his fists and sat staring at his beloved horses in the stable. 'There's always been something wrong with that boy' he said to them.

CHAPTER 16

Jack

2008

Hearing crying from her brother's room, Gracie knocked on his door. 'Jack' she cried out. She rushed in without waiting for him to answer. 'Let me help you sit up?' She rushed to his side and propped him against his desk. 'What has he done to you? Wait, I'll get the first aid kit.' He sat, eyes closed, head spinning, his temples throbbing.

Gracie had a bowl of warm water, a clean cloth, her mother and the first aid kit. Between them, they cleaned and bandaged him up, lay him on the bed. 'I'll bring you a cup of tea and I'll sit with you awhile' said his mother. The swelling had already started. He wasn't a pretty site. 'It's a deep cut. I think you'd better go off to the hospital to have it attended to.'

'I hate him. I hate him' Jack screamed. 'Why can't he love me Mum? He's *never* shown me any love. How the fuck can I live up to his expectations?' Tears welled up in his eyes.

Megan held onto him and pulled him close to her chest.

'I can't answer that Jack. How can anyone understand the likes of your father?' She rocked him back and forth like she did years ago, her head filled with her mother-in-law's words. "He's a chip off the old block, a Dr Jekyll and Mr Hyde"

CHAPTER 17

Gracie & Jack

2008

The following day, the day of the wedding the bruises on Jack's face were all colours, one eye swollen and a bloody bandage covering the deep cut to his head. He heard a light knock on his bedroom door. When he opened it slightly, it was Gracie all concerned. She hugged him. 'Oh Jack' she said, touching the wound to his head. 'Look at you.' He slumped into the chair.

'What's that red mark on your cheek?' he asked.

She thought quickly. 'Going to the toilet in the dark and I went slap into the side of the door. I hadn't even had a drop to drink either.' She laughed and so did he.

'It'll show up nice in the wedding photos.' Jack chuckled. 'Does it hurt?'

'No, it looks worse than it is and I can cover it with thick makeup.'

'I'm not going to Carmel's wedding, not like this.' He pointed to his face, his head. 'My favourite cousin and I'll miss her wedding.' His shoulders rose and fell, and strange noises from deep within.

'Oh Jack, this is terrible.' She held him to her until his crying had calmed. She looked into his eyes. 'Like I said last night, you will need stitches in that wound in your head. C'mon, I'll take you off to the hospital. I know you didn't want to go last night but Jack you need that wound attended to. Mum wants you to go too.'

'It'll be okay. I don't want to go. What will I tell them, more lies?' He stared at his feet. 'And Mum! What would she care?'

Silence filled his bedroom. He pinched his dripping nose. 'Talking to mum is like talking to a brick wall. You know she sides with Dad all the time. Have you noticed the minute he gets into me she vanishes into the garden or her bedroom?' He hung his head. 'I've had enough. I've never fitted in. This is the last time I'm coming home Gracie.' He sat down, looked at her. 'After my last visit, when I went back to Sydney I felt empty. I couldn't pull myself out of it. I was suicidal late one night and I decided to phone Lifeline. The lady on the end of the line told me to make a life for myself and to stay away from any form of abuse. Your life is not safe around him, she told me. Fancy that, coming from a stranger. I was so close to doing away with myself but I decided to phone Lifeline, mainly because I needed to talk to someone. I needed to tell them what my intentions were. Gracie, she actually saved my life.'

'Oh Jack. I'm pleased you reached out but I'm always here too you know that. It's a sad thing that you needed help that bad.'

'I came home this time for Carmel's wedding and to see if there were any changes, but once again I'm leaving disappointed. I'll pull myself together. Once I get back to Sydney I won't ever come back. I've got part-time modelling work. I'll manage, and I'll focus more on my art.'

'Good for you. Live your own life, you need to be happy. Mum is powerless Jack. Don't blame her for her behaviour. Can you imagine what he would do to her if she sided with you? Jack, you need to find someone to talk to, professionally. You were doing well when you went off to the mental unit in Sydney.'

He shrugged. 'I'll manage. Once he looked at my arms he presumed I was still on the drugs. I tried to tell him but his ears were blocked by then.' He rolled up his sleeve. 'Marks don't disappear overnight.'

'He must have gone ape-shit. How can you not blame him I suppose? I used to worry that you'd end up a chalk outline.' He pulled down his sleeves, heavy sigh.

'He wouldn't believe me Gracie when I said I'd given up the drugs. It's been hard for me but I kept trying, mainly to prove it to him. I must admit, the hospital helped me a lot with that too.'

'I'm proud of you Jack, and I'm here if you ever want to talk. For once I agree with you starting a new life, but promise me you'll find someone to talk to. If you do that, you can get things off your chest, it'll be a relief.'

'I can't promise, but I'll think about it.' His head fell to his chest. 'Gracie.' He turned away from her, fidgeting with his lighter, hands shaky. 'I just want a better life, a life with love not abuse. Why *can't* he love and accept me. I'm his only son for God's sake.'

Gracie gripped his hand. 'He's always been fiery and prone to dramatic outbursts, you know that. He flies off the handle the minute he sets eyes on you it seems to me.'

'It's always directed at me. I'm his only son, so why Gracie, why? Wouldn't you think he'd be proud of what I've achieved in the arts?'

She didn't want to mention the hard slap the evening before. She'd hate to think what Jack would do to him if he knew that. 'This treatment from him is not on. In his eyes you'll never be good enough no matter how hard you try.' She moved in and put her arm around his shoulder. His body shook. Time stood still for the twins, little else mattered. She pulled a tissue from the box and wiped away his tears.

She grabbed hold of his shoulders and looked him in the eye. 'Find your own path in life. Make new friends. Leave university if that's what you want. God, you're twenty years old and he still has a hold on you.' She lowered her voice. 'I want you to seriously get help for your problems. It will give you the opportunity to talk about what's going on in your life. Jack, you'll feel better once you talk it over with a counsellor. It'll be a weight off your shoulders.'

Jack pulled her arms away, bent his head and rested his hands on his thighs. 'I'm not at university anymore and he knows I'm gay. He hates me for what I've become.' "What sort of career has a queer got?" he said to me on the last visit. He pointed to his face and head. 'Since he has done this to me he has stayed out of my way. Does he feel any remorse for what he's done? I don't know who I am any more. I've lost my Soul.'

His voice reached a high pitch. He stared at his twin pleading for understanding. After this fresh bout of abuse he knew that this chapter of his life was over. He would leave "Grasstree" behind him. While his father lived he'd never come back.

Gracie wished she could take his pain away. 'I don't know what he thinks. Let me tell you this. Being gay doesn't change who you are inside. It's just being who you are meant to be.'

'Thanks sis. You are the only one who truly loves and accepts me as I am. I still remember the night I told you I was gay. You hugged me and said you loved me more for being honest.' He put his strong arms around her and hugged her tight. 'I think you'd better get ready for the wedding.'

Gracie stood. 'Lock yourself in your room and I'll deal with our father. You know I love you and I'll be there for you. I'll tell them you are driving your own car to the wedding. I think they'll buy that.' She kissed him and rushed to the door. 'Oh God, fresh blood is seeping from your wound. It's running down the side of your head. I haven't got time to clean it up and dress it again. Promise me you'll do it. I'll go get fresh water. The first aid kit's there on your desk. Grab it now?'

She rushed out and came back with the clean water, a fresh cloth. 'I've got to go get ready.'

'Gracie, I love you' he spluttered through fresh tears.

'I know you do. Pull yourself together now. I have to get a move on, see you when I get home. At least I can show you the photos on my phone.' He rubbed his eyes with the back of his hands. He followed Gracie's slim figure to the door, turned the key and leant against it wishing his father the worst.

'A fuckin' street angel and house devil' he yelled into the

room before throwing himself across his bed screaming into the soft doona cover. He eyed the splatters of blood on the legs of the writing desk his father had made him. He remembered the day he and his father carried the desk into his room from the workbench at the back of the garage. He'd spent hours making the desk from the cut down gum trees from the property. It was bolted to the wall under the window. Jack liked the fragrance of the eucalypt all oiled and varnished.

"Now you've got no excuse for not studying" his father had said when he finished bolting it. "Most sons wouldn't get a personalised desk built by their own father, right son!" He'd stood back and examined his work pointing out the drawers and a secret compartment behind. Jack remembers giving his father a hug, staying longer than his father wanted.

It was one of a few fond memories he'd thought of over the years. Something nice his father had done for him. He wondered if he had a kind bone in his body these days, maybe it was hidden behind his friend, the scotch bottle that accompanied him in the study of a night.

Jack lay there in a pool of blood, his eyes heavy. He would smash his father's pride and joy to pieces later.

CHAPTER 18

Gracie

2018

Singing away, Gracie stepped into the shower washing her hair thoroughly. She wasn't quite sure what to wear as she scanned the wardrobe full of outfits. She chose a silk print long-sleeved blouse, black pants and a thick hand-made steel grey shawl made in India to throw over her shoulders for warmth on the winter's night. She stepped into her high heels, grabbed her matching handbag and sat with her book in her lap in the tub chair in the music room, Cindy by her side.

She watched the clock on the wall. Five minutes to go. She checked her painted toes that peeped out of her shoes. Just before 4.30 pm she heard his car pull up in the gravel driveway. She grabbed the corner of the curtain and pulled it back slightly, peeking. As she opened the front door, she stepped to one side and let him in. Cindy jumped up and down pleased to meet the stranger. 'Here Cindy?' she called. Booker wore a multi-coloured tie in place around his neck, a white shirt, dark blue suit, clean shaven. *So Handsome!*

He handed her the array of coloured flowers and she

sniffed them straight away. She remembered as a child picking any flowers from the garden, sniffing at the strong perfume. When the petals of the roses fell onto the lace cloth she collected them all and placed them in her hard-covered book. After weeks they were no longer soft but brittle. Then she remembered folding the scented oil through them in the basket her Granny had given her.

'Thank you Booker, they are lovely.' She giggled like a teenager before rushing to the side cabinet. Peering inside, she found a crystal vase. After filling it with water, she allowed them to fall naturally.

He stood back a bit, watching her movements. 'I know most women love flowers.' When she shouldered her handbag, he took hold of both her hands. 'All set for a lovely evening?' He leant in and kissed her on the cheek.

'Yes, all done and ready to go. Did you have a problem finding the cottage?'

'No not at all. Mind you, I did cheat.' He grinned. 'I used the GPS.' She raised her eyebrows before turning away, busying herself with her handbag again, checking the things that she already knew were in there. She turned to face him jingling the house keys in her hand. 'Now I'm ready to go. You might think I'm a bit strange, but I always like to double check everything. Because I don't need the key to lock the front door on my way out, it's become a habit to over check.' She did have a key hidden high on a beam at one end of the verandah. 'Okay Cindy, you've got to go outside.' She closed the gate on the way out making sure Cindy was safe to roam the backyard.

CHAPTER 19

2018

Twenty minutes into the drive, Booker pointed to the sky. It was an inky colour mixed with streaks of pinks, oranges and yellows. 'I think we'll make it in nice time for the sunset. We're almost there.'

'I love this time of day just before the sun goes down. Granny and I used to watch it from the front verandah. She was a lover of nature and taught me to love it too. She used to pour a Sweet Sherry and sit and sip while the sun sank into the west. It was her time to sit and relax, reflect on the day. Even if it rained, she sat there watching it fall.'

'Nothing better…I do agree with your Granny.' He turned into the narrow dirt road.

Lake Emily and "Zen" restaurant was about twenty five minutes west of Gracie's cottage off the main tarred road. He'd ordered a table facing west and a view of the large lake. 'Almost there. Sweep around this corner and it's about two minutes.'

'I don't think I've ever been on this dirt track before. Of course, I usually go in the other direction, east.'

'I love going for drives with James on weekends, and this

day I thought I'd see what was around the area and low and behold I found this sign leading down a dirt road to this cute little restaurant and B&B.

He parked close to the entrance and led her down the mossy-covered brick path, Mondo grass either side. The flicker of lights in the trees looked magical. They were led to a table with a view of the lake. A slight wind led the waterlilies into a dance and the birdlife swam and dove for food. 'Have a closer look' he said. 'You can see the little turtles near the rocks.'

'Oh wow! So I can. They are cute.'

He moved her out onto the verandah to get a clearer view. They held hands as they watched the sun slide behind the mountains. Reds mixed with bright oranges.

'What a wondrous sight. We just made it in time' she said. 'I'll take a photo.'

Staring at the sky, absorbing the silence, he pulled her in and trailed his fingers down her arm. Her body melted into his. She took a photo of the colourful sky her memory of their first date.

"Listen to the silence, it speaks volumes" she remembered her Granny saying often.

A feeling of melancholy invaded her. Being here brought back memories of when Pa Banner took her to the mountains to do exactly that, watch the sunset. Pa was her mother's father and he lived in Beechwood, a town about seven kilometres west of Cloverdale. He was a gentle man and loved nature like her granny. He used to tell her to be grateful for all those precious things in life. Money wasn't what happiness was all about he'd told her often. It was more about nature that bought you peace and happiness. "Walk amongst the trees and flowers." I guess he was right because she was always drawn to these things.

When they walked back to the table, Booker ordered their wine from the waitress. 'We'll sit with our wine for a while before ordering' he said to her. The two of them chattered away as if they were old friends. He told her how beautiful she looked and she could tell he meant it. He talked about his life, the ups and downs and where he'd lived in England until he was eight years of age. She did the same, feeling at ease. She knew not to reveal everything about her life. *That was private. Family secrets she would take to her grave.*

'Sounds like you had a wonderful loving childhood spending time with your Granny.'

'Oh yes. I loved coming to stay with her when I was a little girl. I'd often come and stay with her when I came back from boarding school too. She was such a kind and wise woman. I learnt a lot from her. If I had words with my mother or father I'd run like a hare down the hill to spend time with her. She would meet me with a bear hug and there I'd stay until someone came to get me.' Her Granny had told her about her son, Harold. "He has a short fuse and I avoid him where possible." Gracie had grown up seeing his abuse especially with Jack and her mother, Megan.

'Your relationship you had and the memories with your Granny will stick with you the rest of your life. And having that close bond from childhood is something others don't get a taste of.'

'I have so many fond memories of those years. As I grew older, I was intoxicated with her presence. She was everything anyone would ever want a human being to be. She was one of a kind.'

'Hello again' the short blonde-haired waitress said. 'I'll leave the menus with you and come by shortly. Would you like more wine?' She wore a pretty multi-coloured top, black skirt and comfortable shoes. 'Are you warm enough here?'

'Yes, it's cosy and there's plenty of warmth from the fire.'

'I'll have another white wine. House wine will be okay' Gracie said.

'Scotch and dry.'

'Thanks, I'll be right back with those. It's such a beautiful evening. Enjoy the view.' She walked away leaving them in peace.

'What a pleasant waitress' said Gracie.

'It makes all the difference. It sets the scene for a relaxing stress-free evening.' He leant back in the chair mesmerised by her beauty, her long blonde hair falling in soft curls over her ears.

Gracie scanned the menu. 'Oh, it's hard to choose. I think I might order barramundi with steamed vegetables.'

'Would you like some soup first?'

'No. I'd never fit it all in.'

He sat up straight eyes glued to the menu. 'Right! A steak it is for me' he said, patting his chest. The drinks arrived and they placed their meal orders. 'It is a beautiful spot isn't it?'

'It is. I would never have thought something so beautiful would be found on this dirt track west of Cloverdale. I suppose they would get a lot of people staying overnight in the B&B.'

'I guess they would.' He leant back in the chair. 'Tell me more about your family?' He began to visualise the two of them huddled together in one of the rooms beside the fireplace.

'Geez, where do I begin?'

'At the beginning, I guess.'

'Okay then...back in 1981, at age twenty six, a guy called Harold Jack Lawson met Megan Banner in an English pub. He was working for a top law firm in Sussex, England. She was travelling with a concert tour through Europe. As the story goes, she was about to have two months holiday before returning to Australia when she met him. She fell in love with the good looking one hundred and eighty eight centimetre tall lawyer. Within weeks, they both travelled around Europe together before coming back home to live in Australia.' Megan Banner was a City girl and Harold Lawson a country lad. So Megan, at twenty three years of age, six weeks after arriving back home in Australia, became Harold's wife and settled with his parents in the homestead at "Grasstree."

'Wow.'

'Is it boring so far? I know the whole history of the Lawson family, so stop me if it's all too much.'

'I'm enjoying it, go on?'

'Granny told me that her son was keen as mustard for Megan to start a family straight way. He opened his own private law practice in Port Macquarie, mid north coast a short walk from the local courthouse. He also flew regularly to the Supreme or the Family Courts in Sydney when necessary to represent his clients.'

She paused to take another sip. 'Did you know that Port Macquarie was named by the explorer, John Oxley after the governor of NSW, Lachlan Macquarie in 1818?'

'Yep, knew that and taught that to my students. It's the two hundredth year anniversary so there are a lot of celebrations going on in the area at the moment.'

'Wow, so it is, gosh, two hundred years.'

'Long story short, Megan gave birth to twins on the 3rd March 1988 in Port Macquarie hospital. The girl was born first, eight minutes later the boy. You are looking at one half of a twin.' She burst out laughing. 'Mummy named me, my father named Jack.'

'Wow, so you are a twin. Do you look alike, think alike.'

'We do think alike.' She put her finger to her chin. 'Perhaps we have the same colouring. Well I won't bore you anymore. I might get another drink. All that talking has made me thirsty.'

Booker called for the waitress. 'Do you want the same Gracie?"

'Yes, I'll have the same. Thanks.'

'Your parents, do they still live on the property?'

'No they don't. My parents separated in 2008 and when the divorce came through a year later, my mother re married and moved to the UK.' She began to laugh. 'I facetime her before I go to bed every Sunday night. It's become a ritual now. She's happy with that. My father lives in Sydney.' She thought it easy to lie. She doesn't know where her father is and she doesn't care. *Please don't ask me about him.*

'Have you been over to England to visit your mother?'

'Yes, I have, once.'

'And tell me more about your Granny?'

'Oh, once again, where do I begin? I loved her and I loved her stories she used to tell me about her childhood.'

He raised his eyebrows. 'Do tell?'

'Oh gosh, there are so many. I remember one of the things that stuck out from her younger days. Only because I think it is so bazaar.' She chuckled. 'She told me that every Monday her mother kept her home from school to help with the washing, because she happened to be the eldest daughter. Monday was always washing day.' She shook her head, her hair flicking from side to side. 'Crazy! She said her mother lit a wood fire in the back yard and boiled the clothes in a huge copper.'

'Yes, I have read stories about those days.'

'Anyway, after that, the clothes were placed on a scrubbing board, scrubbed by hand, wrung out by hand then placed in water with a blue bag. What the!'

'Yes, what the hell is a blue bag?'

She laughed. 'God only knows. Then they were wrung out and hung on the wire line to dry. Can you imagine that?' She put on her silly face.

He leant back in his chair, laughing. 'I have no concept.' He shook his head. 'They had it hard, didn't they? It would have been the depression years then too.'

'Yes, it was. So many stories she told me. She had eight children and she said in those days the town's folk mother's stayed in hospital for ten days or more after the birthing. Of course in the country some of them elected to have them at home with a midwife's help.' Her body shook. 'God, it seems unthinkable. I know people today who go home within twenty four hours.'

'I wonder who helped out with all the other children at home. They all seemed to have lots of kids. Mind you, they didn't have the contraceptives like today. It was a tough life.

No electricity in those days either. Thank God we live in these times. I think the best times.'

'Here's your meal' the waitress said, balancing two large plates.

'I could eat a horse and chase the rider' Booker said to her, sparkling eyes.

She laughed. 'I hope you enjoy your meals.' She set them down and whisked away.

'Bon appetite' he said. He delved into the basket of garlic bread after passing it first to Gracie. 'Wow, this looks amazing. Look at the size of it.'

'Look at mine too. I should have asked for a small portion.' They both got stuck into their meals, idle chatter.

'Well that certainly filled the hole' Booker said.

'I'm surprised I ate most of mine. It was delicious.'

'Okay, I'm ready to hear the rest of your stories.' He picked up his drink and leant back in the chair again.

'Geez, are you sure?' She moved her plate away and picked up her wine glass. 'When I was a small child, before all these stories, Granny used to tuck me up in bed and read me stories from her old books she found in the camphor chest at the bottom of the bed. She would fluff the pillows and prop me up to look at the pictures. When it was time for sleep she'd tuck the sheets in tight and kiss me goodnight. I used to lie in bed wondering what I would do with my life when I got older. Listening to all those bed-time stories, I thought I might become a writer. Well that never happened.'

He took her hands. 'Never say never...what *do* you want in life, Gracie?'

'Nothing more than I have really. I love my job, my little

cottage.' She went to say friends until Jayde popped into her head. 'It'd be nice to have a good male friend in my life.' There, she'd said it.

'I've not set out with any great intent to find a companion since Sylvia and I split up, but meeting you makes me want to see a lot more of you.' He put her hands to his lips and kissed them. 'Would you like to see me again Gracie?' He lifted one eyebrow, waiting for her answer.

'Yes, I'd like that very much. Friday night for the last month I've met up with my friends so other than that and Wednesday night when I play tennis, I'm free. Oh, and Sunday night I need to be home to connect with my Mum.' She laughed. 'It's not set in concrete though.'

'Beautiful. I play golf most Saturdays, sometimes Sundays. Depends if we are playing out of town or not. I think we might have a lot in common. What do you think?'

'I guess we might.' She looked into his piercing blue eyes. 'I'd like to let you know…' she looked down, fiddling with the pattern on the linen tablecloth, quiet voice. 'Well, early on in my relationships…well, I like to take things slow. I've learnt over the years. I have many friends who live side by side in dull relationships and of course I've been one of them…'

He put his hand up. 'It's okay and I've witnessed it too.' He leant back in the chair as if waiting for Gracie to continue.

'Thank you.'

'I think that's sensible and I like your honesty.' He gave a half smile as he leant in to take hold of her hands. 'Thank you.' He stalled for a moment. 'Because I haven't sought permanent company, I need to tell you that I've been no angel. I'll be honest with you. I have had the odd woman for sex now and again, but they're not the keeping types.'

Gracie looked at her empty glass, blew out a breath then inhaled short breaths. Did she need to hear this?

He looked around the restaurant. 'It looks like we are the last to leave.'

Silence!

'Gracie, that was before you. I like to be upfront then you know where I'm coming from.'

She looked up at him, watery eyes. 'I'm just being silly. Of course you are right. It was before you met me.'

'That's right Gracie.' He searched her face. 'It was. Shall we go?' he said, small voice.

He threw her shawl around her shoulders. 'It's been a wonderful evening. Thanks Booker.' They stood together by the long glass window for a moment looking at the reflections in the water. With the light from the moon and the little Tiki torches, they were guided to his car.

'I've totally enjoyed myself tonight. It's been magical' she said. She glanced up at the stars spilling across the sky like fairy lights. 'It's such a beautiful spot. My grandfather used to take me to a little café in the mountains for a milkshake and we'd wait for the sun to go down. It was magical as a child, but I still get a fuzzy feeling today too.'

'There's something beautiful about watching the sun sinking slowly into the west. Do you realise, that somewhere in the world right now, it will be someone's sunrise?'

Gracie turned, looked up at him. 'That's so true.' She pointed to the moon and they both gazed until the clouds moved across, making it dark again. She pulled the shawl tighter around her shoulders. 'This is such a beautiful spot, so pretty with the lights.' Gracie loved the moon and she knew how easy it was for her to fall in love on a moonlit night. She was a romantic at heart.

'I thought you'd like it. The whole place is tranquil.' He folded her in his arms swaying like the branches in the wind. When he leant down to kiss her softly on the lips, he felt stiffness inside his trousers. 'I think it's time to leave this oasis and head on home before you turn into a block of ice.'

'Yes' she said, pulling away. At her front door, Booker gently rested his hands on her shoulders gazing into her eyes. 'Would you like to go for dinner and the movies through the week? I'll have a sitter look after James for a few hours.'

'Yes. That would be nice.'

'If you decide to opt out be honest and say so? I've been let down before as I'm sure you have.'

Gracie nodded. 'Once you get to know me, you will find out that I'm not the type to let people down. If I say I am doing something, I will do it. And if I am unable, I will call you.' She tilted her head and smiled, mouth closed.

'How does Thursday evening sound?'

'It sounds good to me.' He had listened earlier when she said tennis on Wednesdays, the girls on Fridays. She gave him a tick.

'I'll call you before then to confirm.' He gave her a lingering kiss at the front door before leaving for home. In the car he adjusted his trousers, his mind consumed with thoughts about mysterious Gracie and her beautiful looks and body. How lucky could a man be to find everything in one package? He didn't want to ask about her past relationships yet or pry into her family: too soon.

Gracie danced around the kitchen with a bottle of white wine in one hand and a full glass in the other. She pulled her granny's chenille dressing gown tight around her and sat out on the back stairs thinking about the night, wondering how she would ever get to sleep. She should have invited him in for a drink…next time maybe. She was besotted by his looks, his impeccable manners and how easily the conversation flowed over dinner. He seemed to be one hell of a catch. Put that in your pipe and smoke it, Jayde Carlson. Gee that saying was a past memory from her Pa.

Later, in her bedroom, she swallowed down her medication, slipped into her nightwear and pulled the covers over her ready for sleep. She'd keep their meetings to herself as she knew Jayde took a great interest in the guy at the bar. Well there you go control freak Jayde Carlson, I've got the man of your dreams.

At high school on Monday after the early morning meeting, Booker realised Gracie was seeping into his thoughts. She'd been in his thoughts a lot over the weekend, especially since Saturday night at the Zen restaurant. He hadn't even remembered the drive home after dropping her back at her cottage. Ok, snap out of it Booker, there's classes to be run.

CHAPTER 20

Abby-Lee Park

2018

Abby-Lee Park rushed around doing the housework as her parents were arriving to stay with her for the next ten days. They insisted on hiring a car once they arrived at Port Macquarie airport. It suited her. She was looking forward to seeing them as it had been almost two years since her sister's wedding in Adelaide when she flew down for it. She was close to her father, he'd taught her a lot during her lifetime. Her mother, well, that's another story. They were at blogger heads most times but these ten days she was determined to make it pleasant for them both and she would hold her tongue.

Her father was a retired judge. He was reaching seventy and her mother was coming up sixty eight. Sam, her brother, was nine years older and lived with his wife in Germany. Her mother had told her often that when she arrived in the world it was a shock as they'd only planned on the one child. "One boy to carry on the name" she'd repeated often. I guess in some way, hearing that, put a wedge between mother and daughter. Later in life, her father had told her she was a blessing in his life. "You kept our marriage together Abby. If it wasn't for you coming along later in life I don't think our marriage would have survived. And to top it off we have this wonderful bond, you and I."

Yes, she loved her father and he taught her much, but her mother, well Abby reckoned that she was jealous of her and her father's close relationship. She also knew that blood ties were no guarantee of a functioning relationship. She'd heard of some families where it'd worked out well, but in her case within her family, it hadn't. She chose not to concern herself. She got over it and moved on. Her life was busy bringing up two children, Aaron and Penelope and her nursing job at the hospital. The children were with friends for the day and would be home for dinner.

When the house was neat and tidy she pulled the old wooden chair away from the shade of the mango tree and sat it in the sun. So far the windless day held enough sun to sit comfortably and enjoy her cup of coffee, book in hand. The day was warm, winter warm. Most of the trees had lost their leaves and lay waiting on the ground for raking. Her father loved doing little jobs around the place. He liked to be kept busy, mostly to keep out of her mother's way.

It's funny how the mind works. She didn't think of it often but since her parents were visiting it brought the past to the fore. Abby knew when it happened. The second time Slade Peterson had come to her parent's holiday house at the beach, that's when it happened. Years ago, his mother and Abby's mother played netball together and had kept in touch since. Abby and Slade went to different high schools but she could tell he looked at her in a different way since she started to develop. She had just turned fifteen and he, sixteen. They had separate bedrooms but they met on the back deck, he carrying a pillow and a thick blanket for comfort on the hard splintery wooden decking. She curled into him on this moonless night the sound of the goods train with screeching brakes in the distance. After the train, in the silence, she could hear the odd bird call. When he pulled her in and kissed her she pulled away. She had never been kissed before but had practiced on the mirror attached to her dresser. She wasn't sure whether she'd like flesh to flesh. Of course she'd seen plenty on TV, perhaps too much for her mother's eyes.

'Is this your first time?' Slade asked.

'Sorry, first time for what?'

'Kissing, touching. You know....playing around.' He lay his head on her chest and felt the thumping of her racing heart. He breathed out hot air. 'Can I feel your breasts?'

She thought for a minute. 'Okay.' No one had ever touched her anywhere before. It wouldn't hurt, surely. He had rough wandering hands that massaged the soft flesh of her breasts. He felt her nipples harden into his hands. He bent his head and sucked, tender at first, then hard. He met her lips and pulled her on top, dragging her winter night dress over her head. 'Oh Abby, Abby, you gorgeous thing you...'

She felt something hard beneath her. 'Stop Slade, stop, please...don't.'

'Don't you like it Abby?'

'We shouldn't be doing this.'

'Oh yes we should young lady. Has anyone else told you how sexy you are? I know of quite a few mates of mine who think you're miss hot pants.' She rolled off him and grabbed in the dark for her nightdress. He pulled her into him and kissed her hard finding the moist area between her thighs. She pulled away. 'Slade…stop, please' she said, louder than a whisper. 'I don't want to go any further. You and I both know we shouldn't be here doing this.' Abby's heart raced faster. She needed to get away from him.

'You're just a little tease.' He ripped at her panties, pulled his jocks down and thrust his hardness into her pressing his rough hands hard on her buttocks. 'I'm going to make you into a woman.' He ignored her whimpering. He went on and on calling her name. 'Abby, Abby, this is what you've been waiting for.'

'You're hurting me. Please Slade, stop?' She bit into the cloth of his top, muffling the sounds. She'd never experienced pain like this, but he didn't care. Everything was running through her mind right now. What if her mother heard her or went to check on her in her bedroom. She sobbed, tears falling down her cheeks soaking his top. Oh God, when will this end, I can't cope with this horrendous pain.

He rolled her over so she lay flat on the blanket. 'Oh' he called out. 'I'm coming. Oh Abby…Abby, sexy Abby…'

She lay like a slab of stone waiting for it all to end. She thought she would die. 'You're hurting me. Stop…Slade, stop?' He rode her until he climaxed then shoved her aside feeling his way in the dark for part of the blanket to cover their bodies. He attempted to nestle into her but she groped for her nightdress, panties and slipped away finding her way in the dark to her bedroom. She sat on the bed pulling her nighty over her head. She held her head in her hands, her body shaking. She held back her cries in the quiet night. What was she going to do? He had taken her without her consent: he'd raped her. She stepped under the shower not sure why blood seeped down her legs, bleeding like never before. The pain where he had thrust his hardness ached like hell. A ball of anxiety formed in her stomach.

Even after her shower, she could smell the faint smell of mothballs from his rough woollen blanket and the stink from his breath after eating the pasta dish full of garlic his mother had made for dinner. Why the hell did she allow him to do this to her. She should have screamed out. She covered her head with the blankets and sobbed.

Abby felt the winter chill on her arms. She moved the wooden chair further into the sun. Tightness moved to her chest. Although it was many years ago, in her mind it was like yesterday. At fifteen when Slade had raped her she was not much more than a child. The smell of anyone with bad breath or mothballs today was a trigger to the memory on that moonless night. And the sound of the screeching brakes from the train in the distance. It always amazed her about triggers to past memories and what it did to the body. She'd turn up her nose as soon as her granny opened the wooden chest where the linen was stored, scattered mothballs amongst them. The smell brought all those memories back into the present moment. Cindy poked her head in the air, barked and ran to the gate. There was no car in sight but Cindy knew, like all animals do.

A small dark blue car pulled into the driveway. She locked the long-ago secret away into the deep recesses of her mind.

She often wondered about secrets. Do people take them to their grave or do they have a confidential friend to spill to? She knew she would never tell a Soul, how could she? As far as she knew she, Slade and her father were the only ones who knew about that night on the hard wooden floor in the dark. Her body shuddered as she walked ahead to greet her parents. *Shake the past away.*

'Hello sweetheart' her father, Patrick said, in a low gravelly voice, like a smoker's. She noted his sloping shoulders, his pale-coloured skin as she went to hug him. He was skin and bone. She kissed his old face affectionately. Her mother, Peg, pulled them apart. 'Well I don't come all this way and not get a hug too.' Abby kissed her on the cheek before the three hugged.

'Come on in? Here, let me help you Dad with those suitcases?'

'He can carry them' her mother called out as she headed for the front door.

'You go on in love. I've got it.' Abby wondered what had happened to her father in the last couple of years. He looked sick, not well at all.

When she went inside, her mother had filled the kettle with water, stood on tip toe looking in the cupboards for the good china. *Shut your mouth Abby. Just zip those lips.* She hated what she was thinking, but she wanted her mother gone already.

When Abby was fifteen, her parents tried everything with their daughter. Something was terribly wrong, her grades had dropped off at school and she listened to loud weird music in her earphones in her bedroom. Gone were the long conversations they used to share. She was totally isolated from family and friends. She'd locked herself away. She slammed the bedroom door in her father's face when all he wanted to do was talk some sense into her. He wanted to help his baby daughter get well. They thought maybe drugs to begin with but when they looked for signs, there were none.

Depression descended on Abby like a dark cloud. The feeling came, a churning sensation in the pit of her stomach. She lay in her bed staring at the walls, wondering what would become of her.

When she turned eighteen and about to begin university, her doctor who was treating her for depression, suggested she see a psychiatrist. Abby, after many years of illness, depression and strange behaviours she went ahead with the appointment. She wanted to break away from the dark days and find some joy.

For the first time in her life she let out the big secret she'd lived with ever since the moonless night with Slade Peterson at the age of fifteen. She let it out to the kind Doctor Mary Burgin, the doctor who sat opposite her asking leading questions, listening.

Many tears were shed during the visits but in the end she had shared her feelings, something she hadn't been able to do with another Soul. The counselling sessions continued right through the first year of her studies and in the end she could hold her head high and say, "This was not my fault." Of course she still has depressive days but with her doctor's help and medication, Abby has managed to handle it.

She met Pete, another student, when she was nineteen.

She confided in him about the night with Slade. He got it and took things slow, gentle. They married two years later and began a family. They were madly in love. Pete made her laugh and she felt alive again. He knew every joke in the joke book she reckoned. They rolled off his tongue one after the other. She belly-laughed and began to live again.

One day, she confided in her father about that night with Slade. He hugged her tight. 'I'm sorry you felt you couldn't speak up back then darling.' Father and daughter had a closeness that the mother and daughter would never share.

CHAPTER 21

Gracie & Booker

2018

Booker took Gracie to dinner through the week and after watched the movie, "Christopher Robin." He grabbed hold of her hand as they dashed across the road in the rain to the car. 'I think I'll take James to see it. I'm sure he'd love it.'

'If we knew we were going to see it, we could have brought him along. A beautiful movie, I loved it.' He squeezed her hand as he pressed the remote to unlock his 4WD. He opened the door for her then ran around and hopped in behind the wheel. 'Home James' he said, grinning.

She rolled her eyes.

'It's a running joke with me and my son, James.'

At home, nestling into the sofa she hugged her knees to her chest. They talked until just after midnight. She loved listening to the stories about his travels, the many places he'd been to in the world. He had a great sense of humour too. He made her laugh which she hadn't done in a long time.

'I won't be able to see you this weekend or all of next week because the brood are gathering for my father's seventieth birthday before he heads back to the UK. I have lots of aunts, uncles and cousins and some are coming from different parts of Australia, flying in. We're actually hiring out one of the rooms at a resort in Port Macquarie as it's central for everyone. It'll be hectic but I'm sure a lot of fun.' He clasped his hands staring at the carpet square in the middle of the room. He looked towards her, straight faced. 'Will you keep the following weekend free? I was thinking perhaps I could meet you in town after you finish with your music students on Saturday morning. I'd like to take you to a mysterious destination for the weekend.'

Gracie loved surprises and took hold of his hands, moving in to kiss him on the cheek. 'That sounds interesting.'

'Mind you, I'll miss seeing you in all that time.' He looked at her, smiled, then checked his watch and stood ready to leave. 'What time is your last student then?'

'I'll be finished around 12.30.' She started counting on her fingers. Friday, Saturday, Sunday. So I'll see you in nine days. I put in for a week's leave as from the Monday. I have things to catch up on at home.' She was busy writing her memoirs.

'Oh if I would have known we could have spent an extra day by the sea. Mind you, it's nice for you to have time on your own too. I know I'll miss you but at a guess, I think the time will probably fly. I'll be rushing here, rushing there, airport pickups. Oh, and remember to bring an overnight bag.'

She jerked back when he reached for her. Ignoring her reaction, he gathered her close holding her tight. She held back a little but before long her arms were around his neck.

He cradled her head. He pulled away first then kissed her lightly on the lips.

'Perhaps explain about the overnight bag. I haven't agreed yet' she said. 'And if I do, there's no hanky-panky.' She waved her finger in front of his face, half meaning it. 'My mother used to say before a date, "No hanky-panky" but I had no idea what it meant back then.'

'I'm taking you to a place with breathtaking views of the ocean.' He held up his hands, grinning. 'Okay, no hanky-panky, if you say so.'

'Okay. I'll remind you of that.' She escaped his embrace. 'No hanky-panky.'

He laughed out loud. 'I'll look forward to seeing you in about nine days time. I think you are going to enjoy the getaway.' He could feel her hot breath as he leant in to kiss her on the cheek.

She found his lips and kissed them tenderly before nestling her head into his chest. Her heart was beating, quick beats. His kiss was different from all the previous men who'd kissed her. It was full of tenderness. She moved her hands up and down his back, a feeling of calm spreading through her body.

He fondled her breasts one at a time. He thought about their weekend away so he pulled back. He could wait. He bent down and kissed her forehead. 'Perhaps we could save ourselves for our weekend away?'

She raised her eyebrows. 'An overnight bag you said…and no hanky-panky.'

He smiled. 'Well, the place I'm taking you to is approximately four hour's drive away. Something you can't do in a day.' He'd booked a house right by the beach at

Byron Bay, on the NSW coast. Booker had been there many times in his youth when he did a lot of surfing with his mates. They organised the meeting place at around 12.45 pm the following Saturday. 'They say absence makes the heart grow fonder. I will miss you Gracie, even though I'll be busy running around. I've been given a lot of tasks and Dad's looking forward to celebrating the big birthday. I'll see you in nine days. If you change your mind, call me?'

'I doubt it.' She stood on tip toes and kissed him on his lips.

Gracie found it hard to contain her excitement. She really liked him but wondered why someone else hadn't snapped him up. Like he had said though, he settled into the role of principal at the high school and kept busy doing things with his son. Then again, he could have problems with commitment. He had told her he had women for pleasure only. Well, she'd soon find out.

CHAPTER 22

The girls

2018

Jayde began to think of the Friday night hunk. She hoped he would be there again this week. She'd been fantasising about him at times during work hours and when she went to bed at night. She hadn't had much luck with partners. Often some of the men wanted to own her and others only wanted sex. At this stage in her life, she was a free spirit and wanted to stay that way. That was before she saw the handsome one. He could be the settling type.

Jayde walked into the Hotel on the Friday evening and sat at the same table waiting for the girls to arrive. She scanned the room hoping to find him. No sign. She scrolled through her phone while she waited. When she looked towards the bar there was still no sign. She sighed. *Bugger!* She saw a couple of good lookers at a table drinking, laughing. *Not bad.* She might check them out later if handsome doesn't show.

'Hi Jayde' said the gang in unison. They all hugged then Jayde took the drink orders and went to the bar with the money from kitty. As she passed the table of two, one of the guys gave a soft wolf-whistle. She turned back, raised her eyebrows, smiled. After searching the bar she carried the full tray back to the table, another wolf whistle. 'I was hoping that hellishly handsome bloke would be here again. No sign of him.' She let out a long sigh. 'It's my life story…'

Gracie pricked her ears, putting on a vague face. 'The one that was with the older guy last Friday, you mean?'

'Yes. Wasn't he gorgeous? Don't find good lookers like that anymore. I think he likes me' Jayde said. Gracie inwardly grinned.

Lara interrupted. 'Okay, let's get on with organising our trip. We've all got a copy. Shall we go through it to make sure it's what we all want?' Touching glasses, they all nodded. She'd have to keep Alex off her mind tonight. He was persistent in wanting to see her through the week but she'd held off. He had another week left of his holiday staying with his parents in Cloverdale. She didn't want to betray Brad but Alex was the first person on her mind when she woke and the last as she went off to sleep of an evening. She knew it was purely lust. She wondered if she went through with it, would it get it out of her system. *Perhaps it was the chase.*

'I can't see anything out of place. It's what we all agreed on. The hotels sound flash. Pricey too, but we wanted posh didn't we?' said Abby, smiling.

'Nothing but the best for this foursome' said Lara, holding her glass up to toast. She knew she'd have to hide some of the costs from Brad because if he knew, he'd blow a fuse. She started planning a secret stash twelve months ago so that she wouldn't go without on this dream holiday. So far she had over a thousand dollars in a safe place at the boutique.

'Getting back to the luggage' said Gracie, soft voice. 'I don't know whether I will be able to do it. I have so many outfits, with shoes to match.'

Jayde levelled a glare. 'Look, no one knows us over there so what does it matter to wear the same outfit a few days in a row. We'll be able to wash our clothes of an evening. I gave a lot of thought to this during the week. I agree that we all take cabin luggage which means taking less. Who else agrees?' She could do sarcasm but she had better things to do rather than kicking Princess Gracie off her high horse.

All hands went up except Gracie's. 'Well Miss Gracie, majority wins.' Jayde called out louder than she meant to. 'Just think Gracie how easy it will be…just small bags to pull along. And we won't have to wait when we get off the plane. We'll all grab our cabin bags and go straight through customs.' Jayde did a sweeping action with her arms resting her eyes on Gracie. 'Okay, now that that's settled, let's move on?' Gracie cast a furtive glance at Jayde, but couldn't meet her stare for long. She put her hands under the table, clenched her fists. Finally, they rested on her lap but she felt the heat build on her cheeks, her lips in a straight line.

Jayde shrieked with laughter raising her hands in the air. 'Oh for God's sake put a smile on your dial. We're not in a bloody morgue. Anyway, getting back to the suitcase…you can do it. I've had a practice already and although I had to sit on the bag to close it, it can be done.'

Gracie held an image of Jayde sitting on her luggage bag with that big fat arse. She pulled her shoulders back. 'Look, I'm not getting into an argument over it all. I'm not in the mood tonight.' She stood, sculled her wine, and grabbed her handbag. 'Great start this is. Not one of you has left room for a discussion on this. I'm going home. I just don't think this trip is going to work for me.' Moisture built on her forehead, acid milling in her stomach.

'Gracie, sit down? Let's talk about it, c'mon, Gracie, please' cried Lara. 'Don't go off upset.'

'Sorry Lara, but I think you have all made up your minds.' She searched their faces. 'Yes, easy to see.' Tears were forming. She needed to get out of there. 'Don't worry about what I think.' She rushed towards the front entrance trying to catch her breath. Lara went to follow but Jayde put up her hand.

'Look, we all know that Gracie is a spoilt brat but this decision I am not backing down from. Can you imagine if she took a large suitcase? We'd all be waiting for her to collect it. Cabin luggage and we'll be out of the airport in no time. Let's take things that don't crush, it's easy. God, why can't she see that?' said Jayde, red faced.

'Gracie finds it hard to see anyone else's point of view. She likes things her way. You know that Lara' said Abby. 'What about the time when Fay came with us to NZ. Gracie was the only one to take a large suitcase and we had trouble finding room in the 4WD we hired. I had to put my bag between the two of us in the back seat. No, this time I'm not backing down either. And don't forget how long we all waited in the car while she finished applying her makeup. We always had to wait for Gracie. You haven't witnessed it yet Jayde.'

'Look, let's leave it for now. She'll probably come around to our way of thinking' said Lara. 'Are we going to book tickets to shows online or wait until we get over there? Hands up if you agree we do it from here?' Everyone raised their hands.

'Lara, are you happy to do the bookings once we've decided, or do you want one of us to do it?' asked Abby. 'It's okay. I'll look into it over the weekend.' Her head was still filled with the way Jayde treated Gracie. She didn't deserve to be treated like that.

'Oh, but what about Gracie' said Abby. 'We'll have to find out if she wants us to do it for her. Why can't she just fall into line and go along with all of us. Grrr!'

'She's bloody annoying. That's what she is. Miss high and mighty' said Jayde. She flicked her shoulder length honey blonde hair away from her face. She felt her face redden, her chest tight. Why the hell can't people listen to common sense?

'I'll call her on the weekend' said Lara quietly. 'She'll see it our way I'm sure. She listens to me.'

Jayde searched for the two men who were drinking earlier, no sign of them: just her luck. 'Don't bet on that. She's been a spoilt brat all her life. It'd be much better if she didn't join the foursome if you want my opinion.'

CHAPTER 23

Jack

2008

Jack Lawson didn't know how long he'd been asleep but when he looked at the clock it was 4.39 pm. The wedding celebrations would be in full swing by now. He felt groggy but he knew he had to get out of that room, maybe get some help. First he had a job to do. He went to the kitchen and made himself a beef sandwich and poured himself a coke, unsteady on his feet.

When he looked in the mirror in the bathroom he noticed copious amounts of blood had seeped through the bandage. He grabbed a clean tea towel from the kitchen, filled the bowl with water and after removing the bandage he dabbed at the wound. Blood spurted into the air. He applied pressure attempting to control the bleed. He hated his father even more right at this minute. He sat on the side of the bath holding a clean washer against the wound. He should have been sensible and gone off to the hospital. If he wrapped his head again in a fresh bandage it should do the trick. He'd do that. The blood kept trickling. This time, he pressed a cushion against it but parts were soon covered with blood. After holding it for some time it seemed to ease. He had to keep his wits about him, he had to focus. He'd get this job done then tend to his wound, maybe go to the hospital, even call the paramedics. He bound the bandage tight around his head.

He headed for the garage. In the back was his father's tool shed. He found the axe and stumbled his way back to his bedroom. With the little strength he had, he let the axe fall on his father's precious piece of work. He got a rhythm going, up, down. Splinters of wood flew across the room. With each movement, he pictured his father's head being smashed, stroke after stroke, bits of flesh flying in the air. Within no time at all the sculptured wooden work desk was smashed to smithereens. He'd be well on the road to Sydney by the time his father sights the mess. Wouldn't he love to be a fly on the wall, see the look on his father's face? He'd be shattered.

Pulse thrumming in his temples, he sat back in his chair and smiled, laughed, elation filling his lungs until his shoulders slumped and tears fell. All he ever wanted was a father, a father who took notice of his son, a father who shared his son's interests, a father who accepted him for who he was, a father who followed his progress in the arts. A little part of him still loved his father but he wondered why.

He grabbed his notebook and pen and went into Gracie's room and began writing at her desk. Weariness took over. *Focus.* He wrote a page, another. He spilt his feelings, his wishes that hadn't come to fruition. All he wanted was to be accepted by his own flesh and blood. He wrote about his abused mother, the mother who locked her Soul in a dark place.

Weakness came, tiredness, eyes heavy. *Keep going, keep writing.* He told her how much he admired her and to keep following her dream, like he would do. He wrote about his intentions, about starting a whole new life, a life without violence. He looked at the clock, 6.04pm. Outside it was dark the winter night had set in. Tears blotted the words on the paper, became illegible. He talked about their sibling bond, their love.

He placed it in the top drawer of her desk. She would know exactly why he couldn't ever come back to "Grasstree."

His legs, heavy as lead, found their way down the hallway to his bedroom. He fetched the axe, glanced around the room and stumbled out the door pulling the axe behind him. He looked back and smiled. *Good job Jack.* Dragging the axe down the hallway, objects blurry, vision minimal. "C'mon, put the axe away, put it where it belongs." He could hear his father's gruff voice, see his red face. "If you borrow my tools, return them. You know the rules. Respect other people's property." Yea, well you never respected me, Jack thought. He grabbed his father's thick coat from the hook, buttoned it tight across his chest. His shoulders shuddering, tears streaming down his face, he stumbled down the hallway, ignoring the searing pain in his head. If he felt the pain he knew he was still alive.

He gripped onto the back door frame for support figuring out the quickest way to get to the garage. Should he go via the tank stand or on the track which would take him much longer? Tank stand he'd decided, but could he make it? There was no light and his vision was weakening, things blurry. He knew it was a long walk to the garage. *You can do it Jack.* He tripped on the step, fell, picked himself up, and kept going.

Lift the leg, just one at a time. Jack, you can do it. Do it for Gracie, mother. *Put the bloody axe back?* With every step as slow as it was, hatred was building towards his father. Why would Jack call him his father, he never was. Dr Jekyll and Mr Hyde was the new title for his father from now on. Once he made a new life for himself in Sydney, he'd block his father from his mind.

He leant on the rusty tractor, his frame weak, eyes heavy. *Get the bloody axe back where it belongs. Do the right thing.* Rant, rave, rant, rave that's all Jack ever heard. He dragged the axe behind him on the dewy grass finding his way in the pitch black. When he heads back to Sydney, he's going to stop off at some of the beaches on the way. Water was a sign of rebirth and he's sure starting a new life, a life without his rotten father. Of course he'd always be in touch with Gracie and his mum.

Weakness overtook him as he saw the opening to the garage. *Come on Jack, you can do it.* There's nothing to hold onto. He used the axe like a walking stick but he toppled on the uneven ground. He fell but when he went to pick himself up he fell back once more. He crawled to the open doorway, pulling himself up. He leant his back against the wall, slid down landing on the cold cement floor. He couldn't find the strength to move. *The axe, where's the fucking axe?* He crawled back to where he came from feeling in the dark. He felt it, lying in the dewy grass.

Eyes heavy, lifeless body, nothing to cover his cold body, he guessed it was a good a place as any to rest. He'd replace the axe when he gained his strength. *Don't worry father, I'll get the effing axe back where it belongs. All your effing rules I'll be happy to live without.*

CHAPTER 24

The girls

2018

'You're not eating?' Lara asked Gracie.

'No. I'm skipping one meal a day. I want to lose a few kilos before we go on our trip.' She wanted to look good for Booker too. One part of her was excited about their weekend away and the other not so. She hadn't been with anyone since Troy and that ended over a year ago. She enjoyed shopping for some lacy underwear in Cameron Street through the week and looked forward to watching his face when she pranced around.

'I don't think that's sensible Gracie' said Lara as she cut into her steak. 'You'd better go light on the wine if you're not eating. You know how the cops have their secret spots. Brad was telling me they booked over twelve in the spate of an hour last Friday night. Remember, his brother is a cop.'

Gracie shrugged as she took another sip.

Jayde searched the bar. No sign. She wondered whether she'd ever see him again. This was the second Friday night he hadn't turned up. The girls were busy chatting and their glasses were almost empty. 'I'll go get the next lot of drinks. Want the same everyone?'

'Ah, yes.' Abby looked at the others. They all nodded. Jayde wandered to the bar and stood waiting for the barmaid to look her way. She scanned the bar, around the corner, but no sign. Perhaps he *was* a ring-in after all. He was probably a salesman servicing the country areas. She walked back to the girls, down-mouthed. She should have made her move the first night she saw him. How could she be so stupid to let the hunk of the century go? Just one night with him would satisfy her.

'Remember, Lara and I will be flying off to Sydney in the morning Gracie' said Abby. 'We'll be back for next Friday's meeting. Try not to get upset with her.' She pointed towards Jayde. 'Have a go at the cabin bag and see what you can fit in. You can always take a large handbag and stuff things in.' Abby put her hand on Gracie's arm. 'Have a go love?'

Gracie gave a small smile. 'She's just a control freak. I don't think it's too much to ask to take a large bag. Anyway, I promise I'll give the small bag a go.' She squeezed Abby's hand.

'Here everyone, Lara has printed a copy for each of us. Would you peruse it and mark anything you don't want or want changed' said Abby.

'Jayde, I've tried numerous times to fit everything into a cabin bag. Why have you made me feel bad because I want to take a large suitcase?' said Gracie. She crossed her arms waiting for Jayde to answer. Inside, she felt like screaming.

Jayde shot back. 'When you've got a minute, Miss high and mighty, it's like this. When we get off the plane we can grab our cabin bag and head off to customs. If you take the larger one, we'll all be waiting around unnecessarily for you to go and fetch your bag. Do you get it?' She took a bite of her toasted cheese sandwich before going on. 'Talking to you is like talking to a child. Have you ever thought of cutting down on things?'

'Just thinking it through, why don't we all give some thought about taking the larger bags then we'll still all be together.'

'Gracie, don't make this little thing into something big. For God's sake, it's not hard to minimise.' *Jesus.* Jayde hissed through her teeth.

'Moving right along' said Lara. 'How about we check the itinerary and make sure there's nothing there that one or more of you want changed and we'll get back to the baggage shortly.'

'No Lara. I want it sorted now. I can't go with cabin luggage. We are away for three weeks. What about our dirty clothes?'

Jayde sighed. 'Gracie, you wash them out at night and they'll be dry in the morning. Have you not travelled before?' She glanced towards the bar. No sign of him. Concentrate… get back to business. God he was gorgeous and she'd let him slip through her fingers. 'Are you for real' said Jayde. 'It's such a simple request.' Abby and Jayde turned and stared at Gracie. Lara stared down at the paperwork.

Gracie's breathing quickened. 'If you don't all agree to take a large bag I may as well not go. Perhaps you can find someone else to make up the numbers. There are four of us to wash our clothes every night. Then they have to dry.' She could feel her eyes welling, a sob rising in her throat. She'd wanted for so long to go to Europe. Ever since she was a young child she wanted more than anything to go to the Eiffel tower in Paris. She used to paste pictures into her picture book of Paris or anything French. Her breathing quickened as she glared at Jayde. She'd be dammed if she's travelling all those weeks with a small suitcase.

Lara spoke in a whisper. 'Yes, why don't we all take large suitcases?' she looked from one to the other hoping they'd all agree.

'Give me one good reason why three of us have to bow down to one selfish bitch.' Jayde took a deep breath before going on, eyes directed at Gracie. 'Think about it? It is such a small request and all you've got to do is say, okay, I'll take a small bag. It's not fair that we all wait for you while you stand in line looking for your suitcase with the rest of the world.'

Gracie welled up but determined not to cry in front of Jayde. 'I believe mine is a small request too. Find someone else that'll fit into your unreasonable idea Jayde?' Gracie sculled her wine, picked up her bag and pushed her chair in with force, her final act of rebellion. She rushed towards the exit sign. The three girls sat dumbfounded.

'Holy shit! That was an outburst out of the blue. What do we do now?' said Abby.

'Actually, I'm about to see if I can find Mr Handsome. I need some cheering up. Sort it out girls?' said Jayde. She carried her empty glass across the wooden floor to the bar. She had all night, but something told her he was not coming. The barmaid poured her another wine. She lingered for a minute then headed back to the round table.

'Well here I am girls' said Jayde. 'Have we all calmed down after Gracie's outburst?'

'Well I guess the only thing to do is all agree to take a large suitcase' said Lara, stony faced. She spoke slowly, sounding like a robot.

Jayde stood, hands on hips. 'I was given a mouth and I'm gonna use it, so listen carefully girls?' She swallowed down half a glass of her wine. 'Have you all gone batty? You know what she's like. She's stubborn and a spoilt brat. I'm not bowing down to her wants. Why the hell should we fall into what she wants every time? It's three against one. Majority wins.' She slammed her fist on the table.

Lara grimaced. 'Why don't we make it easy otherwise this whole holiday will be a nightmare? Let's take the large suitcases and be done with it.' Her lips quivered. She wondered where Jayde's cruelty came from and her words full of venom. Her stomach churned her hands clammy. She was beginning to get a picture of this overseas trip, and it wasn't pleasant.

'Look, I don't mind either way' said Abby. 'If it means that Gracie won't go because of the baggage thing, won't it be better if we all agree to take the large suitcases?'

'Well, I don't agree' Jayde shot back. 'You give into her now, can you imagine the power it will give her. She'd love it and would expect it the whole bloody trip. I say No!' She stood, walked back and forth. 'Not my bloody night tonight. The handsome one didn't show up two Friday nights in a row and miss goody two shoes has stormed out. Some bloody holiday this is going to be and we haven't even sorted the itinerary yet.' She threw her arms in the air. 'Fucking hell.'

It's Lara's turn to glare at Jayde. 'Wouldn't it be amusing if three of us decided to take large suitcases, then it can be left up to you to take cabin luggage? Hey, that might work.' Lara was being smart now but it's true, turn it around and see how Jayde likes it. Abby almost spat a mouthful of wine all over the table. She nudged Lara and they both fell about laughing.

'You're a sick pair.' Jayde picked up her glass, bag and waltzed up to the bar.

'Abby, look at her, she's mad as hell. She's shitty because the guy hasn't turned up tonight.' Lara couldn't control her giggling, Abby just as bad.

'Oh wah! We're a sick pair' said Abby, straight faced then fell into uncontrollable laughter.

'Oh my God, I need to find the ladies quick before I pee my pants.'

CHAPTER 25

Gracie

2018

Gracie ran towards the car park like a hare, as though a murderer was after her with an axe. Beside the car, she took a deep breath in the crisp winter's air, perhaps hoping it would clear her head after the upset with the girls. Her stomach tightened as she lowered herself into her sports car, tears forming. She wished Booker were here to cheer her up. Better days tomorrow, her bag was already packed and in the boot.

She dabbed at her eyes before punching the accelerator of her new Mazda MX5. She sped down the street. It was chaotic in the traffic, some sort of street fair going on tonight. It seemed worse too with the light rain. She'd go home, open a bottle of wine and think about things. Was she unreasonable? Maybe she was. Did she want to go with those bitches? No, correction! Jayde was the bitch, the others following like sheep.

She liked Lara she had a good heart. Even at school she was always the one to help everyone in class. She fumbled in her bag and grabbed her medication and swallowed it down with her bottled water. Tears were threatening. Her breathing quickened with every sour thought. Who does Jayde think she is? I should have gone for the throat with that bitch. *Of course you wouldn't Gracie Lawson…who are you kidding?* She wiped her palms on her skirt, her mind going to a dark place.

The wipers were going full blast, the demister working overtime. She hated driving in the rain, especially at night on these country roads, no street lights. Blast, she missed the turn…too much on her bloody mind. She did a U-turn. Out of nowhere, headlights appeared. Her hands gripped the steering wheel, eyes big as saucers, mouth ajar.

CHAPTER 26

Booker Harrington

2018

On Saturday, just after lunch, balancing his umbrella, Booker Harrington waited by the town clock until 2pm slightly pissed off. He'd left heaps of messages on Gracie's mobile phone. He walked up and down the main road filling in time. Perhaps something came up and she was going to be late.

She'd told him she had taken a week's leave from work. Perhaps she'd gone off on her own, maybe changed her mind about their weekend away. The rain pelted down and it forced him to wait in the car. He glanced at the esky in the back seat. He'd spent some time choosing the best cheeses, fresh bread, apricots, olives, figs and champagne. It had happened to him before and when he'd seen a therapist he was told he perhaps moved too fast in relationships. He really liked Gracie but right at this minute, he didn't like her at all. On the other hand, he figured something wasn't right. Even if she wanted out he had a strong feeling she would have let him know. He'd already asked the young girl at reception which room Gracie used for her music lessons but the girl was of no help.

At 2.35 pm, he started the engine of his 4WD and drove out of town onto the country road. When he arrived at *Rose Cottage*, there was no sign of life and her car wasn't parked underneath the carport. The dog raced to meet him. Booker opened his umbrella and looked around. Five bowls of water filled to the brim, one empty and plenty of bowls of dried food. He peered into the windows. No sign of life. She'd provided for her animal as if she was going to be away for a few days. Where are you Gracie? Call me?

He sat in the car and pressed her numbers again and left another message. Maybe a family matter arose. Surely she'd have the decency to call him. Nah, he was convinced. She dropped him like rubbish in the street. *Maybe he was rubbish.* He put his foot down, the mud splattering in the wake. 'Bloody women, when am I going to learn?' He still had a niggly feeling that something was wrong, because he remembered how excited she was about their weekend away. Why he wondered. Why hadn't she contacted him? In his mind, everything seemed to stop but the rain. He'd be patient. She had to come home sometime with an explanation.

Like his father had always said, the only person you can rely on is yourself. After closing the gate, he drove down the dirt road heading for Beechwood road, faster than the speed limit. After he drove through Cloverdale, he headed straight for the highway on his way north to Byron Bay. Gracie had his mobile number he'd leave it at that and go and do a bit of surfing or perhaps even have a bit of fun.

CHAPTER 27

The girls

2018

Through the week in Sydney the two girls were concerned. 'She's not answering her mobile phone. It's going straight to message bank. What are we going to do about the excursions? Should I just go ahead and book them or wait to hear from Gracie. Surely she's still not carrying on. We might have to wait for our Friday night meeting.'

'Lara, let's just leave it and enjoy our holiday? See if she turns up Friday night for our meeting. Of course you can contact Jayde if you like.' They both laughed. 'I doubt whether she can coax Gracie.'

'Anyway, Gracie knows our numbers.'

'Yes, let's forget about her. I'm ready for a brisk walk along the sand.'

'Me too.'

***

On Friday night, Lara and Abby went straight to the hotel after they touched down at Port Macquarie airport. They reckoned they both needed a holiday after living the high life in the big City. They both knew that wouldn't happen once they collected the children from relatives. When they got there Jayde was sitting on her own, no sign of Gracie. They all discussed the excursions they might be interested in.

'There's still no sign of the bitch. Does it mean she doesn't want to join us then' said Jayde. 'It's what she was indicating when she left last time.'

'She's got a name Jayde, show a bit of respect? I'll give her another buzz now' said Lara. She pressed the numbers and waited. 'It's still going to message bank. I don't believe she's ignoring me.'

Jayde flung her hands in the air. 'Well you all know she suffers with depression.'

'You don't have to announce it to the world. Keep your voice down?' said Abby.

Lara sighed. 'Do you think we can call over after our meeting?'

'It's a hell of a drive on that country road and what sort of reception will we get?' said Jayde. 'I say no, not interested.' She looked towards the bar and there he was staring at her. *Oh my God, he's back.*

'I'll get us another round.' She grabbed the money purse and headed towards him all smiles. She was swanning around like Marie Antoinette, giving her best smile, fluttering her lashes. *Why was he drinking alone tonight?*

'The same all round love' said the barman, all cheery. 'Where's the other one tonight?'

'I think she's pissed off with us.' She laughed. 'She suffers deep depression. When she's like that, we all leave her alone.'

'Gorgeous girl, I hope she comes out of it.'

'Yes, the same all around please.' He busied himself with the concoctions. She felt the guy's eyes on her. She turned to face him, broad smile. He nodded, giving a tight smile before turning back to the football game on the TV. Time went slow. She wished she could've been swallowed up as she waited for the barman to finish mixing the drinks.

'Thanks' she said, as he placed the drinks on the tray. She took hold of it, glasses rattling. The bloody table seemed forever away. She wondered if his eyes followed her. Geez, she hates it when people go all hot and cold. If he came onto her, she knew she could give him a night to remember.

'What's the go?' said Abby to Jayde.

'What do you mean? Nothing's the go. I went to get our drinks.' She felt the knot in her stomach. He turned his back on her, so obvious. There's plenty more fish in the sea. 'Where are we up to?' The three of them went through the excursions that they were positive about and marked those that Lara would look into further.

'Gracie's a problem. I'll try her once more' said Lara. She pressed the phone to her ear while staring at her iPad. 'Nup, it's still going to message bank.'

'Leave another message. Ask her if she wants in or out' Jayde said, nostrils flaring. Lara phoned back and did just that. They all discussed if it was worth trying to find someone else if Gracie opted out.

'Surely we can all get along together the three of us. I know sometimes they say three's a crowd but we're all adults and we'll just have to deal with it' said Abby.

'Hey, getting off the subject, my cousin Neil called me

while I was in Sydney and told me that one of his neighbours rolled his car the other night. He was high on ICE apparently, twenty five years old. Anyway he killed himself in the accident' said Lara.

'Where did this happen, in Port?' asked Jayde.

'No, it happened close to his parent's house in Beechwood. Apparently he went to our high school way back when.'

'Where's Beechwood' said Jayde shrugging her shoulders.

'West of Cloverdale' Abby said. 'That bloody ICE is everywhere. We see shocking things at work due to illegal drugs.'

'It's only asking for trouble if they get on that stuff' said Lara.

Jayde interrupted. 'C'mon, do we care. Let's get on with business?'

'I might take a drive out to Gracie's on Sunday and see if everything's okay. If she doesn't want to answer her phone she can't just ignore me when I turn up' said Lara. 'It's been too long surely she's still not shitty.'

'I'll go with you if you like' said Abby. 'As long as it's in the afternoon because we all go to church as a family in the morning.'

'Okay. Let's do that. I'll pick you up say 2 o'clock. It's about a thirty minute drive from your house. It's nice out there in the country. Hey, remember when Gracie and her twin brother Jack celebrated their 20th birthday. We could make as much noise as we wanted to as the nearest neighbours were miles away. We couldn't even see another light accept for the homestead, "Grasstree" on the hill. Everyone gathered around the fire, her brother Jack playing his guitar and everyone trying to sing. Jack really got stoned and we were all half pissed too. All the tents scattered around the property and you, Abby, were so drunk you had to crawl into your tent, but you had trouble finding it. We were all in fits of laughter.'

'No one has ever let me live it down either' she said, screeching with laughter. 'Someone filmed it, how embarrassing.'

'She was so much fun then but these days, well, I guess we're seeing the worst side of her' said Lara.

'Remember though, that was before…….' Abby trailed off. She didn't want Jayde asking too many questions.

CHAPTER 28

Abby & Lara
2018

Abby and Lara travelled out of Cloverdale onto the country road towards the cottage where Gracie lived. Nice old trees spread shade in the warm afternoon sun. It was 2.35 pm on Sunday when Lara drove on the gravel driveway towards the wrought iron gate. 'I'll open and close' said Abby. 'It's so quaint her little cottage isn't it.'

'It's lovely but too far out of town for my liking, and far too quiet.'

'It wouldn't do me either. Wonder what sort of night life there is.' They laughed together. 'Geez, I don't like our chances of getting hold of her because her car's not parked under the carport.' Abby waited until Lara had driven through the gate then closed it so Cindy, the dog, wouldn't escape. After parking, they both walked to the front door.

'We'll knock on the door and if no answer maybe we'll leave her a note' said Abby. The dog jumped up and down, barking like he hadn't seen anyone in years.

'Here Cindy' said Lara. The golden retriever jumped up and down, seeking attention. 'It feels eerie, don't you think?'

'Yes, too quiet. The dog's going crazy around her food bowl.' Abby walked over and noticed a few scraps left and a little water in one of the bowls. 'It looks like she's provided bowls of water for her. I'll clean them out and fill them with fresh water.' She walked around the side to find a tap. The dog straight away lapped it up. 'He needs food, the poor thing.'

'Geez I hope nothing's wrong. If she's gone for a Sunday drive why did she leave her dog here? I know how much Gracie loves animals and there is no way she would not take her dog with her.'

Lara picked up her phone and tried calling Gracie once more. 'Still no answer I'm sure she wouldn't stay shitty with us for this long. Go stand by the front door and I'll call her number again? Listen out?'

Abby ran over and put her ear to the door. 'No, can't hear a thing.'

'I feel as if something is not right. You know how she suffers with depression. What if she's done herself harm. Do you think we should call the police?'

Lara thought for a moment as she looked around the yard. 'I think that's a good idea. Something's not right at all and poor Cindy, she's got to have food. How long's she been without I wonder? I know where the key is, but I'm not entering the property to get some.' Lara had this strange feeling. What if she has hit her head and fallen inside. Stupid idea! Of course, the car's not here in the carport. Gracie can be stubborn and she knew that she was playing games with the girls. She wanted her way and she took the path of flight rather than fronting up and working it through.

Abby interrupted Lara's thoughts. 'There's no car and no sign of life. I think I will phone the police at least they can search the house. I have a feeling Cindy hasn't been fed for a while. I'm not feeling good about any of this. It's spooky and with us being here could be quite dangerous. What if she's inside being held up by a prison escapee?'

'Don't be stupid. Remember, her car is missing' said Lara.

'I hope your suggestion is not right about doing away with herself…we all know how depressed she gets. I've read stories about people taking themselves off into the bush to end it all. They take pills or put a gun to their head.' A shiver went through Abby's whole body. 'You don't think Jayde has something to do with her disappearance do you?'

'What…what are you thinking? That's absurd.'

Abby shrugged. 'Well she seems to have it in for her. I'm going to check the chicken coup.' She heard the squawking as she got closer. All the water containers were bone dry. She grabbed the hose and filled them one by one. 'Geez how long have you all been without food and water?' They all scratched around following her every move. Two fat geese were pecking through the chicken wire. 'Alright don't answer me.' Abby knew something bad had happened to Gracie. There is no way she would have left her animals without nourishment. 'Let's get back to the car. We'll stay parked outside the gate and wait for the police to arrive.' Cindy followed them so Lara put her in the back seat. It took a good forty minutes for the police to find the cottage. Lara and Abby left the car and walked towards the cops. She did the introductions.

'My name is Sergeant Carole Harris and this is Sergeant Jack Franks.'

'I hope we haven't wasted your time but something seems odd here. Two Friday nights ago, the lady who lives here had an argument with us and we haven't heard from her since. She's not answering her phone and now when we came all this way to talk to her she's not answering her door and her car is not underneath the carport. Also I have a feeling her animals haven't been fed for ages either.'

'What's her name?' Harris asked.

'Gracie Lawson' Lara said. Sergeant Harris had smooth coffee-toned skin, tall with jet black short hair. She'd never met an indigenous cop before, softly spoken, easy smile, showing a beautiful set of white teeth. 'It's unusual for her not to take her dog with her.'

'Okay we'll take a look around.' The girls and the dog followed them through the gate and down the track to the front verandah. The cops rattled at the front door before taking off around the side of the building.

'I'm feeling nervous' said Abby, kicking the dirt with her good runners, head down.

'Me too' said Lara running her hands through her hair.

'Nothing strange there. We'll have to break into the house' said Harris.

'I do know where she keeps the key.'

'Well, that makes our job easy' said Franks. Lara walked along to the end of the verandah and put her hand on top of a beam and handed the key to the sergeant's outstretched hand.

'You girls go and sit in the car and we'll do the rest. Take the dog and give him some attention. I think he'd like that.'

'I wonder if they are thinking the worst' said Abby, walking to the car. 'I am.' She did have a bad feeling but having the police check the house would hopefully give her some relief.

'Stop it, you're making me scared.'

In a short while the two cops appeared with a tin of dog food. Sergeant Franks tipped the contents into the dog's bowl and the golden retriever scoffed it down, one eye on them and one on his food. Franks walked around the area as if searching for something.

'The chickens haven't been fed either' Lara yelled from the car window.

Franks went back inside and came out with a bucket and wandered down to the chicken coup. He went back inside and brought three tins of dog food and a can opener.

'I'll leave these on the shelf at least they're out in the open so whoever turns up they can feed the dog. There's a full bucket of food for the chickens too.'

'I guess there's nothing more we can do' Franks said to Harris. They closed the gate to the property and Sergeant Harris put her head near the open car window. 'No sign of her. I'd say she's probably out and about. Top marks for calling us because the scene could have been ugly. Especially when she is quite isolated like she is.'

'Should we contact the hospital in case something has happened? It is odd for her not be in contact with us as we meet every Friday night at the local pub. She didn't show up two Friday nights in a row and we just thought she still had the shits with us.'

Silence.

'I need to tell you Sergeant Harris, this lady suffers with depression.'

Harris got out her notebook. 'What about parents, family, her workplace?'

'I believe her mother lives in the UK. Gracie teaches music at the Catholic School. It's opposite the Country Club. I think there's only one Catholic school in town' said Abby. 'We didn't even think to call the school. Now I feel stupid.' She slapped her forehead with her hand.

'You had no idea' said Franks.

'Most of the houses on the property here all belong to family, like cousins, Aunts, Uncles etc. but Gracie sticks to herself.' She waved her arms indicating the vast land. 'You see how the main track branches off. Each of the roads lead to somewhere, it's just that you can't see the houses from here.'

'Look, we'll chase everything up and get back to you. I'll take your full names and numbers?' Harris wrote everything down and with a smile she reassured the two of them that Gracie would probably arrive home later that day ready for her working week. 'I've replaced the key' she said, with a smile.

After the police left, Lara and Abby took the dog back inside the gate and made sure she was settled. Lara gave her a few reassuring pats and she bounced around ready to play. Abby re-filled the bowls with fresh water and they both agreed if they didn't hear from the police or Gracie by the next afternoon they'd drive out again after work.

'The police didn't seem too concerned.'

'They don't know her like we do' said Abby. 'I don't feel good about her disappearing like this. We both know her story better than anyone.'

CHAPTER 29

Lara

2018

At Lara's fashion boutique, "Three Little Birds" in High Street, Cloverdale, opposite the Department Store, the two police officers came through the front door.

'Hello' said Sergeant Harris.

'Hi.' Lara had more or less been waiting to hear from them. She didn't have a good feeling. The look on their faces told her so.

'We thought we'd come by and tell you in person this morning. Both of us have just spent two weeks in Sydney on a course and we're still trying to catch up. We had the accident report back at the station. It didn't click with me that it was the same person until I read Gracie Lawson's name. The accident happened on... He looked at his notes. 'It happened on Friday the 3rd August. She was obviously on her way home after being with you girls at the hotel. Sorry to say, but the young guy who ran into her died at the scene.'

'Oh no.' Lara sat down on the leather chair, clutching her chest.

'You might like to get in touch with the Port Macquarie hospital. I'm sure she'd love to see you.'

Lara slapped her hand to her mouth. 'This is terrible news.'

'We went to report the news to her workplace and while we were there the principal told us she'd taken a week's leave and hadn't returned. He'd made numerous calls to her mobile phone. He thought she may have been unwell. He was pretty shocked to hear what had happened. He had heard of the young man dying out at Beechwood and a young woman taken to hospital but there were no names mentioned of either of them.'

'Gee, she hadn't told us she was going on leave. If we knew that, we wouldn't have even been so worried. Anyway the story is different now.' Lara tsks. 'Abby and I went off to Sydney on the morning of the 4th August. We were away for a week. Needless to say, we heard nothing about an accident back here.'

'Get in touch with Abby and maybe you could go and see your friend.'

When the officers left, Lara sat in the tapestry covered stool in the change room, staring at her phone. 'Shit, shit, shit.' She wrapped her arms around her body, rocking back and forth tears falling. She reached for a hand-towel and wiped her forehead, her cheeks. *OMG! This is shocking news. Poor Gracie!* When she settled, she phoned Abby and Jayde telling them what had happened to Gracie. They agreed to meet and visit her after work that day. Lara held back her tears. This was devastating news for them to hear. Counting today, she worked back the days. It would've been the night she went off in a huff. Then she remembered her cousin, Neil, calling about the accident at Beechwood, the guy on ICE who died at the scene. She rushed to the bathroom emptying her stomach.

From her boutique, Lara phoned the hospital but they didn't give her many details. Just short visits the receptionist had said. When she arrived home from work she told the children what had happened and to stay indoors. 'Watch TV until I get back. You know the rules and you have my mobile number. You can have an ice cream each and I'll organise dinner when I get home.'

'Yea' they yelled in unison. She headed towards the car and onto the road to collect her friends.

CHAPTER 30

Gracie

2018

At the beginning of her night shift, Nurse Katherine Plummer found it hard to stop her tears forming as she examined the beautiful woman's face filled with multiple stitches, swelling and bruising. She had been monitoring Gracie Lawson closely along with Doctor Neil Thomas since day one. She dabbed at Gracie's cheeks with a soft cloth. The same afternoon, after seventy two hours the specialist had ordered cessation of Propofol and Katherine hoped she would observe some signs of movement from Gracie before her shift had ended.

On the 7th August the fourth day after Gracie's accident, she stirred. The day nurse, Samantha Knight, rushed to hold a dish in front while she heaved over it. Gracie was confused, agitated. The nurse mopped her forehead, wiped her mouth. Gracie soon slid into the land of dreams.

***

It was 2.26am on the digital clock the following day when Gracie stirred. 'Help me? Where am I?' she screamed out into the black night.

'The overnight nurse, Katherine Plummer ran into the room. 'Shush.' She switched on the lamp giving a soft glow. 'You are in good care Gracie.'

'Help me. Where am I?'

'You were in a car accident and the doctors have mended you.' She mopped Gracie's forehead with a cool cloth brushing the hair away from the wounds. Katherine knew it would be a long journey, not only her healing but having to face the news about the death of the occupant in the other vehicle.

'What have they done?' she cried out, pulling at the bed covers. 'What are these?' She tugged at the tubes, disoriented.

'The tubes have to stay there, now lie down, you need to rest. The doctor will see you when he's on his rounds about 10am and he'll tell you everything. Would you like anything at all Gracie?'

She started to whimper. 'I want…my Mummy.'

'Your mother will see you shortly.' Gracie wept like a baby her body shuddering. Katherine pressed the emergency button. She dabbed at Gracie's salty tears before they reached her wounds.

'Hello beautiful one! I see you're back in the land of the living' said Sister Marion Adams as she waddled into the private room. 'Would you like to sit up?'

'How long have I been here? What happened? Take these things out? I hate them.' Gracie noticed the plaster on her leg and arm. 'No!' She tried to remove the covers but Sister

Adams pulled them up and tucked them into the side of the bed, tight.

'Later in the morning your doctor will see you so that will be up to him to decide' said Sister Adams. 'C'mon now, let's prop you up a little bit.'

'No, I don't want to be propped up. I don't want to be here. Take me to Mummy's house now? I want out of here.' She shook her head from side to side pulling at the IV from her arm. 'I can't see. I must be blind. Get Granny Maud she will know what to do?'

'Let's rest. Nurse, take over for a minute?'

Sister Adams came back and administered the injection. 'There, that will help you relax beautiful one. Try to get a little sleep now.'

Gracie's lips moved slightly. 'Where's my Mummy?'

Nurse Plummer wet Gracie's dry lips with the soft cloth then covered them with paw-paw ointment to keep them moist. 'You'll see your mummy soon.'

'Yes please' Gracie whispered. She closed her eyes and wanted to go to another place. She hated the smell in the room and all the tubes connected to her. 'Everything's blurry. I'm blind, I must be blind. I hate it here. I want to go home to Granny. Where's Granny?'

'Your eyes are a little swollen at the moment. Once the swelling goes down you'll be able to see more clearly' said Sister Adams. Gracie let her adjust the pillow before flopping back resting her head into the hollow, her eyes heavy. 'Mummy, Granny' she cried out. 'Where are you? I wish you would come and take me out of here.' Within no time at all, sleep had taken over Gracie's confusion.

CHAPTER 31

Gracie & Megan

2018

Gracie opened her eyes slightly. The doctor had told her the swelling would go down soon and then she would have better vision. She was confused about everything. What accident? She doesn't even remember the accident. The last thing she remembered was leaving the girls at the hotel, heading for her car. The doctor said not to worry about trying to remember. 'It's not important right now' he'd said.

Megan Lawson, Gracie's mother, had arrived from the UK and sat in the hospital chair in the warmth of the afternoon sun her knitting needles resting in her lap, eyes closed, wondering if part of her daughter's memory was gone forever. She thought it might be a blessing after all.

Gracie wouldn't have any idea of dates or times. She is still in another world. Today, the 08.08.18 is exactly ten years after Harold Lawson left "Grasstree." It was the day when all their lives had changed forever, the day that Gracie's father, Harold left the family home. That part of their lives would be best forgotten, just bypass that memory completely. It's difficult to forget the date because of all the eights. Now another date will be stuck in Megan's mind forever, the 3rd of August.

'Mummy' Gracie whispered. She tried to get up but the bedding was tight around her. Megan became alert at the sound of her daughter's voice. She walked over and took hold of her hand. 'How are you feeling my darling?' She doesn't answer. Just shakes her head as one fat tear snakes down her cheek.

'Where have you been?'

'I've been here all day waiting for you to wake. C'mon I'll help you sit?'

'No, I want to lie down.' She hit out at her mother when she went to help her. 'Stay away from me?' Her vision was limited from one eye and she was sick to death of everything, hated being closed off from the world, her sick bed.

Megan sat in the chair beside the window. She hated to see Gracie this way. Never in a million years would she expect this behaviour from her beautiful daughter.

After a short doze, Gracie looked across at her mother. 'Have the girls…been to see me? Overseas trip.' She tried to think of their names.

'I just arrived today darling.'

She had a vision of the bitch, and her breathing took a different direction. Quick fast breaths she couldn't control. 'Bitch Jayde' she yelled out. 'Help me, somebody help me?' Her mother pressed the buzzer hoping a nurse would come pronto. 'I can't…breathe' she cried out.

The nurse hurried in and straight away called for help.

Gracie went crazy, yelling, arms flapping in the air. 'Bitch, fucking bitch...'

'Please wait outside?' the nurse said to Megan. Gracie's words shocked Megan. She'd never heard words like that from Gracie's mouth before. When the Doctor came he gave instructions to administer an injection to calm her. He realised he had perhaps taken Gracie Lawson off Propofol too soon. Perhaps he should've kept her in an induced coma for a little longer. Within no time, Gracie had closed her eyes, her breathing slower, quiet voice.

'What is it...what's wrong?' Megan asked Doctor Thomas when she met him in the corridor. 'She asked about the girls, the overseas trip and mentioned something about the bitch, Jayde.'

'Perhaps a little shock setting in, perhaps a memory of the accident, a girl's name overtook her for that moment. Any memory might be confusing. It will take time for her recovery. Something right now has clearly upset her. If you wish to sit in the room to be with her that's okay, but perhaps not talking will give her the rest she needs.' Her mother understood. She had her knitting to keep her company. 'Thank you Doctor.' She sat on the chair holding her knitting bag, took deep breaths to centre herself. Poor Gracie, what will become of her darling daughter?

Megan stayed in her daughter's private room red-eyed. She sat with the sun on her back thinking about when Harold was first married and as keen as mustard for her to fall pregnant straight away. Over the following five years she had three miscarriages and she wondered whether she would ever have a baby. She visited a gynaecologist to see if there was a problem. After a few tests, she sat opposite doctor Jillian Stanton and listened. "I think you need to relax more and drop all expectations" she had said. Megan went home and did just that. She learnt meditation and became a new woman. Then it happened. The doctor gave her the news. Once again, Harold couldn't contain his excitement. 'Twins' he yelled down the phone to everyone.

She remembers, like all mother's the day she gave birth to the twins. At the time, she wondered how she'd manage. Of course all mother's manage and thank God she did too. She and Harold were happy back then. He was a good provider but hopeless at doing anything for himself. Virtually, she had three children all her life. She dabbed at her eyes remembering the dreadful arguments and bashings her son Jack endured. If things didn't go Harold's way or to his liking, Jack copped it. How could Jack live up to his expectations? Of course she copped it too, but she might have deserved it, but not Jack. Harold was quick tempered and her son didn't deserve the treatment her husband dished out. He never really appreciated the wonderful artwork Jack produced and the roles he played on stage, his culinary skills, musical talent. That creative load of garbage, as Harold called it, was recognised by the local art galleries and he was even commissioned to do a piece for a gallery in NZ. Success comes in all different forms, but would Jack's father see that. No, never.

One of the best days of Megan's life was when Harold Lawson walked out of her life forever. It was the only time she felt free after twenty seven years of marriage. The memory of being a famous concert pianist seemed an eternity ago. After her second marriage in 2009, a year after Harold left, her husband purchased a grand piano for her and had it delivered to their home in England. She enjoyed playing for him each day. How could one not, with happiness oozing from every particle of her being. They held a soiree once a month in different friend's homes. Megan was alive again. Gone were the headaches, swollen lips and bloody noses.

CHAPTER 32

Doctor Thomas

2018

Doctor Thomas sat Gracie's mother, Megan down adjusting a cushion behind her back to see her comfortable.

'It was shocking news for me being so far away. She is my only daughter. As I've said before, I can stay as long as she needs me.'

'That is wonderful news, nothing like close family.'

'True.' She fiddled with the strap of her handbag.

'Megan, Gracie is suffering PTA. Post-traumatic amnesia. It's not unusual with victims after car accidents. Since she's been awake she's confused and disorientated. You might also notice that she's finding it hard to remember things, especially simple words. As times passes, these responses typically subside, and the brain and other body systems will eventually become stable. It could be that certain areas of the brain remain damaged, but time will tell. So if there is permanent damage, don't be surprised if Gracie has challenges in her life down the track. Of course, we hope that is not the case.'

Megan teared up grabbing her cotton handkerchief in her handbag. 'Her face…'

'It is amazing how something that might look so terrible today, but in six months, her face could possibly be healed… to a certain extent, that is. There will be a time, perhaps months away, when I can put her in touch with a good plastic surgeon. I will start her on a cream, Mederma, which will help reduce the scars, a little. The scars will be a red raised ridge but over the next couple of months, this will gradually flatten. Finally, the scars will weather and fade. Remember, I did say the word fade, not gone.'

'She's always been such a good looking woman, beautiful skin. In the past she's done photographic modelling. I don't know how she'll handle the face. I prayed to God once I found out that there was no permanent damage to her hands. The broken wrist will heal. She is a concert pianist you know, so having the use of her hands is vital.'

'That *is* a bonus. I want you to know that she has had around the clock care, been in good hands here. After seventy two hours I decided to bring her out of the induced coma, and that was six days ago. She has been slow to come out of it but that's quite normal. Don't be surprised with her behaviour, as quite often they can become quite aggressive and sometimes that can frighten loved ones. She will be disoriented and like I said, her memory won't be up to scratch for awhile. That's all to do with the PTA. She is on strong medication too and sometimes that can blur the mind.'

'Yes, I've witnessed her behaviour.' She smiled. 'Do you know anything more about the accident?'

'If you want to know any details about the accident, I

think the police will fill you in on all that. They will have all the details. The main thing is to be here for your daughter with the least stress as possible. I will keep you up to date with her progress.'

'I only pray that she will come through this with a full memory.'

'The results may take time, Megan. Let's not get our hopes up too soon. She's got a long way to go.'

CHAPTER 33

The girls

2018

Around 6pm the girls bundled into Lara's 4WD and headed towards the hospital. When they walked into Gracie's room, Megan came up to them and introduced herself. 'I've flown across from the UK, I'm Gracie's mother, just call me Megan.' She told the girls what she knew about the accident and how she had flown immediately from the UK to help where she could. Gracie was asleep but they still spoke in a whisper.

Lara went weak in the knees when she looked at all the stitches on Gracie's face before casting her eyes on the plaster on her right elevated leg, a deep wound around the ankle area. All the bandages, the neck brace, the shoulder sling, the wrist. She found a chair in the corner and took deep breaths.

Abby rocked on the balls of her feet staring at the floor. 'We didn't know' she said, voice low. 'We'd had a tiff and assumed Gracie was still mad at us. Oh, this is terrible. I feel sick. And we found out that it happened not long after she stormed out of the pub.' She found a chair, pulled it in and sat down, her head in her hands.

Megan went and put her arm around Abby's shoulders. 'Don't blame yourself? You didn't know about the accident and you didn't know she was in hospital. How could you?' Abby's shoulders shook at first then she took a deep breath and dried her eyes with a handkerchief Megan handed her. Jayde sat in the corner spending time on her mobile phone.

'Megan, can you tell me anything about the accident?'

'I can tell you what I know.' She pulled a chair in and sat down. 'Gracie was unconscious when the ambulance arrived at the scene late at night on Friday the 3rd August. The first responders found her slumped over the steering wheel, face down, shallow breathing.

'This is terrible and all this time we had no idea.'

Megan patted Lara's arm. 'How could you? The paramedics placed an endotracheal tube in her trachea and transported her to Port Macquarie hospital, where she was admitted to the ICU. She received medications to elevate blood pressure, ventilator support for breathing, and IV fluids for hydration, all of which was necessary to support the brain and the body so that the brain could recover from any injuries. He's keeping the ventilator on for a bit longer yet.'

'Oh, this is so terrible, poor Gracie.'

'A CT scan showed a little swelling of the brain. The neurologist, Doctor Melissa Lee, evaluated her. I had a word with her too.'

'What will be the effects of that then?' Abby asked.

'We'll have to wait and see. Doctor Lee will be monitoring all that. Gracie has broken her right leg as you can see, and her right wrist. She has a deep cut just above the ankle on the broken leg and that's why the contraption is fastened securely to this.' She pointed to the metal piece holding the leg into a secure position. 'They can tend to the wound at that height and it stops Gracie from moving the broken leg. She thrashes about a lot.'

Lara sniffled. 'Will the broken wrist affect Gracie's piano playing?

'A flexible wrist is one of the main pillars that hold the entire "piano performance" structure. Her students watch her movements carefully and that is how they learn, by example. I myself used to play in the Sydney symphony orchestra and we had our eyes on the music teacher at all times when learning. The doctor seems to think it will come good. See the stitches on her cheek? He told me that the cheek bone was broken and of course the glass from the windscreen has cut her face in many places, some of them quite deep.'

'Her face looks like a crossword puzzle. I hope it all heals for Gracie' said Lara, all concerned.

'And of course I do too. Doctor Thomas told me that she was put in a medically induced coma because of her serious injuries and also, it gives the brain time to heal. I have an appointment with her surgeon, doctor Nagle, at 1pm tomorrow to discuss everything.'

'It's intriguing to me as to how they contacted you all those miles away but none of us knew' said Lara.

'Apparently, like the obedient trained daughter that she is, they found all the details in the glovebox of her car.' She chuckled. 'I had drummed it into her once I left Australia to live overseas. I told her to always have details of her next of kin handy.'

'Good on Gracie' said Abby. 'She's such an organiser.'

'I'm sure you can imagine how I felt when I received the call from the police in Port Macquarie. I was beside myself. I packed my bag and I was soon on a plane over here.'

'Where are you staying Megan?' Lara asked.

'I've got a room at a hotel in town. The same publican I knew from years ago.' She grinned. 'It's comfortable and I get taxis to the Hospital daily. I've been constantly praying for healing. I've been told it will take some time but I'll stay as long as she needs me.'

'Would you like me to take you to Gracie's place and maybe stay there? Perhaps you could rent a car. From the Hospital it is probably only a fifty minute drive. And she has her beautiful dog, Cindy and it needs looking after. Then there are the chickens too. I'm sure you'd agree it's a comfortable cottage to live in and quiet too' said Lara.

'Yes, I know the cottage well. It belonged to the Lawson family before the property was subdivided. I had thought of going there but it's been a bit touchy for Gracie, so I thought the comfort of the hotel would be easier for the time being. Besides, I'm not sure how comfortable I'd be living way out there in the bush by myself these days.'

Abby overheard, her body shuddered. She thought of how awkward it might be for Megan to go back there after what had happened ten years ago.

CHAPTER 34

The girls

2018

It was dark outside when the girls left the hospital carpark. They all piled into the 4WD ready for the drop offs. 'What are we going to do about the overseas trip then?' said Abby. 'To be honest, I seem to have lost interest now. This has really thrown me.'

Lara shook her head. 'I think we'd better give it some thought through the week and meet on Friday night as usual. We can discuss it then. I'm not in the mood to even think about it at the moment. In the meantime, let's take it in turns to visit Gracie. What do you say?'

'That goes without saying' said Abby. 'We'll get a roster going.'

Jayde sat behind the driver, a feeling of guilt arose, her breath sour. If she hadn't been so dammed head-strong that night, Gracie wouldn't have left the hotel upset. She pushed her thoughts down into the deepest part of her being. She stared out into the black night.

On the other hand, if Princess Gracie had fallen into line

with her perfectly good idea she wouldn't be lying in hospital connected to tubes, broken bones and stitches covering her model-like face. Jayde's face features altered: a tight smile. She's not going to put her name on any roster. Not my problem, deal with it Princess Gracie.

CHAPTER 35

Gracie

2018

The nurse, Erin, pressed a button and the top half of the hospital bed rose until Gracie was in a sitting position. She winked at Gracie. 'That's better darlin'. Now take deep breaths?'

'It hurts.' She winched. 'Mummy, it hurts.'

'I know darling' said Megan.

Erin knew that Gracie was not in a good place emotionally right now. 'Doctor's on his rounds and it's nice if he sees you making an effort. C'mon let's dry those tears.'

Gracie squinted. Nurse Erin Harris was written on the name badge sitting on the top of her pocket. 'The best feeling ever was someone pulling out that bloody feeding tube...I hated all those tubes.' Gracie let out a heavy sigh. 'When can I go home?'

'I knew you'd be relieved once we got rid of them. And as for going home young lady, that will be the doctor's decision.' Erin fluffed up the pillows and filled her glass from the drink container. She slipped away when she saw Gracie's doctor coming through the door with his nurse.

Doctor Thomas dragged the heavy visitors chair across and sat beside the bed. Gracie tried to focus but the weeping started. From the other side of the bed her mother comforted her. Gracie didn't want to know about all the stitches on her face and her injuries. It was too much to deal with. She wanted to sleep until they were all healed.

'You were a very lucky girl' he said. 'These injuries will heal but it will all take time. The nursing staff will take care of your face and the rest of your injuries. They'll keep up with the Neosporin to help with any infections.' He touched her face lightly. 'The swelling and bruising will take about two to three weeks to disappear.'

Gracie stared at his grey hairs protruding from his nostrils. His face had deep lines and creases, like her Pa before he passed away. Her granny had told her that he was a hard worker all their married life. He worked mainly out in the hot sun, tending crops and cattle and he'd had many cancer spots cut out or zapped. He had one downfall, she'd said. He had a short fuse…often.

'When can I get out of bed? I hate lying here day and night.'

'I'll be the first to let you know, this has to come off first.' He tapped the cast. 'Then down the track, when I think you are up to it, I'll send you down to Rehab and the staff will help you get around using a frame at first, then, by the time you go home you will be well enough to handle crutches. Right now, rest is what you need. Especially the pelvis where it was broken, that needs total rest. Now girlie, if you do as I say now, it will pay off for you later.'

'Can I have a mirror to see my face?'

'Not at the moment. When you get stronger we'll get you up for a shower but until then I want complete rest. Your body has been through a lot of thrashing and it'll take weeks to settle down. Have you got any other questions at all?' He looked at Gracie then the mother.

'I'll be staying as long as necessary to help my daughter.' She leant in and smoothed Gracie's hairline.

Gracie ignored the tear that rolled down her cheek. By grabbing a tissue and wiping it away would draw attention. 'Why can't I remember the simplest of things? Sometimes when I am talking, I stop midstream. I just can't remember what I was talking about a second ago. Then there are other things I know parts of, but that's it, I don't remember all the things I should.'

'I think you are expecting too much too soon Gracie. Let's give it time.'

She juts out her chin. 'I don't want time, I want my memory back' she screamed.

Doctor Thomas stood. 'That will take patience, Gracie. I'll check on you tomorrow. I want you to get plenty of rest and keep the visitors to a minimum.' He walked out of the room, the nurse trailing behind.

Her mother moved beside her to take hold of her hand, bear the brunt of her outburst. 'It'll all come good, you'll see.' She hated her daughter's behaviour it wasn't like her at all.

'What would I do without you Mummy? The first person

I called out for was you. Thank you for being here. When is granny coming?'

'Soon darling.' Granny had been dead for a number of years but Megan knew it was no point in bringing that up and upsetting Gracie right now.

'Mother's never stop being there for their children darling. Now you just shut your eyes and wait for the nurse to bathe you. I'll head on down to the kiosk and grab a sandwich and coffee and will be back in an hour. Is there anything you would like while I'm there?' Gracie shook her head and followed her with tear-filled eyes as she walked towards the door. In an instant, the two of them were separated.

CHAPTER 36

The girls

2018

The pub was packed but the girls found a quiet spot in the corner. 'It seems that Gracie will not be better for a long time' said Lara.

Jayde pulled her shoulders back. 'I think we should continue with our plans. Gracie will get her money back as she's insured as we all are. So what are your thoughts?' Jayde leaned her elbows on the table, her chin held high glaring from one to the other, waiting.

'I don't feel good about it but what can we do. We had planned this trip and the only one who wouldn't agree to this luggage thing was Gracie. So maybe it will be easier now.' She crossed her arms. 'I'll go along with continuing with our trip' said Abby.

'What about you Lara, do you agree with Abby and I?'

'I need time to think about it. You know we can always wait until Gracie has healed. So what if it's another year.'

Jayde drew in a deep breath. 'Are you crazy? Like hell I'm waiting another year. She caused this accident herself. She left here in a huff, and her alcohol reading was over the limit. Over my dead body I'm waiting another year. Maybe it'll end up being just the two of us on this trip, Abby and me.' She glared at Lara waiting for a response, perspiration dotting her forehead.

CHAPTER 37

Megan Lawson

2018

Megan called for a taxi. Ever since she'd been back in Port Macquarie, she wanted to check out the family homestead, "Grasstree" west of Port Macquarie. It was a good forty five minute drive. At the top of the hill, she stepped out of the cab, handbag clinging to her arm.

'I won't be long' she said to the driver. She stood looking towards the front of the house shading her eyes from the bright winter sun. They'd taken away the balcony off the living area, built a carport with a raised roof blocking the window. Stupid idea! The garden that used to be covered with blooms every season was gone and replaced with children's play equipment. Where once the family of four had congregated in the family home that Harold's ancestors had designed and built had now disappeared: No trace of it. Someone in the Lawson family with young children had purchased the house, moved in and had made many changes to the place. Of course, she knew it was their right.

Harold's ancestors long ago had built it after spending

some years living in a tiny cabin while they raised their children, the tiny cabin where eventually her in-laws lived, Granny Maud and Pa who named it *Rose Cottage*. She'd often heard people say to never go back. She knew it was a big mistake. Trudging through the unkempt yard, she walked around the house looking for signs of her days there but it was all alien to her now. From high up on the hill, she could see *Rose Cottage* in the valley, Gracie's house now.

'You lookin' for someone' a gruff voice called out.

'Just reminiscing…my family built the homestead many years ago. I wanted to have a look. I'm sorry to intrude.' A tall young well-built woman dressed in jodhpurs, check flannel shirt, cigarette hanging from her mouth waved her away and went back inside. Megan had never had an interest in keeping in touch with Harold's family, far too many of them. She knew that when the property was subdivided the houses were sold to the Lawson family alone, no outsiders. There were seven houses on the thousand acre property.

Dare she glance towards the garage? The place where they used to house their two cars to protect them from the red dust. The day her heart had sliced in two. And months after, spending day after day swallowing Valium! No, she couldn't bear to look. She turned around and headed towards the cab unsteady on her feet. She stopped to look at the vista. Even that didn't have the same beauty. *Mistake, mistake…big mistake,* she mumbled under her breath as she stepped into the cab. She'd wanted to see "Grasstree" once more, but God only knew why. Good riddance to all the rotten memories of Harold Lawson. It's time to bury them now.

She watched the family home shrink in the distance as she

looked into the side mirror of the taxi. Good riddance to all of it. She knew she wouldn't be back to see where she raised her family. The visit today gave her a sense of closure but she left with a hardened heart. She realised she fell in love for all the wrong reasons back in '81. Successful man, good looking, knew what he wanted. She wasn't part of what he wanted right from day one. At the time, she was ready to settle down, have babies. She married a monster, someone who wanted to control her life. *And all along, she stayed to honour her vows.*

The cab driver drove down the steep dirt road sensing his passenger wanted silence. He spied a look in the revision mirror. The attractive bright-faced woman thirty minutes ago now showed a stony face, lips tight.

CHAPTER 38

Gracie

2018

At the hospital, the room fell dead silent, like a morgue. The morning sunlight streamed through the large window. Lara's shoulders fell and her face froze at the site of Gracie's face. She looks without blinking. Gracie's face was like softened wax, multi-coloured bruises standing out against the bone-whitish skin.

'Gracie. It's Lara' she said. 'How are you this morning?'

Gracie opened her eyes slightly and allowed her fingers to crawl along the stiff sheet to meet her friend's. Lara took hold of her hand and smiled. 'We've missed you. Tell me, how are you?' Gracie's perfect pink bow lips stood out minimising the stitches across her face.

'Like shit. What's my face look like?' She spoke slow and precise. 'Please be honest with me Lara?'

'I can't really tell much because you have some of your face covered…probably so that the wounds won't get infected. You only have a bit of swelling.' *Little white lies.*

Gracie grimaced, closed her eyes and tightened her mouth.

She remembered the times when she was alive, aware, focused. She'll never have that again she's sure of that.

Lara shifted her weight from one foot to the other. She hated the silence. Then she saw a teardrop slide down Gracie's cheek and in that instant her stomach tightened, her cheeks burned. Another teardrop followed.

Out of the four girls it had to happen to Gracie. She was so vain and the scars would send her into a deeper depression once she looked into a mirror. Lara moved closer and gripped Gracie's hand.

***

The police arrived to interview Gracie but were told ten minutes max. She felt the blood drain from her face as they introduced themselves. 'Detective Dean Monroe and I am Sergeant Julieann Pierce. It looks like you've had a rough time Gracie? Do you mind if we ask you a few questions?'

She shook her head. 'I don't remember anything, I'm sorry.'

'Tell me what snippets you do remember?' said detective Munroe.

'The last thing I remember is storming out into the street after a disagreement with the girls at the hotel. I remember running to the car. I also remember being upset, really upset.'

'And do you remember what the disagreement was all about?'

A small smile appeared on her marked face. 'Something stupid…I wanted to take a large suitcase on our overseas trip and the others didn't agree.' She drew in a deep breath. 'They wanted to take a small case. I became upset and left in a huff.

I remember all that, but sometimes I can't even remember the girl's names. I do remember that one of the girl's was quite nasty to me. Her name was Jayde.'

'I guess in the scheme of things it was a stupid argument but hey! What's done is done. We can all get caught up in silly disagreements, us girls.' Sergeant Julieann Pierce laughed. 'Do you remember getting into the car Gracie?'

Gracie paused to savour her coffee her mother had placed by her bed earlier. 'I've tried so often to think back. I just can't remember a thing after running to the car. Waking up here in the bed is the only thing I remember, full of tubes and plaster.' She envied the cops beautiful clear skin. She hoped one day her skin would clear up and look as smooth as hers.

'That's alright. Sometimes things come back later' said Monroe. He stood still, freckled arms folded across his chest. 'We'll leave you rest up a bit and perhaps call back in about a week's time.'

Gracie leant forward as if in pain. 'I want my mobile phone. It was in my handbag. Someone's got it.'

'We have it at the station. It's wrapped in a plastic bag, but unfortunately it's smashed to pieces.'

'All my phone numbers…I need to call someone' she screamed out.

'It's unfortunate. I'm sure once your friends know you are here they'll come and see you in person. Your phone's no good to you at all.'

She lay back into her pillow, sniffling. 'I'm over everything…no phone, an ugly face, broken limbs.'

'It will all take time to heal Gracie.'

'Was anyone else hurt? Did I hit anyone? Did I run into a

tree? Tell me, what happened?' He scratched the back of his neck and looked across at Pierce, she nodded.

'Yes' he replied.

She went to sit up. 'How bad….' He went all quiet, looked across at his offsider.

'A young twenty five year old man was in the other car.' He sighed, quiet for a while except for the cracking of his knuckles. 'He died at the scene. It was instant, but I want you to know it wasn't your fault. He came out from a side street. Gracie, you were in the right. He just headed straight for you.'

Pierce had read the toxicology report. There were significant amounts of alcohol and ICE in the dead man's system.

'No' she screamed, her head shaking from side to side. 'Oh no…please…no. I killed a man.' She covered her face with her hands. She pulled the sheets away, tried to move but her right leg was in traction and her body secured by a few tubes. Two nurses heard the screams and quickly rushed beside her bed. They tried to coax her to lay back into the pillow but she was determined to get out of bed.

Nurse Luca Browning raised her voice. 'Please Gracie, lie down? You must relax?' Gracie pressed her fists hard over her closed eyes until it hurt. She screamed at the nurse, her breathing fast. 'No…no…no. Get me out of here?'

'Please you must leave' nurse Luca said to the officers.

Detective Munroe quickly pulled the nurse aside. 'She asked if anyone was hurt in the accident and I told her about the young man who died.'

After the officers left, nurse Browning called for assistance. Gracie was clearly distressed. Sister Adams arrived. 'I'll get her meds.' She rushed out the door, came back a few minutes later and handed Gracie the tablet and a glass of water.

'It's okay sweetheart. There's nothing you can do about it. The accident wasn't your fault.'

Gracie swiped the glass away the contents spilling over the bed linen, the glass hitting the floor. 'I don't want the tablet.' Her face was contorted, her arms flinging in the air. She hit out at Sister Adams, fiery temper.

Luca Browning fetched another glass, filled it with water and forced the tablet down Gracie's throat.

'I hate it here, I want to go home' she cried.

'C'mon let's have a little rest. Lie down Gracie?'

'I want to go home. Where's mummy?' Luca stayed until drowsiness took over and Gracie's eyes closed. Within twenty minutes Gracie showed no sign of trauma eventually drifting into another world.

***

The following morning, Gracie had a fleeting memory about a guy, but her mind was foggy. She had a vague recollection of his looks, or was that just her imagination. She'd seen someone on the TV who she thought reminded her of him, but she still couldn't think of his name. With her head pounding, she wondered if her full memory would ever come back. Just flashes of things, then they're gone. She'd think of something then it was gone. What was happening to her mind? She let out a loud scream.

She slept fitfully.

CHAPTER 39

Jayde & Booker

2018

There he was leaning against the bar. Eagerness filled Jayde's being. 'I'll get the drinks. Do you want the same?' She pointed to Abby and Lara. They nodded.

Please don't ignore me this time? She hurried across to the bar. The two locked eyes and swapped a smile. 'Hello' she said to him, high pitched. The barmaid took her regular order. She turned back to him, 'Nice to see you.'

He turned to face her. 'Yes, lovely to see you too. And what is *your* name?'

'My name's Jayde.' She thought she'd gone to heaven. He had the most beautiful sky-blue eyes, white teeth, bushy eyebrows and a gorgeous smile. This was the first time she'd been this close to him.

'And your name is?'

'Booker, Booker Harrington. Would you like to join me for a drink?' He sidled up to her.

'Yeah, I'd like that.' *I'd like that more than you think.* 'I'll just take the tray back to the girls and I'll be right back.' She took her drink from the tray and popped it on the bar.

'Okay, I'll wait right here. Then we'll find a nice comfortable place to sit.' When she returned, he led her to the far corner of the room, pulled out the chair for her. They chatted on about their workplace, a bit about their travels etc. He leant back in the chair looking beneath the clothes, thoughts about bedding her. He knew she'd be easy she was all over him, like a rash. Attractive buxom blonde: easy. He knew he was on a good wicket with this one. He had an early start in the morning, playing golf. It was a good hour's drive north. He looked at his watch. 'I'll need to head off now. I have a huge golf day tomorrow. Would you like to have dinner tomorrow evening?'

She wondered about the sudden change. 'I'll have to check my diary.' She gave a laugh, her honey-blonde hair falling about. She moved closer, touched his arm. 'I'm only kidding! I'd love to have dinner tomorrow night.' She leant into him. 'What are you suggesting?' She was now close enough for him to get a good view of her cleavage.

'I know somewhere nice in Port Macquarie to take you. It has a nice view. I'll make a booking. Is six o'clock a good time for me to pick you up Jayde?' He stalled, reached for his phone. 'I'll need your address.'

'Umm...yes.' She watched him punch away as she called it out to him. Then he asked. 'What's your last name?'

'Carlson.'

'Lovely. Thanks Jayde Carlson. I'll put your address into the GPS and I'll look forward to a night out with you, perhaps tell me a little bit more about yourself.'

'Well that won't take long.' She looked back at the girls. They were all staring at her. 'I'd better get back to my friends. See you tomorrow night then.' She leant in pecking him on the cheek.

'Sure. The place is a little posh, so no casual gear.' He knew her type but he was lonely and hurt. Gracie had shut him out but he reckoned he was guaranteed a good night with this one. No attachment is what he was more comfortable with. Women seemed to let him down the minute he got too close. Then again, it could be more to do with him.

Jayde was sure her face had turned red. She walked slowly back to the table, a huge smile. 'He's asked me out on a date tomorrow night. Please don't look his way because he'll know we're talking about him.'

'What! And you said yes. You've only known him two minutes' said Lara. 'You don't know anything about him. You be bloody careful.'

'Well, life's for living and I intend doing that.' The girls raised their glasses not saying another word.

It didn't take Jayde long to picture the two of them huddled together on the sofa after an all-night lovemaking session.

CHAPTER 40

2018

Jayde stood in the kitchen listening for the sound of Booker's car. She had been ready for over an hour rumblings in her tummy. She found it hard to believe that he'd asked her out on a date. The last time she had a full-time relationship was over a year ago and that only lasted twelve weeks. Thomas Lucas had picked her up on everything she said, criticised her friends and the clothes she wore. He wasn't worth hanging onto so she gave him the flick. Of course, she'd had plenty of one-night stands since. She hoped this hunk lasted a bit longer than that. She'd put clean crisp sheets on the bed, fluffed the pillows.

She loved clothes but didn't follow the latest fashions. She held herself tall and wore outrageous things that smaller ladies couldn't wear. Her honey-blonde hair was shoulder length but tonight to be different, she pulled it back and clasped it with a small silver clip on top. She was overweight but some men preferred voluptuous women.

Most men since her relationship with Thomas had any want for sentimental attachments but that suited her at the moment. It left her wondering about this one. More than likely he was out for a good time too. She adjusted her breasts, making sure the cleavage was inviting. She had a feeling she was in for a good night with Booker, but that had nothing to do with dinner.

When he knocked on the front door she took one last look in the hall mirror, flicked a strand of hair back away from her forehead, and checked her lip gloss.

'Hello.' He handed her a small bunch of cyclamen.

'Why, thank you. They are beautiful. I'll have to find something to put them in.' Searching the cupboard she found a tall cut-glass jug. 'This will do.' Filling the container with water she threw the flowers in and fiddled until they sat evenly. She stood and looked back at her artistry.

'You've done a great job' he said. She took the jug and placed it in the centre of the kitchen table. 'That is where they belong.' She took hold of his hands and looked into his eyes. 'May I kiss you…for the flowers?' She leant in close, pushing her breasts hard into his chest. Her kiss lingered when he went to pull away. She went back again kissing him as if she hadn't done this in a long time. This time he responded.

She led his hand to her right breast. She felt his hardness.

He felt dizzy with excitement. His hand found the soft flesh inside her bra. He bent down to reach the full-blown nipple. Jayde's head jerked backwards, hands digging into his back. She led him to the couch her lips stuck like glue. Small moans crept in, soft at first then louder, her breathing quickening.

'Oh my God, you are so sexy. Shall we continue before heading out or shall we wait?' He blew in her ear.

She lifted her head and looked into his blue eyes. 'You've

started things now, perhaps a little entrée. Main meal and dessert later, what do you say?' She placed her hand at his groin.

He twisted her nipple gently then pulled her breast out of her bra cup and kissed it tenderly.

'Please' she said. 'How can you begin something and not finish it? Take me to my king-size bed?'

He wondered if he were dreaming. He could stop it right here but he was ready and she was flaunting her body right in front of him, no urging needed. He lifted her up. *Why isn't it you Gracie in my arms. Holy shit, she weighed a ton.*

'Down the hallway and to the right' she said. He could see the outline of the bed from a sliver of light coming through the narrow window.

As he placed her on the bed covers, Jayde found the lamp switch. He pulled her top over her head, the bra next, throwing them idly on the floor. He knelt down and kissed her neck, breasts, stomach. He pulled her loose slacks down over her buttocks. She arched her back to aid him. He took a quick intake of breath when he noticed her bare bottom. He wanted her there and then. He fiddled with his buckle and his pants fell to the floor. In one sweep, he kicks them away with his feet.

He stood staring at the figure in front of him. He stood beside the bed, grabbed hold of her hand, guided it. He closed his eyes dreaming of what was to follow. He longed for touch as it had been a few months since he'd been with a woman for sex. He thought of Gracie for a second and wished it was her that was touching him. He'd have to let her go but maybe not in his mind.

Jayde opened the top drawer of her bedside table and handed him a pair of handcuffs, pink fluffy balls attached.

'Ooh, that's my girl' he said, clasping them around her wrists, attaching them to the bedhead. 'You've done this before I see.' He'd never encountered anything like this before, except in porn movies. His head was spinning.

She opened her legs, writhing, moaning while he teased her. He found other spots that sent her wild.

'Booker, I'm bound by these handcuffs. You can do anything to me, but first, kiss me?'

He found her mouth. He tried to shake the thought of Gracie out of his mind. He moved his mouth over her breast, flicked his tongue across her erect nipple. Mouth again. He pictured Gracie's face. It was her he was making love to in his mind.

Her body convulses at the touch of his tongue dashing like a lizard. It sent her into another world.

'You are so sexy' he whispered, hot breath.

She called out his name. 'Booker, oh Booker, I want you. She'd always loved sex but there'd been a lack of it in the last few weeks. She had her vibrator but it wasn't the same as the real thing. The touch of a man is what she loved. Flesh to flesh.

'Later, I'll handcuff you to the bedhead. You'll go wild with what I can do to you and you can't do a thing about it.' She let out a screech of laughter. She thought of the can of whipped cream in the fridge. Men went crazy with that spread all over their body parts. Then she could also dress in her leathers using the whip. That sends them wild.

Booker's imagination began to run wild. He was about to

orgasm and she got ready too. She called out his name and he called hers. More foreplay - went again, multiple orgasms. After, he lay on top nestling into her neck his breathing heavy. 'Oh…oh…Jayde, you've worn me out.'

'Oh Booker, that was fantastic. I feel great. Are you going to leave me attached to the bedhead or set me free?'

He laughed out loud, fetching the key. 'How about going on our dinner date?' he said, rolling off the bed.

'Dinner…Oh, I'd forgotten.'

CHAPTER 41

2018

They showered and left for the restaurant both looking as fresh as a daisy. In the background Ed Sheeran's music played softly.

When they arrived, Booker apologised for the lateness as the waiter showed them to their table. It overlooked the sparkling lights of the town. 'May we have a bottle of Chardonnay please and we'll have the menu while you're at it.' He pulled the chair out for Jayde then sat himself. 'We'd like to place our order as well.' Jayde liked how he took over. He knew what he wanted in every way.

'Yes Sir.' The waiter bowed before walking away briskly.

'It's beautiful Booker. I've not been anywhere like this before. It is kinda posh.'

She ordered sealed alpine salmon with coriander, coconut and lemon cous cous. He ordered Rib eye fillet.

Although Booker could fill the night in with Jayde's company, his thoughts were still on Gracie. His mind began to wander. Her kindness, tenderness, yes, he wished it was Gracie sitting opposite tonight. Sex satisfied him earlier but it was with a player, he could tell she would grab anyone to fill her needs. It was easy to see that she was out for a good time and any man in trousers would do. Well, he started the whole thing.

'What family have you got living around here Jayde?'

'No one here, my family all live in Victoria. And the less I see of them the better.'

'Some have them.' He chuckled.

'And you?'

'Well we have the same parents, the same upbringing, but we're not close at all. We are all living in different parts of the country, one in New Zealand.'

'I live my own life. And when I say live, I mean live.' She threw her head back and laughed out loud. She reached over and touched his thigh.

'Right' he said.

Jayde told him about all the jobs she'd had, about her father getting too close to her when she was just a little girl and her mother not listening. Instead, she hid behind the bottle.

The meals arrived, the chatter went on, but he had very little interest in the woman sitting opposite him. They had nothing in common but he'd see the night out. He glanced around the restaurant. Fingers moved over mobile phones. He wondered what it would be like in another fifty years. Expressionless faces, like robots sitting opposite each other not a word said.

He stared out the window looking down into Town Green, watching lovers stroll by the river, boats ferrying tourists. He's lost his Gracie but he refused to put her out of his mind. He pushed his plate away, satisfied.

'Booker, did you hear me?'

'Sorry, I was miles away.' He rubbed his eyes with his fists.

'I was saying, do you want me to sit closer and touch me? I'm without knickers.'

He laughed, raised hands. 'Would you like something to drink before we make a move? Perhaps you'd like a coffee, liquor maybe.'

'Not really. I can make you something at home. If you are coming in that is.' She raised her eyebrows.

'Actually Jayde, I think I'll give it a miss. It's getting late and I have a busy day tomorrow.'

She pouted. 'Can't keep up with me…'

'Shall we go?' He stood, pulled her chair out. She grabbed her glass and swallowed the last of her wine. He had an urge to go, get away from her.

'I'll go freshen up while you fix the bill' she said, walking off briskly.

He handed over his credit card. Before long she was standing beside him. She took hold of his hand and they made their way to the lift.

'That was a beautiful evening Booker, thank you. I hope we can do it again real soon.' She leant into him. 'Have you ever made love in a lift before?' She tried a laugh.

'What the!' he snapped, drawing any conversation with her to an abrupt end.

CHAPTER 42

2018

Jayde pestered Booker the following day. 'How about coming for a drink somewhere? Please' she pleaded.

After the second call, he broke down. 'Okay, what time and where?'

'Say two o'clock at The Town Green Inn.'

'See you there' he said, uninterested. Why did he agree to go and why was he pretending that he liked her? She was a sex kitten but he also knew that she was an easy target for him and anyone else she pursued. Today it'd just be a drink he decided. She's no keeper.

The pub was crowded and everyone seemed to know Jayde Carlson. He had a feeling she was showing him off. He knew a few of the blokes he'd run into since joining the golf club in Cloverdale. Not mates, just people he'd met on the green. Not Jayde, the blokes were all over her. She'd probably had sex with most of them. He wanted out of there. Before he had a chance, she led him to a table at the back of the room. He'd have one drink and he'd be gone.

'You can smoke here Booker. I couldn't get to sleep last night thinking about what we could've done in bed together' she said. She held up her phone. 'Smile.' He smiled without much thought.

'I hate selfies.' He pushed her hands away but she'd already snapped the photo.

'Sleep, I don't even remember my head hitting the pillow.' Not quite right he thought. He did have Gracie on his mind.

They touched glasses. 'Here's to a fun afternoon.' He pulled a cigarette from the packet and offered her one. She took it. One drink, one smoke and he'd be gone.

'Did you know that one of our four friends, Gracie, had a serious car accident after one of our meetings and is not doing so well? Lara and Abby are a bit concerned about her. The doctor's seem to think she'll pull through. The worst part is that she'll be quite disfigured.'

Booker shifted in his seat, his breathing quickening. *OMG, Gracie, the one who consumed his thoughts since visiting the lake restaurant, ZEN, the movies. No wonder she didn't turn up for their weekend away.* Clammy palms. He couldn't concentrate, his mind travelled everywhere. He put his hands in his pockets to conceal the shaking.

'A young bloke died in the other car. She could be up for murder. Well I say she deserves it. She'd had far too much to drink, over the limit. She had the shits with us that night and stormed out of the pub. I reckon she caused the accident.'

Booker pulled his hands out of his pocket to wipe his forehead with his handkerchief.

'Are you okay Booker, you've gone all pale-like?'

'It's a shock…the poor girl.' He wiped his palms, backs of his hands on his trousers. Beads of sweat built up at the back of his neck, his forehead. *I've got to get out of here.*

'Out of all of us she is the one who will not be able to cope. Her face is full of stitches. I'd hate to think how disfigured she'll be. I call her Princess Gracie because that's what she is. Everything Gracie wants she gets. Not with this little duckie though.' She pointed to her mid chest, laughing.

Booker reached for his sunglasses in his sachet. How could he forget the model like figure, manicured nails and stunning clothes? She looked a million dollars. Yes, she was one beautiful lady. His stomach hardened remembering the constant unanswered phone calls. He looked around the pub with unseeing eyes his head full of confusion. 'What hospital did they take her to?'

'Port Macquarie and she was placed in an induced coma for quite a while. She's awake now though and talking. We went to see her but her mind is frazzled. Her memory is fucked.'

His knuckles turned white as he clung to his beer glass. He'd change the subject. 'Have you ever lived in the country?' asked Booker blankly.

'I was brought up in the country until about twelve years of age.'

'I thought you were brought up in Sydney or Melbourne.' A trail of cigarette smoke headed upwards.

'Nah, I like the City life now, but I had my taste of the country. I love the feel when I step back in time. Even now living in Port Macquarie I still go back to Cloverdale. I have lots of friends there.'

Booker had ants in his pants. He sculled his drink. 'I'm about ready to go on home.'

'So early…I'm enjoying being here with you.' She moved

her chair closer. 'Wanna touch me Booker? And do you like threesomes?'

'Ah, no is the answer to both.' He forced a tight smile. 'I have a lot of lessons to prepare for tomorrow so I need to get back home.'

'Do you want to come to my place for desserts before you head back? I've got a surprise for you.' She gave him a wink. 'I came without knickers today especially for you.' She reached over and took hold of his hand. 'Touch me?' she whispered.

He pushed her hand away. 'I'm going Jayde.' He stood, grabbed his sachet and headed through the pub and out to his car.

I want time alone, time away from you Jayde Carlson. He wished he'd never met the girl. Poor Gracie, I've got to get more information.

Jayde searched the room looking for someone to play with for the afternoon. Aren't I the lucky one, there's bloody Travis. She hadn't seen him in a while, he worked out bush. She strutted up to the bar all keen. 'Hey Trav me mate.' She slapped him on the back.

He turned. 'I'd know that set anywhere.'

'Up for a bit of fun Trav?'

'I'm hooked up with Gabe here but I reckon we can work something out, the three of us. What do ya reckon Gabe?'

Gabe looked Jayde up and down then came in close. 'Not a bad set there. We could have one each hey Trav.' Gabe bent down, kissed one then the other.

'Hey, give us a go?' said Travis.

'Why don't we head off to my place, more private?' suggested Jayde.

'Geez, let's not waste a minute' said Travis. 'C'mon Gabe, we're in for a bit of fun with Gracie for the arvo. I know what Jayde's like, she'll give us an arvo you won't forget. Still got plenty a toys?' he asked, slapping her arse.

CHAPTER 43

The girls

2018

The three girls laid the itinerary out on the table, drinks in hand. 'It all looks fantastic. No changes for me' said Abby. 'Shirley Valentine, here we come.'

'I'm looking forward to Rome and Venice' said Lara.

'What about Florence? This is a dream come true. I'm so looking forward to this trip. Bring it on?'

'If we would have listened to Gracie's reasoning a bit more, this accident wouldn't have happened. I'm not putting blame on anyone I'm just making a point. Be aware in the future how we deal with people. In hindsight, it would have been easier if we all agreed to take the larger suit cases. Abby you know how she takes everything but the kitchen sink when we travel' Lara said. 'This whole thing has turned into a nightmare. I feel for Gracie, I really do. And it wouldn't have hurt us all to consider taking the larger luggage. It wasn't such a biggie.'

'Looks like you're pointing a finger at us Lara. Remember, Gracie was the one who stormed out because she couldn't get her own way. She was the one behind the wheel. She's the one who was over the limit. I'm not taking any of this on board' said Jayde. She raised her glass. 'Here's to dysfunctional friends.'

'Me neither' said Abby, sighing. Abby leant back in her chair and folded her arms. 'I don't know about you lot, but for me, this whole trip has lost its excitement. What have you both decided about getting an extra person in Gracie's place?' She looked from one to the other. 'If you want my opinion, I believe it would be much better travelling with four instead of three.'

'We can all get along surely. I don't see the sense in grabbing another person just to make the group up to four' said Lara. 'Like someone we don't know.' She screwed her face before letting out a long sigh. 'I think we should give it all a rest for a few weeks. We all need time to think about things. Seeing Gracie in hospital with all those wounds has obviously upset me, and right now, I'm not thinking straight.'

Jayde threw her arms in the air. 'Oh for God's sake! She put herself there with her bloody tantrums. Everyone has always bowed down to what Gracie Lawson wants. Well this time it went too far. As you both know, she was over the limit. Three wines on an empty stomach would certainly put anyone over the limit. And the other thing is she left here in a rage so the whole thing is her own fault. She deserved what she got. I for one wouldn't have missed her if she'd died in that accident.'

CHAPTER 44

Gracie

2018

Lara noticed the large framed water colour paintings hanging on the wall in Gracie's private room. She thought it was more like a hotel room than a hospital. She recognised them straight away, they were Jack's paintings, yes his signature. Lara had purchased an abstract from Jack some years back. Someone must have hung them for her. She hadn't noticed them when she visited Gracie the first time, but it was dark then. Gracie would love admiring her twin brother's work. Shafts of sunlight spilled in through the huge window.

When Lara took a look at Gracie, her mouth fell open. Her beautiful face a few weeks ago was now a patchwork of large red raised ridges. She knew the colour would fade in time but the marks would be left for all to see. Lara openly studied Gracie's face, her cute nose, her natural long blonde hair, bow lips. She would talk to a nurse to see if there was a salon at the hospital as Gracie needed her lifeless hair to have a good shampoo.

Until Gracie made a move, Lara decided to sit by the

window with the winter sun warming her back. She pulled out her novel. It was peaceful in the room but she hated the smell. She closed her eyes and said a prayer for Gracie's healing, physically and mentally. And when she opened her eyes she glanced at the crystal angel watching over her friend.

She had spent over two hours reading her novel before Gracie opened her eyes. She saw her smile, a tight smile, consumed by some private emotion. She went by the bed and laced her fingers through Gracie's. 'How are you my friend? Is there anything you want?'

Silence.

Although a wine hadn't touched Gracie's lips, her head pounded and thick with what felt like a hangover. She grabbed the wet cloth she kept close by and wiped her forehead, under her armpits. She stared at Lara, the ceiling, hoping a nurse could come soon to bathe her and give her something to relieve her pounding headache. She had no control over the falling tears.

'I want to die' she whispered.

***

The physiotherapists had worked with Gracie on a daily basis. It had been just over three weeks since the accident and the surgeon had chosen today to hand her a mirror on his rounds. She made a mental note of the time. It was 11.11 am on Monday 27th August, the time and date that would be imprinted on her mind forever, just like 08.08.08. At first glance, Gracie wished she would have died too in the accident. Her screams could be heard in the corridor and the nurse rushed to close the door. They were silenced thirty minutes after doctor Nagle ordered a strong sedative.

'Perhaps it was too soon' said the doctor. 'She's obviously not emotionally equipped yet.'

Once in a deep sleep, the nurse dabbed Gracie's face with a damp cotton ball. How could she know how the patient would feel? She couldn't imagine going through this herself. She held Gracie's hand looking down at her chipped nails. She would see to Gracie's care. This girl needs to at least look her best, if not her face, at least her hair and nails. She remembered Gracie's friend, Lara, requesting personal care for her friend. She would follow it through.

The next morning, Doctor Elizabeth Green, a psychologist, sat by Gracie's bed and got her to open up about her feelings. Tears formed as Gracie talked about the damage to her face and the rest of her body. The doctor realised after a while that there were too many questions too soon and Gracie wasn't up to it yet. 'I'll come by every few days to see how you are. Will that be okay?'

Gracie studied the Doctor's face before speaking. 'Yes, thank you' she said, voice weak.

'I've left my business card on your bedside table. If you need to talk at any time, please call my office.'

Gracie knew Doctor Green would not drag the deep secrets from the recesses of her mind. They were there to stay.

CHAPTER 45

2018

Over the course of the next few weeks and lots of tears and talking to Doctor Green, Gracie slowly began to heal, mentally. She wondered how the doctor got her to reveal her secrets. It's like she knew her thoughts and dragged them out. It had been a relief to discuss her past and delve into her depression. She knew it had a great impact on her relationship with her family and her close friends over the last ten years. Her abusive father had a lot to answer for. Doctor Green suggested she confront him but Gracie's body shuddered and she went quiet.

***

'Hello young lady' said nurse Kath. 'Doctor Nagle will be calling by in about twenty minutes to talk to you.' She picked up the rose petals that had dropped onto the bedside table and threw them in to the rubbish bin. 'We'll need to change the water so they might have a little longer life.' She rubbed Gracie's arm, smiling. 'I'll take the vase and flowers and save what I can. How about sitting up and putting on a smile.'

'Thank you.' Roses made her think of home and her

Granny. She wondered when she'd get out of this morbid room in the hospital. She wanted to jump for joy when they took the plaster off her leg and wrist.

The nurses were kind but it was the regimented life she disliked. They woke her at a certain time to take her medication, then breakfast, a shower, off to rehabilitation, rest, and then lunch. After lunch she rested. Then it was time for visitors again. By then she was ready for dinner and sleep. At times she looked forward to visiting time. Her workmates had come by, her tennis friends and of course Lara and Abby. By early evening Gracie's eyes became heavy, her body ready for sleep.

Before the specialist's visit she concentrated on her breath. She needed to focus. It was important to focus on her heart rate, her hands still and dry. Her leg shook involuntary, another nervous reaction she'd forgotten about. She had practiced meditation after that day: 08.08.08. Jack, her twin brother had tried to teach her when they were in their teens but she couldn't relax back then. She closed her eyes, stilled her mind and went into a peaceful state.

As doctor Nagle walked into the room wearing a smile, she became alert and pulled herself to the side of the bed, feet dangling. He had a large frame, over 180 centimetres tall, a noticeable strong jawline, receding greyish hair and blue-grey coloured eyes. She could tell he'd been a good looker in his youth. She reckoned he was in his late fifties, early sixties.

'Got a smile for me today?' said the pocketed-faced doctor. She moistened her dry lips and split them. He sat in the chair beside the bed and checked her face, his offsider clinging to the folder taking in every word. 'Coming along nicely…I'm more than pleased. Has the soreness left?'

'Just twinges, that's all. The skin still feels tight.'

'That will soon go. Kate, the physiotherapist tells me you're keeping up with the exercises since the casts have been removed. That's good. You need to strengthen all your muscles. You've been in here over six weeks now and there will be a lot of muscle wastage.' He looked closely at her face. 'Your cheekbone fracture is going well. I'm happy with the small scar on your temple where I inserted the plates and screws. It will probably take another few weeks to completely heal.' He patted her arm. 'It's all looking good so far young lady.'

Relief pumped through Gracie's veins when Doctor Nagle told her that he could put her in touch with a good plastic surgeon down the track. News like this is what she was hoping for. Her face may not get back to how it used to be but a good plastic surgeon would help a lot. Wait till she tells Lara and Abby.

His hand was on the door handle and he was soon out of sight. She lay there thinking and reflecting about her multiple scars and what Doctor Nagle had just told her. *A surgeon can work on her face to make it look a lot better.* She closed her eyes. She was given life and she would learn to accept the changes she would have to make. Life's plans don't always work out the way you'd hoped, but this time she knew she was given a second chance and she would adjust and fall into place with her new life. She gave thought to all the burns victims, how did they cope? There was always someone worse off. Acceptance is the key she reckoned.

"You've been touched by death, so life now will have a

new meaning." They were the doctor's words as he held her hand weeks ago. "It could have been worse. You could have lost one or both hands" he'd added, knowing what an asset they were to her career.

At thirty years of age a whole new start was ahead of her and she could still continue her career in music. Lara had given her a journal and she had begun writing down her feelings each day. It was cathartic. She was writing when she heard a voice.

'Hello darling.'

'Hello mummy. Come and sit down and I'll share the good news.'

'Well, do tell.' She pulled a chair close to the bedside and waited to hear what her daughter had to say.

Gracie closed her brightly coloured journal and slipped it under her pillow. 'You know my specialist, Doctor Nagle… well he has just told me how pleased he is with my results and he also said that he will put me in touch with a good plastic surgeon when the time is right.'

Her mother reached over, hugged, kissed her. 'That is the best news I've heard all day. I told you everything would work out.' She noticed her daughter's face beam like she had something to live for all of a sudden.

'I feel so alive Mummy. I'm so happy. I don't care how long the whole procedure takes. I will do anything to get a good end result. When I go with the physio through the corridors for my slow walks each day, I see so many people far worse than I am. In the big picture, it has made me realise that my injuries aren't all that bad. Some may never walk again and some have terrible brain injuries and they won't even remember their parents, or friends.' She wiped the falling tear with the back of her hand. 'I feel blessed that my brain damage turned out to be temporary.' She giggled. 'I still don't remember everything but that will happen in time, I'm sure. I've been given another chance and I'm so happy that you have travelled over to be with me. I couldn't have done it without you.' She reached out and held her mother's hand.

'I love you. Of course I'd be here for my only daughter. As a mother it is heartbreaking to see you go through all of this but I've always believed that one must never give up. You've come through a lot over the last ten years, things that were unbearable at the time but you came through.' She rubbed her daughter's arm. 'And you'll get through this too.'

'I haven't told you, but since I've been back living at Grannies house, I've been writing a book. It's my memoir. As you know, I've kept a diary most of my life.'

'That's wonderful. Is it for your own benefit or are you getting it published for the world to read.'

'I'm going the whole hog.' She laughed. 'It's something I need to do. It seems the right time. Our case is not unique Mummy. Thousands are abused daily and I want to help and inspire others by telling them how Jack and I coped with our journey. You might remember how Granny got me into journaling years ago.'

'Good for you, I'm proud of you. And yes, granny wrote everyday herself. I've kept all her journals.'

'Have you? Would you allow me to read them? There might be something I can add to my story?'

'I'll have them posted over. There's nothing to hide but there's certainly a lot of history of the area and daily things that went on at the farm. I think you'll be able to embellish your story, especially the parts about Harold when he was young. Granny reckons he was born a bully, took his first breath and took over everyone and everything. He displayed anger from day one.'

'Well, anger comes from somewhere and I think that would enlighten the reader. I've got so much more to tell now. I can do that while I'm recovering. Doctor says he has noticed a big difference with my memory. I do too. What's your name again?' They laughed.

The lunch lady wheeled the trolley into her room and placed the tray on Gracie's table. 'Lamb and baked vegetables today' she said with a smile. 'And the sweets look yummy too. Enjoy.'

CHAPTER 46

2018

There seemed to be aliveness in each new day now for Gracie. Different memories returned. Her eyes sparkled, her smile genuine. Snippets came back about the guy. If only she could remember his name.

Lara visited and filled her in on the overseas trip. 'There'll be another time for you' she said, patting her hand. 'It'll be a long road for your recovery and when you're well enough I'll take you to a place you've always dreamed of.'

'Paris' Gracie said, grinning.

'Yes, but when I visit Paris this time, I'll be thinking of you. I'll take as many photos as I can for you. I can send some through daily on Face Book.'

Gracie held out her hand and Lara took hold of it. 'You are and have always been a good friend, thank you. Thank you so much.'

'Shall you and I go down and have a coffee in the café?'

'Let's' said Gracie. Lara pushed the walker close to her and they both headed down the corridor.

***

Something woke Gracie early. She sat bolt upright and looked at the bedside clock, 4:44. 'Booker, his name is Booker.' She adjusted her eyes in the dark room. Oh God, his name is Booker. She closed her eyes trying to picture his face. Nothing! She sank back into the pillow. 'It will come' she said aloud in the silence of the night.

After her first cup of coffee in the morning, she sank back into the soft pillow. She opened her eyes on hearing movement. Abby stood beside her taking hold of her hand. She looked at the clock on the wall. 8.10 am. 'Hello' she said in a whisper.

'I thought I'd come before work. You are looking fabulous.' No harm in brightening someone's day. The reddish skin on her face looked much healthier, it had turned pink.

Gracie turned to stare at the angel crystal her mother had brought her. It hung from the corner of the room in a loop of light. A blur of Booker's face appeared. *She had a blurry face to a name.*

'Abby, would you be a sweetie and buy me a mobile phone? I'll get mummy to fix you up with the money. It will fill in my days at least. I can play some games to occupy my time.'

'Of course I will. What sort of plan do you want?'

'Can you please go into the Telstra shop in Port Macquarie and tell them my story. I need the same phone number and I need them to reconnect me. I'll write down my four digit number, they may need it.'

'I'll get it sorted today. Have the best day you can. I'd better get into work.' She squeezed Gracie's hand and leant in and kissed her before whisking away.

Gracie's face opened up with a smile as she secretly thought of Booker. She'd remembered his name in the early hours of the morning and now she had a peek of a blurry face. She couldn't remember if he had kissed her. She couldn't even visualise his face clearly but maybe that would come. In the first week, the neurologist told her little bits of her memory would come back in time. "Be patient" she'd said to her. Maybe she was trying too hard to get a face to a name. Maybe he hadn't even tried to call her. It all seemed like another life time ago. *Let it go. Whatever will be, will be!*

CHAPTER 47

Lara

2018

Lara Saunders realised it had been weeks since that night when Alex took hold of her and kissed her in the garden at Brad's work dinner. They talked privately on Face Book and texted too. When she was at home she couldn't concentrate on anything but Alex. When Brad had days off from work she preferred to walk around her garden, mostly in a daze. She felt alive in anticipation of meeting with Alex tomorrow. She wondered where. How could she tell a lie to Brad? They'd always told each other everything since the first day of their relationship. Then she thought of Alex's dark brown sparkling eyes, his broad shoulders, his dimples when he smiled, the kiss, the touch that turned her on. They had a history, the two of them.

'You seem miles away Lara. What's on your mind?' said Brad after dinner one evening. She sipped on her wine not wanting to answer. Her other hand curled at the edge of the table her knuckles white. 'It's the planning of this trip and of course, I'm concerned about Gracie.'

'You don't want me anymore in the bedroom when I come home from the mines. Geez, a man only gets home a few days a month and I'm all ready to go and you reckon you're too tired. I think it's more than what you're telling me. What's *really* going on Lara?'

She shook her head and gave a grin. 'It's your mind. It seems to be working overtime. Look, I'm tired and I don't want to get into any deep and meaningful discussions right now.' She took hold of his hand. 'Nothing's going on. I've just got a lot on my mind.' She hated it when Brad picked up on things. That's why she should cancel this meeting with Alex. Brad will know. He senses things, always has. That's what's happening now, he knows something.

'I thought you might be interested in someone else. If you ever were, would you tell me? We've discussed this before and we both agreed if it happened we would talk about it. Do you remember?'

'Don't be silly. Look, right now I could do with a good night's sleep.'

'Right! By the way, Alex is still in town and we are catching up for a few beers tomorrow night.' He kissed her on the top of her head and went into the study to check his emails.

Lara sat as still as a statue, her mind racing. She poured herself another wine. How would she get to sleep with all this on her mind? How could she lie to Brad? She hadn't done anything wrong, yet. Her urge to see Alex was strong but you can't go telling your husband that you may be interested in someone. What would he do or say? Would he say something like, "Go ahead and see if you like him better than me?" I doubt if he'd say that and mean it. Her phone buzzed. It was

Alex, a text. *I want U...1 more sleep...g/night sexy...* She sent him a happy face then right away deleted the messages. If Brad knew Alex was keen to bed her, he'd go ape shit.

She swallowed the last of her wine with two men on her mind. She showered and lay in bed thinking, Brad snoring beside her. Brad was a good man and he was her confidant, friend and lover but there was something intriguing about Alex. She put her arms around Brad and in no time, he responded. Soon Brad told her how much he'd missed her in the matrimonial bed and how he'd longed for her. 'I love you Lara baby.'

After, Lara lay in the dark listening to Brad's even breathing. *Think of something beautiful like sitting by the ocean.* She pulled the doona up under her chin and visualised herself walking on the wet sand, alone. It wasn't long before she was holding Alex's hand.

CHAPTER 48

2018

Lara ran a red light while rushing to meet Alex. 'Shit!' The kids chatted for several minutes about what she'd done. 'I'm telling Daddy' Primrose kept repeating.

'You swore and went through a red light' said her brother Josh.

'I didn't see it' Lara said. 'C'mon forget it. We'll be at Nan's in a minute. I hope you've got everything in your bag?'

'Yes mummy' said Primrose.

Why the hell was she doing this? Going through that red light was a sign. Maybe it won't all go to plan. She gripped the steering wheel, her breathing coming in fast. *Calm down you'll have a heart attack.* She had little sleep last night worrying about her plans. It happened to be school holidays and she'd bloody well paid a casual worker so she could go off and sleep with her ex-boyfriend. It's like paying for it but she had no choice if she wanted to see him. Brad had a golf day. He would meet with Alex for drinks early evening.

'Stop hitting me? Mummy Josh keeps hitting me.'

'Guys I'm trying to concentrate. Please don't argue.'

'He keeps hitting me.'

'If you can't behave I'll take you back home and you won't get to see Nan and Pop.'

Silence.

After dropping the children with her parents, she took off, checking the speedometer. Geez, it's not right. If her parents found out she'd told them a down-right lie she'd have to live with the consequences. She pulled a tissue from the box and mopped her brow.

The hotel was in Port Macquarie. She parked in the shopping centre and walked across the road. She hoped she wouldn't run into anyone she knew. He'd given her the room number. Fifth floor but she'd deleted the message. What room was it? She texted him and he texted back.

Her stomach rumbled her head pounded. When she got out of the lift he stood there waiting. He took her in his arms, led her to the room locking the door behind him. It took him no time kissing her, caressing her.

She pulled away. 'Can I breathe first?'

'Okay, drink?' he asked.

'What have you got?'

'I bought champagne. It's already on ice.'

'Cool.' Why was her tummy rumbling?

'Relax. You're safe here.' He poured the liquid into the glasses. 'This is our time together today.' He raised his glass to hers.

'I can't relax Alex.' She touched his glass anyway.

'Let's sit on the balcony. We'll just talk.'

'My friend had her 50th birthday party here and many of us stayed overnight. It is central isn't it? I love looking out at the ocean, watching the boats on the river.' *Shut up, you know he hates idle chatter.*

They finished their drinks and he took hold of her. 'Let's shower together. I'm looking forward to seeing your flesh. It's been far too long.'

'Brad told me you're meeting tonight. I feel guilty being here.'

'Lara, today is for us tonight is for Brad.'

He ran the shower and undressed her. His dreams had come true. Spending time with Lara after all these years had consumed his mind since he caught up with his old mate, Brad.

After the shower, he wrapped the towel around her and carried her to the bed. Earlier he'd pulled the covers back so he could lay her on the crisp white sheets. 'Oh Lara I've been waiting for this moment.' He trailed his fingers around her breasts, kissing them, one after the other. Her mouth found his, arms snaked around his neck. He let go to take a breath. 'Remember when we were teens, the first time.' She giggled, covered her face. 'How could I forget?'

'It was a hit and miss. In the end we worked it out, didn't we miss Lara?' He kissed the tip of her nose. 'After that, we enjoyed the practice.' He moved from her mouth to her breasts, hungry for every inch of her. He took his time, teasing. 'I want to kiss you all over. What do you want Miss Lara?'

'I want whatever you give me, how about surprising me.' She closed her eyes and opened her legs wide, waiting.

His eyes roamed, his tongue slithered like a snake. Her body tingled all over. She called his name, moans loud in the quiet room. He'd found places Brad hadn't been, it sent her to another world. 'Alex, oh…' Her body squirmed, stretched her hand to find his hardness. He moaned at her touch and soon after, guided his manliness into her, slowly at first then rhythmically. She yelled his name like she used to.

'Oh Lara, I'm going to orgasm relatively quickly' he said. 'I'm sorry…let's go together.' His sexy voice turned her on. 'C'mon Lara?'

Lara went to another place in her head, a place without guilt, worry, Brad or the children.

Minutes later, he flopped on top of her his breathing heavy, hers too.

She searched his eyes. 'A lot has changed since our teen days' she said, raising her eyebrows, laughing.

'Hey, I was sixteen. I knew nothing about all these love-making tricks.' He laughed. 'All I knew was about getting it in, climax and then it was over till the next time.' He lifted his body off her and lay beside her, exhausted.

'You're beautiful Miss Lara and you didn't disappoint. I'll get us another glass of champagne.' He pecked her on the forehead and slid off the bed. She lay there thinking about going again.

'After a sip or two, I will really make love to you like I'd dreamed in my head.'

'I think it might be something I can cope with.'

After Lara showered she had her last kiss at the door of the hotel room. 'We lusted for each other Alex but it has to stop here. I've had a wonderful time. It's been great catching up with you. I'm going to leave the whole love-making episode in this room. I don't want to carry any guilt with me.'

'I don't want you to leave.' He held her tight.

'Alex, it's out of our system now. This day can stay in our heads and hearts, but let's just leave it hey?'

He kissed her on the lips. 'What about next time I'm visiting my family, couldn't we catch up then?'

'No. I loved having this time today, but Alex, I'm married to Brad.' With that, she snuck out the door and hurried to the lift thinking of his and Brad's drinking session that evening. She wondered how Alex could front up knowing he'd spent the afternoon with his best mate's wife. She shuddered. *Same for me though.* She walked briskly to the car putting it all behind her. She kept checking in the rear view mirror all the way to her parent's house. She's guilty already. *Put it all behind you Lara?*

CHAPTER 49

Abby

2018

Abby Rose Devin read, the lamp on the table lighting the pages. Now and again she looked away from the pages, thinking about the things she had just read. Her mother had started her reading from a young age and since then she carried a book wherever she went. Today, she was trying to get her mind off her blind date that her sister, Beth, had set up for her. Beth kept telling her, "You need a life." Abby guessed she was right. All she did was work and occasionally meet up for a coffee and a movie with her girlfriends. She wondered why she said yes because she was happy on her own. Abby loved being a mother to her two children. Aaron had turned six and Penelope four. She decided to open her book, and step into another life.

She arrived at the restaurant in Port Macquarie early. She wore a straight dark blue linen skirt below the knee and jacket to match. A string of pearls highlighted her soft-coloured floral blouse. She wore skin-coloured sandals with a heel and a small bag to match. The whole outfit made her feel feminine, a vast difference to her nurse's uniform.

The waiter placed the napkin in her lap. 'Drink madam?'

'No, I'll wait thank you.' She kept her eyes peeled at the entrance hoping to get a glimpse. The napkin was a mangled mess as she searched the room. Couples and groups laughing while she sat like a pimple on a pumpkin. Maybe she could delete stuff from her mobile phone that would keep her busy, but she knew it wouldn't look good. Abby thought the blind date would be fun when her sister first mentioned it but now that she was sitting here all alone, feeling like an idiot, she began to wonder. What if he didn't turn up? She wished she would have waited longer in her car in the carpark. She should've been late, made him wait. Her mother had always said, be prompt, it's respectful. It stuck with her for life.

The waiter showed a short, light ginger haired gentleman to the table dressed in a brown suit and pale green shirt open at the throat. Abby fumbled for words as he introduced himself before sitting down. 'I'm Kelvin, Kelvin Lightfoot. I wanted to arrive first. I'm so sorry. At the last minute, I got a call from a client and I had to fumble through some paperwork searching for what he wanted.' He showed a big open smile, his hand extended. 'What would you like to drink Abby?'

'Hi Kelvin.' She let go of his hand and looked up at the waiter. 'I'll have a strawberry daiquiri thanks.'

'I'll have a gold rush?'

'Thanks. I'll be right back.'

There was a pause before he spoke. 'I feel a little awkward

I've never been on a blind date before.' He shrugged his shoulders, grinning. 'Have you?'

'No, I never have.' Her eyes went to his cleft palate. It was off-putting, like his reddish cheeks and flour-coloured skin. His hair was clipped short showing his cauliflower ears. She wondered why he wouldn't want to find a way to hide them. Her mind raced, wondering why the hell she went through with this. She mustn't be rude he can't help how he was born.

'You look beautiful may I say' he said, open smile. 'I love your outfit, the colours suit you.'

'Thank you' she whispered, staring at his mouth again. It'd been a long time since Abby had received such complements. 'It's a lovely restaurant Kelvin. I've never been here before.'

'I brought my parents here for their fiftieth wedding anniversary a couple of years ago with my siblings. It's great food as well as stunning décor.' The waiter put the drinks down, told them about the specials then left the menu for them to peruse.

Abby was relieved she had something to look at instead of his cleft palate and big ears. Her father always said to look for something good in another person's appearance. He did have a lovely straight set of teeth, and a great open smile. 'Where do your parents live Kelvin?'

'They lived most of their married life in Coffs Harbour, but they have both passed away now. Father first, then Mother. I think Mum pined for him.'

'Sorry to hear that. My Mother and father have had a wonderful life travelling the world. My father was a Judge and during his holidays we wouldn't see them for dust. My brother and I went to our grandparents and they went off overseas. They've slowed down a bit after retirement though. They want for nothing really. They stayed in the same house all their married life until recently.' She laughed. 'I'm not sure how happy they are. I think my mother liked the social life that came with my father's job.'

'Well one never knows what goes on behind closed doors.' He took a sip of his drink, a slight chuckle. 'My parents drummed into us kids to travel while we were young and I've done just that. Have you got siblings Abby?'

'I've got an older brother but I have nothing to do with him. He lives in Germany.'

'Well, we all make choices. Have you been married Abby?'

'Yes and I have two children. Aaron is six and Penelope is four. Their father died three years ago, the horrible cancer. He was only twenty eight.'

'That would have been tough for you all. How are you handling things three years on?'

'We all have our days but we also know we have to move on.' She sipped her drink slowly and he did too. She could sense he had a kind Soul. At least he didn't talk about himself all the time, like most men she'd dated.

'Have you worked out your dinner order?'

'Yes, I'm having the barramundi' she said.

'Same.'

Kelvin called the waiter and placed their orders and at the same time selected a bottle of white wine. There was a short silence. She hated silence. Then he spoke. 'Where are you living Abby?'

'I live south of Cloverdale, a little place called Apple Grove and I live in Apple tree lane.' She laughed as she said it and he joined in too. 'It's my parent's house. I was born in Ireland and we all moved here as a family back in the early 90s. They bought a few acres and built the house and lived there all their married life until they made a sea change and moved to Adelaide. So they sold the house to me and moved away. Of course in Dad's line of work he had to travel a lot, but only within Australia. Mother tagged along.'

He nodded. 'I live about two hundred meters from here. I live in one of those high-rise unit blocks.' He pointed towards the water. My apartment is on the seventh floor with a spectacular view over town green and the Hastings River. I live there mainly because it is close to the airport.'

'How lovely would it be to wake up to that view every day?' The napkin was being mangled again. Put your hands on the table, grow up. She wondered what he did for a job. Will he ask her about her life?

'I can be here today and another City tomorrow with the work I do. I could be invited anywhere really. I love what I do, the life and the people.'

'What is it you do?'

'I'm a motivational speaker. I'm off to the USA next week then the UK before I finish the rounds with a talk in Auckland, NZ. I like to help and inspire which ultimately enriches people's lives.'

God, no wonder he can hold a conversation well, she thought. What the hell did she have in common with him? If she knew this beforehand she wouldn't have bothered to meet him. She shifted in her chair.

'What about you. What are you busy doing with your

life?' He leant in showing his wide smile and sparkling green eyes.

She placed her wine glass on the table. 'When I left school all I wanted to be was a doctor, but I ended up becoming a nurse. I've been nursing all my life and have worked at the private hospital in Port Macquarie for the last two years. I love it more every day.'

He looked into her eyes. 'It's a caring role but not an easy one. You'd see a lot of sadness. It takes a special person to cope with a job like that.' He shrugged, his eyes never leaving hers. 'I don't know whether I could do it. I admire you, I really do…'

She fiddled with the napkin, butted in. 'It's one of those things that you either love or not. A lot of nurses don't last.' Thank goodness the meals have arrived. The waiter set them down, a plate of vegetables alongside.

'Enjoy' he said, smiling.

The barramundi melted in her mouth and the fresh vegetables were just what she needed. She worked long hours and didn't always feel like cooking wholesome meals when she arrived home. She often felt guilty throwing a pizza in the oven when she came home tired, or sometimes a take-away. Kelvin chatted away between mouthfuls. He had a great sense of humour. He seemed to enjoy every moment of his life with confidence plus. He poured her a second glass of wine. When he placed his cutlery across his plate, he wiped his mouth with the serviette, and leant back into the chair. 'Well one thing's for sure, the food is excellent here. What do you think Abby?'

'The barramundi was worth waiting for. Yes, I would

come back here again.' She pushed her plate aside, dabbing her lips with the serviette.

'Do you think you could fit in desserts later?'

'No thank you.' She was silent, staring into her glass. She had to admit he had class, manners, polished voice, well educated.

He leant across and touched her hand. 'How about a coffee or liquor…or maybe a dance?' he smiled a cheeky smile.

She looked across at the dance floor. 'Perhaps a bit later, I thought I'd sip on my wine, and watch the couples dancing for a while.' She'd been watching the couples dancing cheek to cheek, soaking in the whole scene. The place was stylish something she hadn't been to since losing her husband. She'd been on a few dates since he died but they wanted her to change to suit their lifestyle, like far too casual. She had a certain lifestyle and she wouldn't bend to suit them. Mostly they talked about themselves and they never got to really know her.

She started to think about dancing. Would he want to dance cheek to cheek? She hoped not, it was too soon. He chatted easily with her telling about the places he's visited around the world.

'What about you Abby. Have you travelled much?'

'I did some travelling years ago. As a matter of fact I went backpacking in my younger days and I nursed in the UK and Scotland for a few years. It was a lovely experience at the time but that was then and this is now.' She leant forward, showing a smile, more at ease now. She wondered if it was the wine. 'I am a mother now and of course until they grow up I will need to stay put. Of course, finances play a big role.'

He took her hand. 'Do you feel like that dance now?'

'Sure.'

He stood, took her hand and led her to the centre of the dance floor. The top of her head met his. They could have danced apart but he chose to hold her close, slow moves. He felt her breasts brushing against his chest. He bent down and smiled. 'Are you happy?'

'Yes, I am.' When the music stopped he waited for the next song to start. He was happy when she didn't drag him back to the table. As she placed her hand in his, a small tingle ran through him. He smiled down at her, pulled her in and out again, twirling around. The next song was a slow number. Abby's beautiful face turned him to jelly. Her sensual dark-pink coloured lips perfectly shaped, her sharp nose, her perfume sending him crazy. He wondered what she was thinking as he closed his eyes listening to her racing heartbeat.

It was a slow number again. He held her tight against him. He leant down and brushed his lips on hers, teasing. She kissed him back, her breathing quickening. When the music stopped he looked into her eyes. 'You're beautiful Abby and I love how you slow-dance.' She let go of him and wrapped her arms around her waist, as if she was cold. 'I think I'd better get on home.'

He led her back to the table. 'No coffee or Liquor?'

'No thanks Kelvin.'

'Perhaps you would like to come up to my apartment and have a drink before you head off home? Maybe look at the view.' She felt her cheeks flush, her stomach churning at the sight in front of her. Find something appealing about him.

There's got to be something. Yes, his smile and his personality. Abby felt close to him on the dance floor, head tucked into his chest, his face hidden.

'Not tonight' she said. 'Perhaps we can meet up another time.'

'Sure, I'd like that. Thanks for coming this evening. It was a joy to have your company. I'm not sure when I'm back in town but when I do arrive home, can I call you?'

'Yes. I would like that.' Kelvin walked her to her car in the parking lot and when she went to open the car door he pulled her in. She reached up and met his lips without saying a word. He kissed her hard and she responded.

'Are you sure you wouldn't like to see the town lights from my apartment. It's only a short walk away?' She smiled and opened the car door. 'Let's see how things go. I'm not one to rush into things. Tomorrow is a big day with the children's sports.'

He waved to her as she sped out of the parking lot. He'd dated lots of women over the years but they broke it off before anything got started. He liked Abby. She wasn't pushy and she didn't have an ego. He'd hold the black-haired, green eyed Irish girl in his heart until he returned. She was a stunning looker. Yes, he'd keep her in his heart.

CHAPTER 50

Lara & Brad

2018

After Lara reached orgasm with Brad one day when the kids were at her parent's house, she blurted it out. 'Brad, I slept with your mate, Alex.'

Brad stopped right there and flung himself to the side of the bed, head in his hands. There was silence in the room except for the ticking of the bedside clock. When he turned to look at her, his eyes had already watered. 'I don't believe you cheated on me Lara. How many other times have you done this? And with my mate Alex…whose idea was it?' He spoke as if she hadn't just shattered his whole world but she'd broken their wedding vows which they'd always claimed were sacred between the two of them.

Lara couldn't move. She wanted to hold him but how could she. Her body tensed. 'He got a room in a hotel in Port Macquarie. It happened to be the same day when he was meeting you for drinks. I'm sorry Brad.' She leant across and took his hand but he brushed it away. 'It was a one-off thing. I had to tell you because it's eating away at me.' She moved, sat next to him but he got up and left the room without saying a word.

He came back in later after showering. 'I told you I knew something was wrong. You were side-tracked all the time, not wanting me. Remember, I had that talk with you and you said you were worried about Gracie. You fucking lied to me. I'm heading out for the day. I need time to think.' He turned, face twisted. 'Are you still seeing him or planning on seeing him?'

'No, of course I'm not. It's why I had to tell you. I feel guilty for doing that to you. Brad, it was the first time I've cheated on you.'

He shrugged his shoulders. 'See you later.'

Lara lay back in the bed, tears forming. No matter the outcome, she'd let it out. She couldn't live with the deceit. Brad was her man, her everything. All thoughts of Alex had left her long ago. It was a silly thing she did and still finds it hard to fathom why. That was then, and this is now she kept saying to herself.

After extensive talks and promises, Lara and Brad got on with life as a family. They purchased a large motorhome and began taking small trips when he had days off from working in the mines. Lara loved all the adventures and the kids did too. She realised how precious life was and how important it was to live each day, as there is no telling what tomorrow holds. The Alex thing was hard to brush aside but she'd learnt a big lesson. She knew who truly loved her. Brad had rung Alex and had words, final words.

CHAPTER 51

Abby

2018

Lara picked up the phone on the first ring. It was Abby. 'I've just received the results from my father's tests.'

'Oh Abby, do you want to talk about it?'

'He has cancer, they found it too late. It has gone to his bones.'

Lara could hear the cracking in Abby's voice. 'Would you like me to visit, perhaps meet somewhere?'

'Yes please. I'm lost right now and my mother wants all the attention. I can't believe that woman. I don't think he's got long' Abby cried into the phone.

'Tell me where and when and I'll be there. It has to be after I lock up the boutique though, after five.'

'Can you pick me up? I'm a bit shaky and not sure if I want to risk driving. Besides, I might like to have a couple of drinks.' She let out a short forced laugh.

'I'll be there after I close. Try not to stress. We'll catch up then and you can get pissed if you want.' After closing the call, Lara thought of Abby. She's such a giving person, kind and she knew how close she was to her father.

At 5.30 pm they sat in the beer garden close to the open fire. Abby's red eyes were stark against her pale skin. 'You drink what you want and any amount you want. You can drown your sorrows Abby.'

'Thanks. Shall we start on wine?'

'You can have whatever you want. I'm driving so I will limit my drinking, but you, well, I'll take care of you.' She dug Abby in the ribs, grinning.

Abby pushed her hand across to touch Lara's. 'Thanks.'

'Can you believe this? I'm left with mother to take care of. She said she's not going to stay in the house in Adelaide when dad dies. She wants to come and stay in their old house with me. Can you believe her? We don't even get along. She's not the kid's best friend either.' She sighed.

'Let's take it one step at a time. Things can change. Right now, she's probably in shock, confused. She has to grieve, just like you. Everyone grieves differently, you know that. In a few weeks she might change her mind and stay in Adelaide. She has your sister there. Try not to get your knickers in a knot over it.'

'Anyway I have a flight tomorrow. Dad wants to come home here and see his old home and be admitted to the local hospital. He's spent many more years here than in Adelaide. I'll have to suss it out with the doctors. They have paid for a plot here in Cloverdale too.'

'I guess it depends on how bad he is whether they'll allow him to travel. It might take a while to get rid of your mother after.' Lara snorted.

'True. Who knows with her?' She leant in closer, whispering. 'I haven't told anyone, but I'm seeing this guy. His name is Kelvin. You are the first to know. He's nice enough, but a little hard on the eyes.'

Lara laughed. 'Bit of a dark horse eh!'

'Look…I shouldn't even say this but he has a cleft palate, ginger hair, fair skin and cauliflower ears.' She shrugged her shoulders. 'He's a hell of a nice guy and he treats me like a lady.'

'Well, if you like him what are you concerned about?'

'You're right. We always look at what others think. I've gotten used to his looks now but it was hard the first time I saw him.'

'Forget about how he looks, it's how he treats you that counts. What does this guy do for a living?'

'He travels around the globe helping others live better lives.'

'Really! That sounds interesting, but what exactly does that mean. Is he a doctor?'

Abby laughed. 'No, he's a motivational speaker. Anyway, he's overseas at the moment and he wants to see me when he gets back. I'm trying to make up my mind, or an excuse.'

'Abby. You work hard and you're bringing up two children. When do you find some happiness for yourself? You need to find enjoyment in your life, even if he just turns out to be a good friend.' She noticed Abby's mind was far away. 'Are you listening to me?'

'I am, and you're right. I think it's difficult when you have children because they all need to get along but I will never jeopardise my children's happiness because I want to be with a man.'

'You don't have to. Work with it. If you like him, work together.'

'Dad would like him.' She giggled. 'Perhaps not his looks…' She stared at her wine glass. *Why did she say that?*

'Abby.' Lara shook her head. 'Stop it?'

'Kelvin is one clever guy and he is not short of words. I know they'd get on. If I get the chance I'm going to tell Dad so he can die knowing I'm at least seeing a decent bloke.'

'He may get to meet Kelvin if he is transferred to Cloverdale. He may have a while yet with you and your mum.'

'True. Thanks for listening. It's good to run things by with a friend who won't mouth off.'

Lara patted her arm. 'Thanks for sharing with me. Mum's the word.' She put her finger to her lips.

'Listen, Gracie won't be going on this overseas trip and at the moment, I'm thinking I might not go either' said Abby.

Lara pulled back. 'Really! Well I suppose your life is a bit topsy-turvy at the moment with your father's health. I can relate Abby. Gee, everyone's opting out. As a matter of fact I'm not comfortable either, especially now being the one left to travel alone with Jayde. I don't get along with her and I don't like how she treated Gracie.'

Abby laughed. 'She might have to go on her own.' They raised their glasses. 'Here's to Jayde and her solo overseas trip.' They roared with laughter. 'I'm not announcing it yet as I might still go. I'll see how Dad is. Right now, my focus is on him.'

'It'd be funny though, she might be drinking her way through Europe on her own. You do know she's an alcoholic. And what's all this stuff about the guy at the bar.'

'Well she reckons she's been sleeping with him. We all know she'd lay on her back for anyone, male or female' said Abby.

'What! How do you know all this? Tell me more? I love a bit of gossip.' Lara pulled her chair in close to Abby.

'Ah ha! I met a girl she'd been bedding. And it was right alongside the girl's husband. Apparently she gets off on threesomes.'

'A fresh bit of gossip. Geez, what a shallow life we live' said Lara. They both screeched with laughter. 'Let's have another drink?'

CHAPTER 52

Gracie

2018

'Well, who's a spoilt girl then?' said nurse Sara, holding onto a small bunch of roses wrapped in a piece of alfoil. "Roses for love" the nurse read from the card.

'Who's it from?'

'I'd say a secret admirer.'

'They're beautiful. They're like the ones in my garden.' She sniffed them and the smell took her back to her little cottage. Gracie held the roses to her chest. Maybe she did have an admirer. She had so many flowers from her work colleagues and friends. The ward was surrounded by dozens of get well cards filled with beautiful messages. She realised how much she meant to people, except Booker.

'So do you know the names of these particular roses?' asked Sara.

'Oh yes, I certainly do.' She pointed. 'The white one is the Christmas rose, then this is the peach blossom, Rumba Rose and this gorgeous one is called Lady in Red.'

'Oh, so you do know your roses. Mind you, it could be a pack of lies for all I know.' Sara gave a wink.

'I don't think so.' She handed them to Sara, laughing. 'Both my mother and my granny had beds of roses and when I was a child they taught me all about the planting, pruning and their names. These particular ones are the winter roses.'

'They're so beautiful.'

Gracie flopped into the soft pillow. 'I wonder when I can go home.'

'The doctor will tell you when it's time. In the meantime I'll get a vase so you can admire this bunch.'

'I miss my little cottage.'

She felt exhausted after her gym work-out and headed for the shower. The physio's worked her hard but it did wonders. She looked in the mirror as she dried herself and tears rolled down her cheeks. She wondered how long it would take before the plastic surgeon agreed to begin work on her puckered face. She turned away, grief stricken.

She asked the nurse to put the "No visitors" sign on the door. She wasn't in any mood to be pleasant to anyone at the minute.

***

The following morning when she opened her eyes he was standing there with a red rose in his hand. 'Gracie, oh Gracie, I had no idea.' He rushed by her side and took hold of her warm hand.

She knew it was Booker, she recognised him straight away.

Her eyes lit up. 'Hello.' She breathed in his scent. 'Thank you for the rose. Are you the culprit for these too?' She pointed to the vase filled with the roses delivered the previous day.

'I'm guilty, yes.'

She sniffed at the single rose. 'Without my winter roses, the place would have no life. Are they plentiful at the moment?'

'I went and collected this one yesterday afternoon. They are pretty scarce but I will find you at least one of your roses from your garden every day. May I sit?' He tore his eyes away from her face. His heart went out to her. He wondered if she had been given a mirror.

'Yes, please do.' She pulled the covers up, hiding what she could of a deep scar on her chest. He wore a dark blue suit with a light grey shirt which he wore open at the neck. His dark brown hair was cut short, as if he'd just visited the barbers.

He pulled the chair close and held her hand. 'Is there anything you want?' He felt uneasy, she didn't seem like the same person lying there, marked face.

'I'm good.' She looked up at the crystal angel not knowing what to say. He seemed like a stranger, he was.

'I only found out a few days ago about your accident. I waited for you on that Saturday. Remember, the day we were going away for the weekend.'

She shook her head. 'Sorry, I don't remember. The doctor said I may get parts of my memory back in time. I didn't even remember you until a week ago. I woke up one morning and remembered your name.' She grabbed hold of the moist cloth and gently patted her forehead.

'Here, let me do that.' He took hold of the cloth and

dabbed at her face, then leant in and kissed her pink lips. 'I've missed you.'

She moved her hand across his unblemished skin stroking his cheeks. 'I don't remember much, but I had a flash this day. You took me on a date and we watched the sunset together. Then, one morning, I remembered your name, Booker.' She smiled as she said his name.

'Yes, I took you to dinner. We went to a beautiful restaurant called Zen, it was by a lake. Then through the week we went to dinner and a movie. Another night you cooked a meal for me at your house. Then after my Dad held his birthday party we were to go away for the weekend.' We'd arranged to meet by the town clock after your music students.'

She shook her head, tears in her eyes. 'I'm so sorry I don't remember any of that.'

"Don't be sorry, it's okay. I thought at the time that you'd changed your mind. I had no idea.' He brushed past her cheeks and whispered in her ear. 'Now that I've found you I won't let you go.' He knew his eyes were watering and he noticed hers were too. She opened her mouth in a small smile before looking out the window afraid of what he was thinking about all the work the doctors had done on her face. When she looked back he was smiling. 'Gracie, I will be here for you now. I'm so sorry this happened to you but we'll get through this together.' He squeezed her hand tight, like jig saw puzzle tight, determined. 'Finding you Gracie has changed my life. When you didn't show up I thought you didn't want anything to do with me, like you dumped me.' He laughed, his sky-blue eyes sparkling. 'You will find numerous messages on your mobile phone.'

'The police have told me that my phone is in a plastic bag at the station, smashed to pieces.'

'I'll go buy you another one.'

'No, Abby is doing that.'

'I've been helping feed your animals. Lara, Abby and I have a roster. I ran into them the other day at your cottage. I like to go visit most afternoons just to have some life around the place. That dog of yours certainly loves to play.'

She laughed. 'Cindy will drive you mad jumping up and down. She loves it if you throw sticks. I don't know where she gets all her energy from.'

'Well we have a bit of a play, then after, she demolishes a whole bowl of water.'

'I don't know what I would've done without Abby and Lara's help. They've been wonderful friends. And thanks to you too Booker. I'm so grateful.'

'Is there anything that I can get for you?'

'No thanks. My mother has come over from the UK and is looking after me. She gets me what I need.'

'Yes, the girls told me she was here.' He opened his mouth with a wide smile then leant in and kissed her on the lips, lingering, not wanting to leave.

Gracie pulled him in. She felt his hot breath on her neck. 'Thank you for finding me. And I'm sorry about not keeping our date.'

'Hey, it's okay. I've found you now and you can lean on me. I will help you get through this. There's always another time for Byron Bay.' He beamed with pleasure on finding his love.

'Thank you.' She searched his eyes, reached up and kissed him one more time.

'Now I have a class to run. I'll come by tomorrow morning. If you need anything at all, call me?' He wrote his mobile number on a scrap of paper he found in his coat pocket and left it on the bedside table. Their lips met. Soft kisses, just lingering.

When Gracie watched him walk through the door ready for work, she had a huge smile on her face. He found her and he would be there for her. She felt exhilarated for the first time in a long while. Only now could she move forward to the next chapter of her life. Booker found her and wanted to be part of her life. She stared at the hanging crystal angel and thought how lucky she was to find someone so tender and caring. *Booker.*

CHAPTER 53

2018

'So why so happy' asked Lara as she entered the hospital room, Jayde following. This was the first visit when Gracie was smiling, a genuine smile. Lara handed her a box of her favourite Lindt chocolates.

'Happy to be alive I guess' she said, accepting the gift.

'Well it's great to see a smile on your face. You're grinning like a Cheshire cat.'

'Sit?' she pointed to a couple of chairs in the corner of the room. 'Bring them over.'

Lara handed her the itinerary for their overseas trip. 'This is the finished itinerary. You will be there in Spirit Gracie. Every time we see or do something on this trip we will remember you. I'm sorry it's turned out this way.' She leant forward and hugged her.

'Everything happens for a reason. I'm obviously not meant to go.' Jayde was busy on her mobile phone. She sat in the corner of the room. Gracie wondered why she came as they had nothing at all in common.

'That's the girl. As I've said, there will be another time.' She still hadn't made up her mind whether she'd go or not.

A few things she was considering. Abby being one of them, and if she opted out then so would she. There is no way she could travel alone with Jayde Carlson.

Lara pulled her chair in closer to Gracie's chair. 'I've met Booker. What a gorgeous man. He is so obliging. We have a roster at your house to feed the animals. Don't let you-know-who know.' She flicked her head back towards Jayde.

'He is so loving and caring with me. I'll tell you all about him once we are on our own.' Lara and Gracie were close friends and now she could share her news. She gave Lara a huge smile. 'I'm so happy he found me again, just thinking about him brings a smile to my face.'

'Well you just hang onto him.' She squeezed Gracie's hand. 'Your face is coming along nicely.'

'You reckon.'

Lara pulled back when she saw Jayde walking towards them dragging her chair close to Gracie. 'Now that you are alive and well and in a better mood I have some exciting news to share with you.' Gracie looked her square in the eyes, uninterested. She'd tolerated her that's all. She gathered the feelings were mutual. 'Go on?' said Gracie, reaching for her glass of water.

Jayde barged straight in bragging about her new boyfriend. 'Remember the hot guy at the bar in the hotel. Well, I've been having it off with him.' Gracie let out a strange sound. 'You know the one at the bar on Friday nights, the handsome one. You must remember him? His name is Booker. Even his name turns me on. I call him Booker, the looker. That's not all. He's a good lover too.' She laughed, throwing her head back. 'We wear each other out.' She ran her fingertips over her body, indicating her shape. And he has a...'

Lara cut in. 'That's enough. We don't want to hear all the details.'

Jayde put the phone in front of Gracie's face. A photo of Booker and Jayde looking all happy, heads together, smiling faces. 'Saturday we are going off to "Lovers Hide-away" for a dirty weekend.' She flicked her hair back, posing. 'It is this amazing vineyard and I believe, has a massive waterbed, like wall to wall.'

Gracie felt her face burn, her heart race. She dropped the glass, contents spilling, struggling to get her next breath. 'Get out! Get out!' She grabbed the buzzer and pressed it more than once. 'Get out, I said.'

Lara noticed that Gracie was clearly hyperventilating. 'Oh Gracie... calm down love?'

The nurse ran in. 'What's going on in here. Gracie, calm down?'

'I want her to leave' she yelled, pointing to Jayde. 'Get out?'

The nurse shushed, pushing Jayde out the door, closing it behind her. 'What's brought this on?'

'Help me. Please help me.' Her body shook her cries loud. She got out of the chair, strutted around the room. 'No, oh no, this can't be true. Nurse, help me?'

'Gracie, what's wrong?'

Eyes welling up, she looked to Lara. 'Oh Lara, this can't be true.'

Hours later when Gracie had calmed down she gave strict instructions to the staff that under no circumstances were

Booker Ray Harrington or Jayde Carlson to enter her private room. This was something else she had to get over now. How much more could she take. To finally remember him, see him in the flesh, touch him, kisses. On hearing this news about Jayde and Booker together, completely threw Gracie. It was all proving too much. She had to shut it out of her mind and concentrate on getting well. How can she trust this man again? The rest of the day, a scowl replaced her smiling face. *I need to speak with my psychiatrist.*

CHAPTER 54

Booker

2018

Over the phone, Booker listened. 'She's upset, and that's understandable. Right now, she told me she wants nothing to do with you' said Lara.

'Of course, I understand entirely. I just want a chance to explain. It's not what it seems. Jayde's a good-time girl and I was looking for a good time. It was bloody stupid of me. Gracie didn't turn up for our weekend away and I thought she'd dumped me. I couldn't contact her and I knew she'd taken a week's leave from work so I assumed she got cold feet and took off somewhere on her own.'

'She told Gracie that you were both going away for the weekend to a lover's hide-away.'

'Now she's dreaming. I'm not seeing the slut anymore. Please tell Gracie. I have nothing more to do with Jayde.' He wiped his brow.

'I'll have a chat with her again and see what she has to say. Gracie's a great person and at present she has a lot on her mind with all of her health issues. I can't even begin to imagine what she's thinking about her scarred face and what the end results might be. She doesn't need any extra stress at the moment Booker.'

'Lara thanks, I appreciate your help, and the last thing I want is for Gracie to be upset.'

'Look Booker, Gracie has had a lot of stuff going on over the last ten years and since she's been back here in Cloverdale, she's been a lot better. She doesn't need another episode of drama in her life. I'll do what I can but I don't like your chances.' She laughed. 'Gracie can be stubborn…or should I say, she likes to have things her way. You haven't seen that side of her yet, have you?'

He sighed. 'No, I haven't.'

She grinned although he couldn't see her. 'I'll tell you one thing Booker. She did tell me she really liked you.'

Booker went to the hospital. He asked the receptionist to have the rose from Gracie's garden delivered to her room. The rose was a beautiful purple colour with a cream stamin. The name of the rose was Maggie May. On the card he wrote: "Listen to your heart, it knows." He walked back out into the street into the rain, his emotions running high.

Early morning the following day, Lara called by and spoke with Gracie about Booker. 'He's a good man so why not give him a chance. You know what Jayde is like. She probably pushed herself on him, she's a tart. Sometimes if it's pushed in their face, well…men are weak.'

Gracie stared at her friend as if to say "are you mad?" She sipped on her water.

'I'm just saying.'

'Lara, I'm not interested. If a man's that weak I don't want him. Given half the chance, he'd do it again. I'm not going down that path.'

'You have to do what you're comfortable with. Hey, I'd like a coffee before work, do you want to climb out of bed and join me?'

'Great, it'll do me good.'

Having coffee together, they sat looking out at the people coming and going. That's when she saw him, Booker. Her heart fluttered for a minute, face flushed. A security guard rushed up to him stopping him in his tracks. He held a red rose, and a box of chocolates. She nudged Lara.

'What's happening?' Lara asked.

'I asked him to stop visiting me. I don't want anything to do with him. I don't want his visits or his gifts. I wrote him a note and asked the guard to hand it to him.'

'Yes, I saw him hand Booker the envelope. What did you say?'

Gracie sighed. 'I told him to stop trespassing at my house and to not visit the hospital or deliver any more gifts. I said I didn't want to see him. Just stay away from me I wrote. I told him how disgusted I was about him and the bitch Jayde together.' She hated to see his forlorn face after the guard walked away. He stood there staring at the envelope in one hand, gifts in the other. When he turned to walk away, Gracie felt a lump in her throat.

CHAPTER 55

2018

Booker downed another beer wondering what the hell had happened. He should've stayed away from Jayde Carlson in the first place. She was a play thing, nothing else and he knew that from the minute he met her. Blokes can tell who's giving out, who's hungry. A foul taste found its way up to his throat, he pushed it back down. He gripped his chest. It felt like a steamroller was crossing over it. He'd be just lucky enough to have a heart attack, that's how it felt right now.

He thought about his life and how it was slipping through his fingers. Who would he become next year, in five years? Maybe his son would have moved on and he'd be on his own. Would he be with Gracie? He can't think straight, mind confused. He rubbed his eyes with the ball of his fists.

Will he try visiting Gracie again? The nurses stopped him last time, rushing down the corridor forbidding him from entering the room then yesterday the security guard. If he went to the hospital in the evening, different staff, maybe then he might be lucky. He was, perhaps, hoping Gracie would forgive him and call him. He drained his beer and lit another cigarette. He would give up smoking if Gracie took him back. He could tell she didn't like the smell of cigarettes on his breath, and how she brushed the smoke away when he lit one.

He slapped his head, his chest tight with anxiety. He felt mentally and physically shattered, this whole bloody thing smashing his heart into tiny pieces. He wiped the sweat from his brow with the bottom of his T-shirt. He'd have to think of a way to get to see Gracie. Maybe he could talk to Lara again and see if she could convince her. Now he's clutching at straws. His mouth hardened and he immediately reached for a mouthful of beer, another cigarette.

He polished off another bottle. Trembling, he sprang to his feet, the overflowing ashtray smashing to the floor. A rush of anger surfaced. He clenched his fist and put a hole in the kitchen wall. He drank himself silly, stupid thoughts filling his mind. He'd found the right girl and he stuffed it up, just like he'd done in the past.

He was flat on his back, his belly full of booze. He heard his mobile phone ringing in the distance. Where the hell was his phone? Stuff the phone. At the sound of the screeching brakes from the train rattling through the town, he fell into a deep sleep. Soon his snoring would wake the dead.

The following morning after a strong black coffee he found his phone. Numerous suggestive text messages from Jayde. Why not, he thought. Gracie has given up on any resolution. He ran his hands through his hair. Yes, why not, he could go and have a bit of fun. It didn't take him long to arrive on her doorstep. She was having a lazy Sunday thinking about going down the pub at opening time. She perked up when he came through the front door. 'Come in?' Dressed in next to nothing she pulled him through the doorway. Within minutes she set out the sex tools on the end of the bed. 'It's your choice' she said. Fully naked, she writhed on the bed waiting. He shrugged his shoulders, not sure. 'How about I handcuff you to the bed and I choose some of these tantalises.'

'I'm here to enjoy' he said, grabbing hold of her breasts, kissing them hard, anger building within thinking about Gracie. Booker drove home more than satisfied, but Gracie was still on his mind. James and his mother pulled into the driveway behind him.

CHAPTER 56

Kelvin & Abby

2018

It was three weeks later when Kelvin arrived back in Australia. He called Abby and asked her out to dinner. She'd said yes but was confused as to why she said that. While he was away she had almost made up her mind not to see him again. He sounded so happy on the phone that she said yes straight away. She had discussed his looks with her sister over the phone but her sister didn't agree with the way Abby was talking and thinking. 'Looks aren't everything. It is how someone treats you that counts.' When Abby closed the call she closed her eyes, hung her head.

Over the weeks following, Abby was warming to Kelvin. He was charming and funny. He took her for walks along the Hastings River in Port Macquarie of an evening after dinner. They drove into the country stopping off to have lunch at quaint cafes. They laughed together and at times cried together watching a movie. She saw another side to him, his sensitive side. She liked that in a man. It was the little things that showed her how much he cared. When he spoke of his love for her, he said it with real conviction.

It was a Saturday evening when Kelvin knocked on her door holding a bunch of flowers and a bottle of wine. 'You look stunning' he said, bright faced. He kissed her on the cheek. 'Are we all ready to go?'

'I'll set the flowers in a vase first. Come sit down.' As he stepped inside, a small child rushed right up to him.

'What's your name?' She stood, swinging her body from side to side.

'My name is Kelvin. And what is yours?'

'Nelope.'

'Hello Nelope. I like your pretty dress.'

'Mummy bought it from a big shop.'

'Well, good taste, mummy' he said, eyeing Abby. 'And who is this?'

'Aaron. I'm six and Penelope is four.' He stuck his hand out to meet Kelvin's.

'How about on Sunday afternoon we all go to a nice café for lunch then after we will find a park?'

'Yea, can we please mummy?' yelled Penelope. Abby was checking her diary on her phone. 'After church, yes, we can do that.'

'Hello' said a small voice. 'I'm Heather, the babysitter.'

'I'm not a baby' said Aaron.

'No you're not…maybe a child sitter then.' Heather ruffled his hair, laughing.

Kelvin looked around the living room admiring some of the art pieces on the wall. He strained to see the title of the book sitting on the coffee table. "Shaeli of Purple Leaf" by R. L. Aiken.

Abby spotted him. 'Do you like reading?'

'I do. This looks interesting.' He held it in his hands reading the back.

'I'm really getting into it. I'm over half way now. It's the first of a trilogy.' She came and stood by him. 'A local author wrote it and I've always been one to support local writers.'

'I agree. Let me know once you've finished. I might like to borrow it.'

'Okay I will. I see that you also love art' she said.

'I do. I can take you to some wonderful galleries. It is one of my passions.'

'I do art too' said Aaron.

'Do you want to show me?' Aaron rushed off down the hallway.

'How did your latest overseas seminar go?' Abby asked.

'It was amazing. I've got more overseas bookings coming up in three months. It'd be lovely if you could come with me for part of the time. I know you keep telling me you have to work, but surely you could get some holidays.' He moved in close and took hold of her. 'I really miss you when I'm away. I've thought of you a lot lately.' He kissed her, lingered. He pulled away then pecked the top of her nose.

'Yukky' a little voice said from behind the couch. They laughed. Now that the flowers were all standing tall in the crystal vase Abby decided it was time to leave for the restaurant. 'Are you ready?'

'Not before I see Aaron's art.' He squeezed her hand.

'Oh, okay. Aaron' she called out. 'Have you got your art to show Kelvin? We've got to get going?'

When Aaron appeared, Kelvin held the pieces up high. 'I think we have a budding artist in the making. It's wonderful. Maybe next time I'll have a look at more of your work. I love the vibrant colours. Good work buddy.' He patted him on the head. 'I'll see you Sunday.' He shook his hand and waved to Penelope.

'Okay, you both know the rules, behave for Heather. Your bed's all made up Heather, no need to wait up.'

'Thanks. I have a good book. I'll read in my room.'

'Goodnight kids' she called out to deaf ears.

***

'I've not been to this restaurant before but it was recommended to me by one of my friends. I want this night to be memorable. They pulled up outside the bleached-coloured stone building, the climbing vines covering the front walls. He took her hand and led her along the short path. 'It's a winery.'

She stopped, looked at the sign and smiled. She reached up and kissed him on the cheek. 'It's called "Rambling Vines." I love it already.' They walked up the few stairs onto the porch, people chatting away, glasses clinking. 'Oh, this is so beautiful. Look at all the twinkling lights.'

'Your name?' said the tall dark-haired jovial waitress. 'Kelvin' he said. She wore a crisp white uniform and a green-patterned apron. 'This is your table. Someone will come and tend to you shortly. Your champagne is on ice.' Kelvin pulled the chair out for Abby to be seated.

'This is so romantic' said Abby searching the room. She touched the simple white china with the green vine emblem on the side. On the crisp white tablecloth sat pink rose petals scattered here and there. 'Kelvin, look. All the walls are covered with off-white wallpaper with a hint of small green vines scattered here and there. Wow! How clean and fresh. The green and white with pink rose petals. I have to tell you something amazing.'

He leant in, grinning. 'Go ahead, I'm all ears.'

'When I went overseas a few years ago I went to this Hungarian manufacturing company. It's in a place called Herend near the city of Veszprem. They specialise in luxury hand painted and gilded porcelain. I fell in love with one of the patterns. It's called the Habsburg Dynasty. These colours remind me of it. I have quite a selection of pieces now. The colours are white, green, with pink roses. I must show you sometime, it's in my glass cabinet. I use pieces from time to time, but I'm extra careful of course. I buy pieces to add to the collection from Hardy brothers in Sydney, they stock the porcelain china in Australia.'

Kelvin wanted to hear everything Abby had to say. 'It sounds interesting. Yes, I must see it, perhaps when I drop you back home later.'

'Yes, but Kelvin, this is the best part. They held a Herend High Tea in Budapest while I was there. I had to book in of course. I stayed about ninety minutes savouring it all. The most beautiful china I drank tea from accompanied with tiny sandwiches, cakes, and tartlets. It was certainly a most enjoyable experience. I had ninety minutes of bliss, being waited on. I thrive on different experiences, how about you?'

'Well I do too. I don't like any part of my life to be boring. I'd love to take you and the children on adventures sometime.'

'Thank you Kelvin.' She leant across the small table and put her hand on his.

'I wanted something special for you tonight. After being away so much, I wanted tonight to be different, something you will remember. I believe they grow the pink roses all year round in the hothouse in the back area somewhere.'

'Oh, I won't forget this place. It is beautiful.' The scent of the roses filled the air. Kelvin popped the cork on the champagne and poured it into the two waiting glasses. 'Here's to our night together.'

Abby stared into the open fire in the corner of the room, sipping the champagne. French doors led out onto the porch facing an arbour of pink climbing roses, twinkling lights nestled in the trees behind. 'This place is stunning.'

Abby smiled as she looked around at the copper antique lights set into the wall. She was thinking about the two of them, all the times they had spent together and their similar interests, tastes, and all the laughing they did. He had so many funny stories to tell. There is not much laughter in her job at the hospital.

'Do you remember me telling you about Gracie who had that terrible car accident?'

'Yes, I do. How is she?'

'She's coming along nicely and soon she may be able to come home. She lives in a cottage called *Rose Cottage*.'

'Oh, where's that?'

'It's approximately thirty minutes west of Cloverdale. It's so quaint. So roses I get to see a lot of and they are my favourite flower. Lara and I have a roster set up to go and feed her animals for her while she's in hospital.'

'That's great. She'll need all the help she can get. And about the roses, I don't think you'd find a woman that doesn't love them.' He took hold of her hand and kissed it. 'In spring, when they are in bloom, I will make sure to bring you roses.'

The Beef with Shallots and Grenaille Potatoes she ordered for her main meal satisfied her and the French pastry for desert with vanilla cream and fresh strawberries was delicious. She scraped the plate clean. 'That was to die for.'

He laid his hand on hers. 'I do hope this has been an experience you won't forget. I'd like there to be many more.'

'It has been an extraordinary evening. Thank you so much. I'd love to join you again, perhaps try different places. We must come to an arrangement about the bill. I don't want you paying every time.'

He put his finger to his lips. 'Shush. Abby, I've got something to say to you.'

She faced him eager to listen. 'Sure, spin away?'

He took hold of her hand and knelt down on one knee. He pulled out a box from his top left pocket and opened it. 'Will you marry me?' She put her hands over her mouth, gasping. 'Oh Kelvin, that is beautiful but I will need time to think it over.' When she looked around the room after hearing laughter, the staff and customers began to clap.

He stood, leant into her and kissed her on the lips. 'I understand, perhaps it's too soon. I will keep the ring here in the box and hopefully one day you will say yes. There is no pressure Abby. I know though that you are the one I want in my life.'

'Did she say yes?' someone yelled out. Kelvin raised his thumbs. Thunderous applause and happy cheers could be heard throughout the restaurant. 'Congratulations' people called to them. The clapping went on, laughter, people raising their glasses. Kelvin smiled back before he sat down. 'I'll wait Abby' he whispered. 'I know I love you.'

'You know I love you too but this has caught me by surprise. Will you give me a little time to think about it? See how the children are with you on Sunday at the park. I want my children to be happy.'

He looked into her eyes. 'Of course I'll give you time. And yes, a good idea for Sunday. The children are only young and I don't see a problem with them settling in to a change. It'd be good for them to have a father figure. Right now though, how about we drink our liquor and maybe order a coffee?'

'I'll be in that.'

When Kelvin paid the bill he was handed a card, a celebratory card for their first visit to "Rambling Vines." The card had a white background, pink roses and the emerald green vine with both of their names inside.

'How special' Abby said, as Kelvin handed her the card to keep.

He walked Abby to her front door just after 11 pm. When he went to kiss her goodnight, she took hold of his hand and led him inside. 'Remember, I want to show you the porcelain china.'

'Of course, I forgot.'

She kicked off her high heel shoes, reached up and kissed him. 'Perhaps in the morning light we can take a good look.' She kissed him once more. When she left his lips she took hold of his hand and led him to the bedroom.

CHAPTER 57

Megan Lawson

1987

In 1981, before Megan Banner went touring to the UK with the Sydney symphony orchestra, she was dating William Arthur Richards. He played the Cello and taught music students privately in his studio in the suburb of Ryde, Sydney, NSW. It's where the two met, at the Sydney conservatorium of music. Megan broke it off with him after the two lovers had a tiff and told him she'd assess the situation while away in Europe and see where the relationship might go once she came back home to Sydney.

William wasn't happy. He loved her and reckoned they could sort it all out before she went away, but in an English pub in London she met and fell in love with Harold Jack Lawson, who had a degree in criminology and worked for a large law firm in Sussex, England.

In June, 1987, after Megan had been married to Harold for six years, he was invited by his old university mates to a special event in London. He didn't discuss it with her at all, he just came home and told her he'd purchased his plane ticket and he'd be away for two weeks.

She was livered but it gave her the chance to make contact with William. She'd thought of him often over the years and remembered how devastated he was when she told him over the phone of her new love and her up and coming marriage to him. Back then, William's response was not what she was expecting. The first time in all the years she'd known him was the only time she'd witnessed the volcano that raged inside him. His behaviour left a sour taste in her mouth so she never contacted him again.

A few days after Harold left for London, she found his number on the internet and called him. The conversation between the two for the first few minutes was stilted. He told her he'd lost his wife only eight months prior to a rare disease and he was still struggling to cope with her death.

'I have thought of you often' she said. 'I know it was a terrible thing I did. I wanted to say how sorry I was but last time I tried to explain, you went into a rage.'

'Firstly, thanks, I appreciate the call.' He cleared his throat. 'Yes and when I got off the phone that day, I didn't feel good about how I spoke to you either, so my turn to apologise.'

'Thanks William. My husband, Harold, has gone overseas for a couple of weeks and I thought it'd be a good time to make contact with you.'

'Thanks for doing that.' He told her about his sick wife, Pamela, and how he hadn't put paint to canvas since her diagnosis.

'I've noticed you've had some good write-ups over the last five years. Your art exhibitions seemed to have drawn a good crowd. I think you've done well William, I'm proud of you. I love your work but you've changed your style a lot I see.'

'Yes, I guess it's what happens in life. Hopefully we all change our likes over a lifetime. It's called growth.' He laughed. 'I'm not painting nudes anymore. I'm more into abstract now and it's been full-on. I know I'll get back into it down the track.'

'Well I've kept a check on your work over the years and every piece of your work I've seen, I've loved. Of course I've loved some more than others.' She let out a laugh. 'What did you ever do with my nude portrait?'

He chuckled. 'I still have it. I will never sell it because it reminds me of our time together. I'll bet you are still as beautiful Megs.'

'Gosh, no one has called me Megs in all these years. You're the only one.'

'Are you still living in Cloverdale?'

'Never left.'

'How would you like to catch up, like face to face? I'm happy to fly up to Port Macquarie and meet with you. Maybe we could have lunch and I could get a flight back the same day. I'd like that.'

'O-kay' she drew out the word. 'I guess there's no harm in that.'

'Can I get back to you with a date? I'm snowed under this week helping one of the charities but next week I'm free.'

'I'd prefer if I called you. You see, I live with my mother-in-law.'

'Oh. Then okay, you do that. I'll look forward to having a good chat, and see if you've changed any.'

'Same here, talk to you soon.' She placed the receiver in the cradle and went through to the kitchen to make her morning cup of coffee. At morning tea she told her Mother-in-law, Maud, that she was catching up with a girlfriend for the day who was holidaying in Port Macquarie. It was a little white lie, but she knew that blood was thicker than water.

That night, as she attempted to get to sleep, her imagination ran riot. She wondered what he looked like. It'd been six years and she hadn't changed much in that time so she guessed he hadn't either.

Her knees went to jelly when she saw William hurrying from the plane. He rushed to her side and held her tight, longer than necessary, laughing and hugging. Six years had changed nothing, his sparkling green eyes, hair as black as the ace of spades, expansive smile. Time stood still for Megan and William. 'I'm shaking' he said.

'I am too.'

She drove to a restaurant by the Hastings River and they ate, drank and talked. Megan revealed to William that it was a big mistake to marry Harold Lawson. 'I had made my vows and made a promise to stick it out.' William was aghast at hearing this. Over the years he assumed she'd been happy. 'You don't really know someone until you live with them' she said. 'That's an old saying from my parents.' She let out a small laugh.

Having coffee after lunch when he touched her arm, an electric shock went through her whole body. She still had love for him, a love tender and sweet, like she had before Harold.

'Megs, what just happened? That touch sent a shiver down my spine.' He rubbed the back of his neck. 'Whoa!'

'It happened to me too.'

He took her jewel-encrusted hand and kissed it. 'You haven't changed to look at and nor have my feelings. It's just like old times. He gazed into her green eyes. 'I'd love to spend some time with you Megs.'

She figured time wasn't just having coffee and a meal. 'I can't William. I couldn't do that to Harold.'

'Megs, blind Freddie can tell that you are not happy in this relationship with him. Why have you stayed on? From what you've told me already, you have no life of your own. It seems to me that he's a control freak and a bully. All the years you travelled with the orchestra you were bright, funny and always laughing. What has happened to that girl?' He rested his hand on hers. 'Let me book us into a great room with a view and we can spend the afternoon there. Just the two of us like it was before you went away. My flight leaves at seven.'

Her eyes filled up.

'Come here?' He pulled her in and she rested her head in the crook of his neck. 'How would you like a strong drink?'

She nodded. 'I know I'm being silly. It's nice to see you again and we've slotted in where we left off, as if we'd never parted.'

He lifted her chin with his forefinger. 'It was a stupid argument that broke us up. I missed you for a long time after that Megs. Then twelve months later I met Pamela at a neighbour's BBQ.'

She lifted her glass and took a sip before she spoke. 'I have to stay with him William. I can stay and work on our marriage.' She looked at her hands in her lap. 'I'll just try harder.'

'Let's have that strong drink and then I want to make love to you all afternoon. Or if we want, we can spend the evening together. I can go home tomorrow. I will take you to a beautiful restaurant for dinner and then you can spend the night with me. How does that sound?'

'Of course you know I can't, as tempting as it seems. I couldn't do that to Harold.' She looked into his eyes. 'Look, we had some great times and now my life is different. I'm sorry if I hurt you before I left for overseas. I was confused at the time too. Also, I think you know how stubborn I can be.'

'I've been with you long enough to know you, yes, stubborn you are.' He pulled her in and hugged her.

The music in the background brought back memories of when she was a child. Simon & Garfunkel singing "Bridge over troubled waters." She tapped her thigh to the beat. She smiled thinking about those days with her school friends. They all used to sing in the playground. A group of four one day imagining they'd be in a band. Well that went nowhere.

Megan added more about her life since marrying Harold. Like the years she'd spent alone while he attended the courts in Sydney, arriving home late of an evening from drinking with his colleagues. The struggle she had running the property, the staff. Keeping the crops alive, droughts, raging fires, the beatings, she told it all.

William's face reddened, fidgeting in his seat. 'Why are you staying Megs? You *are* free to go. There are no children in this marriage to worry about.'

'I made a vow. I married Harold for better or worse.'

'Oh for God's sake Megs…you've got to ask yourself a question. And you need to be honest about it. Ask yourself why you are still with this controlling man and do you want to be with him the rest of your life?'

The question shocked her. She shuddered when he said it. Of course she knew the answer. She shrugged her shoulders. 'When you and I broke up I had no ties. I was touring the UK with the orchestra when I met up with Harold. At the time, I thought I loved him. We travelled around Europe for three months, it was a wonderful time. We did things together that I wouldn't have done on my own. He took the reins. I didn't have to worry about anything.'

William raised his voice. 'You were on holidays for God's sake. It's always different on holidays. And isn't that a good sign, he took control of everything *and* you.'

'Yes, I know that now.' She touched his arm. 'I got caught up with everything too fast and next thing I knew I was looking after a property and he was pressuring me to fall pregnant. The fact is he's never around at the right time for me to fall pregnant. I did miscarry a few times.'

'Do you want his child?' He moved his chair close to her.

'Of course, I want to have a baby, yes.' She rested her head on his shoulder. 'I think I'll have another one of those.' She pointed to her glass.

William signalled the waiter and indicated two more of the same.

Megan wanted comfort and who would show it better than William. They were both going through different types of pain right now. She thought about sleeping with him while Harold was enjoying himself overseas. Harold could be doing the same, who would know. She never knows what he does on his long trips away to Sydney.

She sipped on her drink, staring out at the water. 'It's such a pretty spot here William. I used to meet up with friends now and again, but then it got busy on the farm with so many things to do and before I knew it, my friends had dropped away.'

'At times our life takes many different turns. People that were once close to us at some stage are now long gone.' He patted her arm. 'That's life, my love. Some people come into our lives just for a season.'

'Why not' she said, slurred speech. 'What harm could… come out of it.' She looked at him, unfocused eyes. 'I've… changed my mind.'

'Changed your mind on what?'

'I'd like to…spend the night with you.' She slurred her words.

'Megs…did I hear you right?'

She nodded.

'We'd better find that hotel room before you change your mind. To be honest Megs, I've missed the closeness, the tenderness that you and I had. Pamela was a good woman but I never did have that same feeling with her as I did with you. Pamela and I had a different sort of love, more like a close loving friendship.'

'I don't want to feel…guilty. I want to walk out of this restaurant and be with you without…hanging on to any guilt. We… both want this, don't we?'

'Before we go, I'm ordering you a strong black coffee. Yes,

we both do want this.' He put his arm around her. It took another thirty minutes before the coffee helped Megan.

'Okay, let's not hang around. I'm ready.' He took hold of her hand and helped her up from the chair. He paid the bill and they headed for the car. 'I know a nice flash hotel. We can do room service if you like, that way we can spend more time together. What do you say?'

'I'm in your hands…William Arthur…Richards.' She tripped and he caught her before she fell. They both giggled as they found their way to the car. 'I think you'd better drive William Richards?'

'I think I need to stop off at a chemist first.' He looked across at her and winked.

***

After showering and opening a bottle of champagne, it was more than an urge to carry her to bed and have his way, he needed her and he could sense too that she needed him. On the king-size bed, his kiss was tender, then deepened, becoming hungry, demanding. William and Megan's bodies hungered for each other. Today was the first day she felt loved and wanted in the last six years since she'd been with Harold. William showed Megan how much he loved and wanted her in the king-size bed in the hotel room overlooking the Hastings River in Port Macquarie, NSW. Megan laid there, satisfied look in anticipation for what was to follow.

'I realise I still love you Megs.'

She looked into his eyes. 'We do have a wonderful

connection. Lying here reflecting, I wish you were my husband, not Harold.' He could see tears beginning to well up in her eyes. 'We can change that' he said, gently massaging her breasts. 'I'm free.'

'I can't do that to him. Since I'm staying the night, I will step outside and phone my mother-in-law. I'll tell her I'm staying the night with my friend.'

'Ooh!' He opened his mouth in a circle. 'Well, it is true isn't it?' She gave him a wink, he closed his mouth. He waited, thinking. What a match they'd make but he didn't hold hope for her to leave her abusive husband. Perhaps another time, she now had a comparison.

In the morning, Megan stood on the balcony in the hotel gown waiting for the sun to rise. William came up behind, wrapping his arms around her tiny waist. 'A beautiful lady deserves to see the sunrise this morning. Did you sleep well?'

'Like a baby.'

'I woke once during the night and spooned into you but you didn't stir.'

'Really! Once I'm asleep nothing wakes me.' She felt at ease with him and didn't want him to let her go.

'Will you stay another night with me Megs?'

'I can't think of a reason not to.' They embraced. 'I think we better buy something to wear. I only have what I've got on.'

'What do you mean, you've got nothing on.' He pulled the gown open, staring. 'Shall we have a shower and make love again before we shop?'

'It's exactly what I was thinking.'

After, they lay in each other's arms, like old times. 'Let's get dressed, go have some breakfast in the dining room and we'll go buy another set of clothes. How about we buy some bathers and go for a swim in the ocean?' Megan said.

'I'll be in that Megs. C'mon, let's go?'

After swimming, they sat skin to skin on the grass by the ocean, a light lunch, coffee. Megan stayed three nights in the Port Macquarie hotel with William. They had no need to leave the suite on the third night. He declared his love and wanted her to think about leaving Harold to have a more peaceful and happy life, perhaps be with the one she loved.

Something told her there would be hell to play if she confronted Harold about a separation. She knew in her heart that William was her choice, but she had married Harold Jack Lawson and that was that. She'd have to live with the consequences. Perhaps she could meet up with William once a month, but that wouldn't be fair on either of them.

He pulled her in, swayed with her a little. 'Can I at least keep in contact Megs?'

'I think that could be dangerous. I'll need to concentrate on my marriage and if we keep in touch, that won't help the situation. You know I love you and I know who I'd rather be with, but I have made a commitment…and he wants children.'

William hugged her tight, body shuddering, a wave of frustration sweeping over him. He pulled away, looked at her. 'It's not what I want Megs, but I'll let you go.'

The hollows in his cheeks seemed deeper, his skin pale. She was torn. She'd left him once and she was doing it again. She let her head fall onto his chest.

'I will find my own way to the airport. I can't bear to

say goodbye to you Megs.' He kissed the top of her head. 'Remember, I love you and if ever you need a friend, I'll always be there for you.' He turned and walked out the door not looking back.

Megan stayed a while in the hotel room gathering her thoughts. They had bonded yet once again. William and Harold were like chalk and cheese but her mother had drummed into Megan, "When you make a marriage commitment you stick till the end."

Harold came home from the UK all cheery and they carried on as husband and wife. He went at it, hammer and tongs and within no time she was pregnant. 'Didn't I tell you woman, lay on your back more often and it'd be sure to happen.' Sure she thought, if he was home more often it would've happened a long time ago. Harold was handing out the cigars to all his co-workers and friends. He was over the moon with joy.

CHAPTER 58

Abby & Lara

2018

Lara's phone buzzed. 'Hi' Abby, what's up?'
'I've made a decision. I'm opting out of the overseas trip.'

'Funny you say that. I've been thinking the same. I've been meaning to discuss it with you. It's not going to work with Jayde. I have no time for the bitch especially how she treated Gracie at the hospital. She is a trouble maker.'

'I *never* liked the way she treated Gracie. I was thinking, how about we wait for Gracie to get better and the three of us go together.'

'Fabulous idea and we can postpone, not actually cancel.'

'I'm with you on that. Wait till we tell Gracie.'

'Do you want to visit this afternoon then we can both tell her together.'

'Yes, let's do that. In the meantime, I'll phone Jayde. She can figure out what she's going to do, but seriously, she's not on my friends list anymore' said Lara.

Abby laughed. 'She's not even on my radar.'

CHAPTER 59

Gracie

2008

At her cousin Carmel's wedding, Gracie missed her brother Jack. She didn't get a good feeling about leaving him behind alone. He promised he'd re bandage the wound. The whole episode put a stale taste in her mouth. There was her father big-noting himself amongst the guests. He had a ponce now from the good life on booze and eating at the best restaurants while his mother became the tiny shell of herself back on the property, tending to the farm, the workers, chores, taking care of the homestead and family.

Gracie loved her mother, but she secretly wished she'd leave the marriage and start a life of her own. She wondered why she stayed, why she didn't go and find happiness somewhere else. She was a prisoner in her own home. Her father never took her anywhere to speak of, perhaps a family gathering, but to nowhere posh, like he went in his job as a lawyer. He had another life away from the land, a life of luxury something her mother would never know these days.

She moved out onto the large patio where others were

gathered in groups, laughing, chatting, and hugging the open fire. Dizziness overtook her, blurry eyes. She tried to focus on the mountains in the background, the setting sun. Jack's face appeared before her. Something was wrong. *Jack, Jack, connect with me. What's wrong?* She flicked her phone open and pressed the numbers. Message bank. 'Jack, call me?' she yelled into the phone. Maybe he'd taken himself to the hospital, she hoped so. It was only early, too early to escape from the wedding reception. Besides, the three of them travelled to the wedding in the one car.

Looking across towards the big shed Gracie's father had the floor, young girls all giggling around him, his raucous laughter. Where was her mother? Their relationship was a joke. Thank God she'd had the sense to make a life of her own after university in Sydney with her music, taking in private students when she could. She wanted Jack to do the same, follow his love in the arts. *Jack, are you alright?* She closed her eyes, focusing on connecting with his mind.

Later, when she checked her phone, it was 11.15 pm and no text message from Jack. Gracie wanted to leave for home. She huddled by the fireplace pulling her overcoat around her. There were fireplaces everywhere and it's where most of the wedding party gathered with a belly full of grog. A lot of the guests had left but there was Mr Big shot Harold, telling jokes to the remaining wedding guests. She nudged him a few times but he said, 'Yea, in a minute.' Megan was eager to leave too. It'd been a big day and some of the relatives from Adelaide were staying over at "Grasstree" for the weekend. She could see them lolling about waiting for the nod from Mr Big shot. It was a long drive home and the idea was to travel together, one following the other this late at night. She knew she had to wait for her father. He'd had far too much to drink to drive otherwise she'd be on her way in an instant. Her father had the floor, he loved it. A man full of his own importance and she sensed that is why his own siblings had left hours ago.

Jack worked tirelessly the previous day organising the bedrooms, preparing the food for the following day. She and Jack were bonded since birth and they sensed things about each other. Earlier in the night her knees buckled and she had to rush to find a chair as dizziness overtook her. *Jack, are you alright?* She didn't get a good feeling. Something was wrong back at Grasstree, she sensed trouble. In her heart, she hoped he went off to the hospital for treatment. *Please Jack let everything be okay.*

CHAPTER 60

2008

Gracie finally got her father to say his farewells to the bridal party and a few stranglers who'd consumed far too much booze, like him. The relatives made a good choice not to travel back with them, instead, they decided to stay overnight at the bride's family home. They got sick of waiting for the big shot lawyer to make a time, always the control freak. Gracie didn't blame them. They were tired, it'd been a big day. They arranged to come by and stay a couple of nights before heading back to Adelaide. 'See you early tomorrow' Uncle Pete called out, Aunty Rose holding him up straight.

Harold flopped into the passenger seat while Gracie drove, her mother silent in the back seat. He had plenty to say all the way home about this one, that one and their obnoxious behaviour at the reception. At other times he burst into song. Megan blocked her ears. She'd heard similar behaviour over the last twenty seven years. He'd been a heavy drinker when she met him in the UK but she took no notice, perhaps thinking he'd change once he settled back in Australia, but that never happened.

Her cousin, Carmel, looked beautiful on her wedding day. Gracie had taken heaps of photos to show Jack. They were both close to Carmel growing up and Carmel was disappointed that he couldn't make it to her wedding. She'd said she'd catch up with him after her honeymoon.

Gracie looked at the clock in the car it was 12.41 am on the 3rd August. She hated it when her father couldn't control his alcohol. Of course she loved a drink herself but she knew when to stop. He always seemed to have a drink in his hand around the house: A bottle of scotch and cigars. He belonged to a men's club in Sydney and she presumed they all sat around drinking and smoking cigars, talking shit. She wished he would shut up, never ending chatter and singing. At least he was happy, but that wasn't always the case after he'd been drinking. She could see why her mother shut her mouth in the back seat. Any antagonism and he'd lose it and her mother would bear the brunt of it.

As Gracie drove towards the garage she noticed the roller door was all the way up. She remembered waiting while the door closed on leaving hours before. It was her father's rule. "I've got lots of valuable tools in the back. Always make sure the roller door is locked into place." It was like a mantra every time they drove the car out of the garage as a family. Of course he was too drunk to notice now.

That's when she saw it, the lights beaming on a lump lying in the wet grass. It only took a second for it to register. 'Jack' she called out. She braked, turned the motor off and grabbed her mobile phone. She ran from the car to help her twin brother, her mother following. No pulse, his body cold, stiff. She called triple zero. 'It's a nightmare' she called down the line. 'I need an ambulance. My brother is not breathing. I can't feel a pulse. Help me?'

Megan fell to her hands and knees and screamed into the dark night. 'My baby, my baby, what's happened to my baby Jack?'

Harold, unsteady on his feet came close telling her to shut the fuck up. 'An overdose, no doubt…he'll be tested. Overdose for sure. I knew this would happen…one day. A day…I always dreaded, mixing with the wrong…bloody… crowd, needle pushers.' When he bent down to look at Jack, Megan caught his fall.

Gracie yelled to him. 'Shut up. Get away from him. Get away.' She pulled her brother across her body and cradled him like a baby. 'Mummy, oh mummy…what's happened to our Jack?' Megan sat on the wet grass sobbing into her cupped hands, her body trembling. Harold rocked back and forth on his feet, rambling on about illegal drugs and how the courts don't take it lightly.

'I said get the hell out of here' yelled Gracie. 'Get out?' Harold stumbled, straightened himself and headed zigzag fashion to the house mumbling under his breath.

'Jack is saturated mummy. How long has he been out here? Oh, Jack I'm sorry we weren't here for you.' Gracie couldn't control her tears or her screams in the black cold night. The car lights shone on his waxen face, bloodied head.

The ambulance arrived first. One of the paramedics tore Jack away from Gracie. They worked on him with all their sophisticated equipment but nothing would bring her brother back to life. His skin was cold, his waxen complexion lifeless under the flood lights.

The police arrived next. Megan could hear them on the phone. She overheard the word suicide. *Not Jack, no he wouldn't do that.* Later, two officers from forensics arrived, sniffing around. Two more cars arrived. Cops were everywhere, the place lit up like a Christmas tree.

Megan took her daughter in her arms, wailing. The two swayed, as if in a slow dance. Gracie felt a tug on her shoulder.

'Sorry Gracie, Megan.' The paramedics knew the Lawson family as everyone did in this small town. 'We'll be taking Jack to the hospital where a doctor will be present. All the paperwork will have to be filled out. They'll probably want to make enquiries about Jack and will more than likely call on you later in the morning. You can get to see him at a later date when the police work has been completed. In the meantime, I'll have a few officers stay here until backup arrives on daylight.'

Gracie nodded. She didn't care what they told her. She only cared about bringing Jack back to life.

The officers, along with Gracie and Megan, cleared a path as the corpse was carried and placed into the ambulance.

Megan struggled to muffle her screams. She placed her hands over her chest her breathing sharp, painful. Her baby boy wrapped up like a mummy. The two women clung together as the ambulance drove away. Forensics bagged the axe and took samples from the blood on the grass, anything that might be of help, they bagged and tagged. 'We'll need to go inside' one of the officers said. Gracie didn't care what they did she just wanted her brother back.

One of the female officers led the women into the house. She sat the pale-faced women down, covered them with a blanket and made them a pot of tea. She found a packet of biscuits and spilled them into a plate. 'Megan, Gracie, here we are I've made your tea. Have a biscuit, try to relax. The tea is sure to help with that.' She set out three cups.

The house was quiet and the two women were with their own thoughts. A police officer motioned for them to follow him into Jack's bedroom. When they arrived, Gracie grabbed hold of the door frame for support, her mother slid to the floor. What had Jack done and why? How could someone so sick and weak cause all of this damage? Gracie knew it was a statement, a final rebellious act. Some of the carpet was thick with dry blood, Jack's blood. The male cop went to Megan's aid. The other one ran to the kitchen coming back with a wet tea towel and a glass of water. Gracie leant in touching her mother's face. Megan gradually opened her eyes and the cop cradled her head in his lap soothing her face with the wet cloth.

'She fainted' said Gracie, stone faced. 'It's not the first time, she's prone to it.'

Forensics took fingerprints, collected more blood samples. The room was out of bounds. An officer would guard the area until everything had been thoroughly checked out one of the cops had said to Gracie while her mother sat in a daze in the morning room.

After most of the police had left and everything went quiet, mother and daughter held onto each other. 'This is the worst day of my life mummy. What happened to Jack while we were away at the wedding? What happened?' They buried they heads together, wailing. Megan pulled away first.

'My head is pounding darling, I can't think straight. He was troubled and all because of the good for nothing bulk inside on the couch.'

The time was just after 4am and although tired, neither could see their way to the bedroom. 'I'll go and make us a drink. Would you like something heavy or another cup of tea?'

'I'll have tea. I'll take a couple of Panadol with it.' Megan walked around in a daze her mind filled with confusion. She walked into the living room, checked herself in the mirror. Her eyes were glazed like a donut. Harold had passed out on the couch, his snores filling the room. Megan had a strong thought of putting a knife right through his heart while he slept. She'd need to be here for her daughter, not held up in a cell for the rest of her life. He wasn't worth it. He'll get his comeuppance in the end, Megan's sure of that.

The kettle whistles and Gracie fills the teapot. She grabbed the tea cosy and put it to her chest. Granny Maud made the cosy with scraps from the twin's clothing when they were about nine years of age. 'Jack' she called out.

Megan and Gracie sat in the kitchen with the door closed, nice and quiet away from the mongrel's snoring. 'My poor darling boy, all he wanted was acceptance and love from his father. I believe he would never have gotten into drugs if his father had shown him some sort of love and support.'

Gracie wiped her cheeks with the tea towel. She kept it on her lap. 'He's a mongrel and he will pay. Big shot lawyer or not, I'll see to it that he takes responsibility for his actions, killing my Jack.'

Her mother reached out and held her hand. 'Let's not

jump to conclusions right now? Let the police do their work Gracie. They will know what to do. I was thinking, do you think someone has done this to Jack, maybe a stranger passing through.' When Gracie didn't answer, she sipped on her hot tea, eyes closed head pounding.

Gracie poured her second cup, hands shaky. 'My beautiful brother who struggled every day and all he wanted was to be accepted for who he was.' She wiped her cheeks. Her heart ached for him. She doubled over in pain, rocking back and forth, weeping, as if all her strength had left her, nothing to hold her together at all.

Megan went by her side and put her arm around her shoulders, the two bodies shuddering. 'Would you like to sleep in my bed Gracie, perhaps we can comfort each other. Being alone is not good right now.'

She dabbed her face and threw the tea towel on the table. 'I need to shower, I feel unclean' she said, sniffling. 'I can't believe Jack is gone Mummy. I knew he should have had that head wound seen too. Something has happened while we were away. Maybe the bleeding didn't stop. My father caused this whole thing. I hate what he's done to my brother.'

Megan patted her hand. 'We can't rule out the illegal drugs darling.' Gracie shot up and flung the chair away and raced to the bathroom, she couldn't believe that her mother was still covering for the monster. In the bathroom, Gracie shook her head, but only to try to clear the images from her mind, like her father's bulky hands. Jack never had a chance. Jack was tall, slightly built, he, bulldog like. She wiped her nose.

"We'll have to keep the front door open for our guests. Once Uncle Pete and Aunty Rose find out about Jack they'll be beside themselves' said Megan. 'Remember, Aunty Rose is his Godmother.' She knew Gracie couldn't hear but she said out aloud what she was thinking. She rocked herself in the chair, back and forth, humming a lullaby to Jack. 'Hush little baby, don't you cry….'

CHAPTER 61

Harold Lawson

2008

Gracie's father, pale as wax as he sat at the kitchen table. Was it a dream or did he witness his son's dead body in the early hours. He curled his fingers, cracked his knuckles. The house was quiet, no one to prepare his breakfast. He switched the kettle on and made a cup of tea.

The whole ordeal seemed like a dream. He peeped into his son's room earlier and that's when he found splinters of wood scattered everywhere. The policeman on guard stopped him from entering. His hand shook slightly as he passed it over his face. His son had trashed the wooden desk he'd painstakingly made. The scene left him shattered. He blotted his wet palms on his trousers.

Weak, he leant against the bedroom door, his mind filled with fear. It was hard to comprehend as to why his son smashed his pride and joy to pieces. For Jack to go that wild, he figured he'd have to be on the drug, ICE. He knew his death was caused by drugs and dreaded this day. The media would soon be on his doorstep. He turned away, hands balled into fists, his expression coldly furious.

The wedding guests, one by one entered the kitchen, sleepy eyed from the long early drive. Harold picked up his cup, heavy coat, beanie and dragged himself down to the stables the only place he knew where he could find peace. His mind was filled with confusion, fear, as he warmed his hands on his cup. He was always right about his drug-filled son and how he would cause embarrassment to the well-respected Lawson family. He hung his head wondering what was next. Today was supposed to be a family day, food, drink, fun. Perhaps he'd hide away finding something to do on the farm but first he'd need to have a private talk to his wife and daughter.

***

Just on 8 am, Harold entered the bedroom. Mother and daughter were huddled together. 'Get out' Megan said, voice high pitched. Gracie stirred, finding her bearings. When she sat up she saw the bulk in the doorway his shoulders slumped, tear filled eyes. 'Don't come near us. Get out?' He definitely looked like a broken man, but Gracie's not falling for it.

'We need to talk.' He sat on the wheat-coloured Louis XV fabric bedroom chair, his head bowed. 'I want to conceal the facts about his death as much as I can. I have to hold my head up in the community and if the word gets out about his drug habit, the Lawson family name will be the laughing stock. I am a respected Lawyer and this could ruin my business if it gets out.'

'I said get out. Mummy and I are grieving it's more than I can say for you.' She laid her head down, facing her mother, eyes closed. Gracie had been awake most of the night going over Jack's past. Could she have done anything to prevent this? Should she have stayed back and re-dressed his wound, made time to take him to hospital. All these thoughts ran around in her head.

'Look, we need to collaborate here. Now you both know he's been into drugs for years. It's pretty obvious that he's overdosed. I don't want any dirty linen brought up in the Lawson family. We've been well respected in the town for years.' He ran his hands through his hair sighing. 'This will be the first bit of scandal using our family name.' He gave them a look of be careful what you say.

'I said…get out. Mummy and I aren't in any mood to discuss all this right now. Neither of us has had much sleep and you come through the door expecting a meeting. This is not your work place so you can't order us around like you do your staff.' She sat up staring at the man she called her father, his hair sticking out like it was plastered with Gel, unshaven and still in his wedding attire from the night before. 'We'll all have our own story when the police arrive. They'll want to know the truth and the truth is what we'll give them, so get out and leave us alone.' Gracie was surprised at her tone of voice, but she knew something had gone from the father and daughter relationship when she found Jack cold and dead early in the morning. Right now she couldn't envisage ever getting it back. What love she ever had, had gone. His behaviour to Jack had ruined all that.

'Gracie, Megan, listen to me? Jack's death was drug driven, nothing else. Okay we had an argument but that had nothing to do with his death.' No one answered. 'Are you listening to me?' he'd raised his voice seeking their attention.

'Dad, leave us be…please. We are both emotionally exhausted and grieving. I'll say it again. We've had very little sleep. Please go and leave us alone, perhaps we can talk later.' Unlikely she thought.

'I don't want any trouble from you two mouthing off. Every family have arguments, ask around? I'm the breadwinner around here woman, remember that. Where would you be without all the money flowing in? Do you think it is all fun for me working all the hours I do, forever travelling to Sydney and back?' He walked into the bathroom and wiped his face, neck, forehead with a wet washer. He took a few deep breaths. He needed to sit down but how could he relax at a time like this. The cops would soon be arriving. He walked around the room, back and forth pleading with his wife and daughter to shut their mouths. 'We'll get a lawyer but until then, say sweet fuck all.'

'Please leave and shut the door behind you? We have guests, so go and look after them' said Megan. He stormed out slamming the door with unnecessary force. Where could he go? He was stuck in his own home surrounded by people he didn't even like.

'What's going on Harold?' Uncle Pete asked from the hallway.

'I don't want to talk about it right now. To be quite honest I think our family needs time alone. So if you pack your bags and leave, it'll please the lot of us.'

'We just got here' said Aunty Rose, surprised look.

Harold ignored them and stormed off into the study locking the door behind him. He laid his head in his arms on his desk, blubbering, fear heating in his blood.

CHAPTER 62

2008

At 9.22 am the doorbell rang. Harold had showered and looked half-way decent. Megan and Gracie were in the kitchen making coffee in their dressing gowns. The guests had left and the house was ghostly quiet. The two women had nothing to say to the breadwinner.

Harold had told the family not to say a thing to anyone. "Shut your bloody mouths the both of you" he'd said, louder than he needed. He knew the law and he made sure they knew it too. "You never say anything without a lawyer by your side. Tell the cops that today. If this goes further, I'll get the best help and we'll fight this thing."

Harold let the cops in through the front door. 'My name is Detective Andrew Symons and this here is Sergeant Alan Hayes.' Of course they'd met many times before in court, but this was different because now it was all turned around, this was all about Harold Lawson's son's death. This was an investigation. Here they were in his house, smiling and shaking Harold's hand as if to say, isn't life just wonderful.

Once the introductions were done, Harold led them to the kitchen. He pointed to the women. 'You know Megan, Gracie?' They both nodded.

'Does anyone want a tea or coffee?'

'No thanks' Hayes said to Gracie.

'Is it okay if we use this room to have a chat with you all?' Symons asked.

'Perhaps the study would be more private' said Gracie. Hayes looked at Gracie and their eyes locked. She looked away first. He eyed her long blonde hair, green eyes, unblemished skin. *Wow, not bad at all.*

Harold jumped in. 'It's not a good idea.'

Detective Symons glared at him. 'And why's that?'

Harold wiped his forehead with the back of his hand. 'It's my workplace and I have confidential papers in there. Can't we block off the kitchen?' Symons checked the openings. He closed the back door and beckoned them to sit. 'This will do nicely.' Gracie put her arm around her mother's shoulders as they sat.

'This is a terrible time for you all. My men are working outside and I have another man guarding your son's bedroom. My team will be back shortly to finish things off.' Symons looked at their solemn faces. He hated this part of his job. 'These are things that have to be done. There could be some clues as to how and why this happened. We'll do our part and when we've finished you can have your house back.'

'What do you believe happened to my son?' asked Harold.

'It's not for me to speculate' said Symons. 'I will have a chat with you one at a time. Mr Lawson, would you like to go first?'

He chuckled. 'Call me Harold?' He looked across at his wife and daughter, gave a nod, turned on a stern face. As Megan got up from the chair, he opened up with a smile but she didn't smile back. The shoe was on the other foot for the lawyer, and he didn't like it.

The women left the kitchen and sat in the morning room with the winter sun on their backs. They sat in silence, eyes closed. Megan grabbed hold of her daughter's hand. 'I am wondering what Jack's last moments were. Did he suffer or did he just go to sleep and not wake?'

'Sit back and relax' Symons said to Harold.

Hayes flicked open a note pad and grabbed a biro from his shirt pocket. 'I'll be taking notes regarding this conversation.'

'Sure.' Harold knew how it worked. Nothing heavy at this stage but if it went further, he'd have legal backup, like his wife and daughter would.

'I want your full name, address and occupation.' Harold squared his shoulders chest puffed out and rattled off the information slowly, as if he were addressing the court.

'What was your relationship like with your son?'

'Probably like most fathers and sons. Sometimes good sometimes not…the arguments I had with Jack was more about the drugs he was taking. He just got in with the wrong crowd at university and well …' He took a deep breath. 'May I?' he asked, pointing to the jug of water on the kitchen bench.

'Sure.' Hayes grabbed a glass and filled it with water. He sat the jug and extra glasses on the table. 'I had a heavy night, we had a family wedding.' He chuckled but no one else did.

'Your son Jack had multiple wounds to the head. Can you enlighten me?'

'Well, the night before we went off to the wedding we had a scuffle. It was all over the drugs again. I guess I lost my cool and hit him but when he went down, he hit the wooden desk on the way. We were both a bit punchy.' He shook his head and blew out a long sigh. 'I was angry and left him on the floor but when I went back in later to check on him, he was okay. We just had a laugh about the punch up. He told me he'd have to go off the drugs as he found himself in a lot of debt. He was worried the heavies would find him and ruff him up some.'

'So why didn't he go off to the wedding with the rest of the family?'

'I think he's stubborn…got it off the ol' man.' He laughed, belly flopping.

'Mr Lawson. Did you make a habit of these so called punch ups?'

'Are you fathers?' he asked, pointing at the two of them.

'We are, but we're here to ask the questions.'

'Why I asked is because sometimes kids can disappoint, and if you have kids you'd know just what I mean.'

'Did you love your two children Mr Lawson?'

Harold pulled back, surprised. 'Of course, doesn't everyone.'

'What do you think killed your son Jack?'

'I have a feeling he got stuck into the drugs after we left. Only a month ago he told me he was really hooked, couldn't break the habit. Even when he told me he'd go off the drugs I only half believed him.'

'Well once the cause of death is confirmed, we'll all know.'

'What time did you leave for the wedding and where was the wedding held?'

'We left before 2pm. The wedding was held on the bride's father's property south of Kempsey, beginning at 4pm. I know the way but don't know the address.'

'At any time did you happen to leave the wedding and come back home?'

'Good Lord no. It's an hour and a half away.'

'Did you check on Jack before you left for the wedding?'

'No because I presumed he was getting ready. Jack had told Gracie that he'd be running late so he'd drive his own car.'

'Do you think it would've been the right thing to check on him since he'd hurt his head?'

'As I said earlier, he was in good spirits when I talked to him after the punch up.'

'A long time though between then and when you left for the wedding. Did you see your son before heading out?'

'No, I didn't. Look, can this whole thing be kept quiet do you think? Whatever the cause of his death, I'd like it to be kept private. It's hard enough accepting his death less alone the news being plastered all over the TV, papers and gossip across the small town. Our name is well respected around here.'

'We have no say in how the news travels Mr Lawson as you would well know.'

'Do you realise how much we are all grieving. We don't need all the media interfering. He's hardly cold and here we are in the kitchen being questioned about how my son has died. I know you boys have a job to do but...it's all cut and clear - drugs are the enemy here.'

The detective butted in. 'Have you got anything else to add?'

'No. Except this is only the beginning of a long length of sadness. I have a wife and daughter out there who are distraught, grieving to high heaven. Next, the finalities with Jack have to be done, that'll be left to me. It's all quite stressful at the moment.' He wiped under his eyes with his fat fingertip.

'I'd like you to read the notes and sign below.' Hayes handed the paper work across the table. Harold put his glasses on and read the notes carefully.

'I'm not signing that. No!'

'Up to you...that'll be all for now.' Hayes nodded indicating the termination.

Harold struggled to get out of the chair limping his way to the door. Hayes followed him and beckoned Gracie in. He didn't want any conversations being passed along so he asked one of the constables to escort Harold outside away from his wife, Megan.

When Gracie sat down, detective Symons was on the phone. She watched him scribbling something down on a bit of paper. She crossed her arms, taking a few deep breaths. She was aware Hayes was watching her. He had green eyes, dark brown hair, smooth hands, manicured nails. He was a big unit. She looked down at her own nails, all manicured with dark pink polish like the rest of the wedding party. The wedding, it seemed so long ago now. Her father got rid of the guests, she didn't get to see them or talk about what had happened to Jack. *Jack, oh poor Jack.*

'Hello Gracie. It's not the best of circumstances to be meeting again' said detective Symons. He was middle-aged, greying hair but soft blue eyes. She'd known him all her life. He was stationed in Port Macquarie but his children went to school with her in Cloverdale where they lived. A nice family!

'Hello Mr. Symons.'

'I'd like to ask you a few questions Gracie. Just sit back and relax. Sergeant Hayes will be taking notes.' Haynes looked at her and nodded, gave a small smile. 'What do you think might have been the cause of Jack's death Gracie?' She looked down into her lap taking short breaths, eyes moist. She wished the steady pounding in her temples would go away.

'Take your time Gracie. You have lost your twin. It must be a terrible time for you right now, like you've lost the other half of yourself.' He could see the pain in her face. 'Would you like a drink of water?'

'Yes please.' She sat waiting, shallow breathing, hands shaky. A ball of anxiety formed in her stomach. She closed her eyes listening to the sound of the birds perched in the gum trees. They distracted her current thoughts for a moment. *Slow breathing Gracie.* She came back to the present moment when she heard Hayes place the glass on the table. She took a small sip before looking across at the two officers. She needed to answer the question.

'In my opinion, I think he bled to death. He had a severe cut to his head. I bandaged it before going off to the wedding.' She took another sip. 'I tried to encourage him to go off to the hospital to seek help but obviously he didn't. I was concerned all night. I even tried to call him I was so worried but he didn't answer his mobile.' Tightness moved to her chest.

Symons noticed panic in her voice. 'What do you think caused the head injury?'

'I believe the hit my father gave him caused it.' She took a deep breath, then another, nostrils flaring, her stomach churning. She wanted to tell it how she saw it. Leave the lies to her father, the father who showed no remorse.

'Wasn't it more like a scuffle?' Symons leant back in the kitchen chair, hands clasped. 'I believe Jack hit his head on the wooden work desk when he fell, so the injury may not have been caused by the blow.' Gracie noticed a smirk. She glared at him, cold eyes. 'Have you got anything to add Gracie?'

'Mr Symons, my father was an abuser. He had a dreadful fight with Jack the day before the wedding. Mummy and I bandaged his head and medicated him to ease the pain. The following day he looked terrible and I urged him to go to the hospital. He told me with all the bruises on his face and the bandaged head that he wouldn't be going to the wedding.' She took a deep breath. 'I didn't blame him.' She was silent, staring into her glass. 'I told him that at least he would see all the photos of the wedding on my mobile phone.' She reached the tear before it settled on her cheek.

'How often do you think Jack was abused by your father?'

Her lips closed up. She hesitated before answering. 'Every time Jack came home from boarding school and then, years later the same thing happened when he came home from university. You see, Jack didn't perform in school the way my father expected him to. So once they got on to the subject of his grades, it was on for young and old.'

Symons leant in, arms on the table. 'Surely this all started as a "kidding around" type of punch up?'

Her skin prickled. She pushed out her chin. 'I witnessed this abuse, my mummy witnessed this abuse. If Jack didn't meet my father's expectations, he copped it.' She fetched her tissue from her pocket and wiped the tears as they streamed down her face. 'When the fighting started I ran to the study and mummy ran to her room or out into the garden. Neither of us could help Jack at all. There was no stopping my father, he was a bully. As I said, in my opinion, he killed my brother.' She let her head drop, shame creeping in. Her tummy was rumbling, bile rising, clammy face.

'I have one last question Gracie. Did anyone go back to the house from the wedding or as you were heading on your way to the wedding?'

'No, of course not because it was over an hour away and I held the keys. Ah…my father drove to the wedding and we waited in the car while he went back into the house to get his licence.'

'How long was he in there?'

'Well mummy and I remarked at the time that he took too long and when I questioned him he said he had to search for his wallet. Later, when I was searching for something in the glove box, I found his wallet.'

'What did you say to him?'

'I said nothing. You have to know my father. I shut my mouth.'

Symons would let her go for now so she could get on with the grieving process. 'Find a quiet spot Gracie and have time alone. I'll see you before we go.' He stood, smiled, mouth closed. 'There's a lot for you to contend with right now. We'll call your mother in next.'

'Thanks. I'd like to tell you, my mother is very frail right now, please take it easy.' She rushed to the bathroom. She held her head over the vanity basin, and soon after, she felt a little better. She sat on the side of the bath the washer over her face pushing her thumbs hard into her temples hoping to ease the pain. It was like a nightmare. She reckoned detective Symons didn't believe a word about the abuse. Symons knew her father well and in situations like this, they stick together. She began to weep. What would she do without her brother? Her heaving began again, temples throbbing, exhaustion taking over as she slid to the floor. *Help me Jack?*

'Hello Megan' said Symons. He rose to his feet and extended his hand. Years ago, he took his wife often to Megan's recitals in Sydney. She was well known of course in Cloverdale and her talent was admired in the small town. Megan's eyes were glassy, deep creases between her eyes. Right now, he reckoned she looked a lot older than her years.

'Hello Andrew, Alan.' She held out her long fingers to each of them.

'Sit back and relax. Let's talk over a cuppa? Would you like tea or coffee?'

She looked around absently. 'I just made a coffee. I think it may have gone cold.'

'I'll see to that. How do you like it?'

'Strong black, one sugar please.'

Megan had known Andrew and Alan since her younger days. Her cousin, Thomas, graduated the same time as Alan and they were still good mates. Alan married and had teenagers. Andrew's children had left home and were now working in Sydney.

Symons placed the hot mug in front of her before he sat down. 'Just relax Megan.' He adjusted a bit of paper work on the kitchen table before he faced her.

'How do you think your son Jack died Megan?' She drew a ragged breath before answering. 'I don't really know.' She glanced from one to the other. 'He did have a real drug problem and Harold said he probably overdosed.' Her eyes were glazed over, a look Symons had seen many times in the early days of shock.

'Harold had an argument with Jack, are you aware of that?'

She considered what he said for a moment. She paused and took a deep breath. 'I think I do recall they had words the day before the wedding. Yes, I remember helping Gracie tend to the wound. It was an accident though. Jack hit his head on the wooden desk and fell to the floor. He lost his balance Harold said.'

'Did your husband and Jack often have spats?'

She pushed a damp strand of hair away from her eyes. 'They did but soon got over it all.' She fidgeted with her fingers, entwining them together, over and over. Hayes observed this. She put the mug to her lips, hands shaky. The liquid was too hot she put it down.

'What was the main cause of the fights?' asked Hayes.

'Jack had problems at boarding school. He wasn't pulling his weight so much.' She took a sip even though it was still too hot. 'His marks were the problem of all the fights. Harold was only trying to help him. Well, one thing led to another and next thing there was a big blue.'

'How did you feel hearing the fights?'

Her lips trembled. 'I never liked it. Jack was only a boy

when it all started, I didn't think it fair.' How could she admit that her husband was a psychopath? She closed her eyes, a tear squeezing through.

'Could you have interfered, like helped Jack?'

She took her hands away from her mug, hid them under the table. 'You can see my size Alan.' She looked at him, shaking her head.

'Megan, I was wondering.' He paused. 'Did Harold ever hit you?' He tapped his biro, waiting for her answer. He could see signs of strain on her pale face.

She looked from one to the other. Maybe she's saying too much. She remembered what Harold had told her. 'I guess I asked for it. If I spoke up about the arguments with Jack, he got angry and hit out at me too.' She remembered the day that Harold stood over her saying that one day there might be an accident because she was worth 1.3 million dollars, money from her insurance policy. Her body shook just thinking about that day, his red face, screaming just inches away from her. She had goose bumps thinking about his violent behaviour. The pounding in her heard overtook her current thoughts.

'Megan, are you okay' said Symons.

She came back to the present moment. 'Yes, yes. Over time, I learnt to close my mouth.' She waved her hands in the air, as if to say, that's all in the past.

The detective began to map out the victim's life in his head. Were all the family where they said they were on the night? Did they have good alibis? Why did Harold take so long looking for his licence when all the time his wallet was in the glove box of his car? What was he doing in the house so long? He'd nail it down and find the one who was responsible for Jack's death. They'd all map it out on the whiteboard back at the station.

He went on. 'We are waiting for the results of the autopsy. Once we get the news we'll call over and let you know. You have a right to know first, you gave birth to your Jack.' He'd remembered how excited Harold was at the time, telling everyone in Cloverdale about the twins, one boy, one girl, he'd yelled to anyone who listened.

She dabbed the tears, shook her head. 'I still can't believe Jack's gone. I wonder how long it will take for it to sink in. He was a loving boy, a good boy. He and Gracie were close. She will miss him as much as I will.'

'And Harold?' he raised one eyebrow.

'Ah…' It was like the words wouldn't come. She took another sip warming her hands.

'What were you about to say Megan?'

'Ah…of course, he is Jack's father.' She made a pillow with her arms and rested her head. She thought her head would split in two. How much more can she take. She didn't want to talk about Jack anymore. She thinks she's said too much. If Harold finds out, she'll cop it. Megan took a few deep breaths then she sat up, and with a tissue, pinched her nose to stop the flow of blood.

'Yes, yes, of course. I've got one last question Megan. Why did Harold go back inside the house while you and Gracie waited in the car?'

'He said he went looking for his wallet. It had his licence in it and he was the driver to the wedding.'

'Thanks Megan, go and find Gracie and look out for each other. Maybe you could do with a lie down. My men are still working here as they will need to confiscate some of your son's belongings, like his iPad, phone, computer and other things that might help with this investigation. They will let you know when they're done.' He stood, waiting for her to move. He touched her shoulder. 'C'mon Megan, you can go now.' She lifted her head and looked at them as if they were strangers.

He took hold of her elbow and helped her out of the chair. 'I'll see you out. Go sit with Gracie. You will need each other. Does your nose bleed often Megan?'

'Occasionally, but it will stop soon.'

'It might be best to put your head between your knees for a while.'

'Thanks. May Gracie and I go and see our Jack?'

'I will see to it for you Megan.' When she went to walk away, she seemed disoriented heading for the back door in error. With her shoulders slumped, detective Symons could see she was a shattered woman. How could a mother cope he wondered after losing a child? His body shuddered at the thought.

CHAPTER 63

Megan & Gracie

2008

'Mummy, I need to see a doctor and you're coming with me. We both need some help to see this through. My mind is all over the place and it's impossible for me to relax. The sadness is all consuming.'

'Doctor Flannery does house calls. I'll phone now to see if he can call in on his way. He only lives a few kilometres west of here. It's only 7.30 he'll still be home.' She dialled his number. He agreed. In no time he was standing at the door. He sat them down and gave them both a pep talk. 'Now I can have this prescription on your doorstep tonight. In times like this you both need help. It's not forever but it will see you through these sad days. It's hard to handle grief alone. I'll subscribe Valium, just a small dose.' He wrote the script for the two of them and placed it in his bag.

'Are there any side effects?' Gracie asked.

'If you stick with the dose I give you in the beginning, then no. Down the track when things have settled down a bit, I'll slowly wean you off the drug. They can be addictive but you are both on a small dose and it probably won't be for too long. We'll keep in touch about how long. I'll call back tonight with the medication, so start taking the dose straight away. It will help you get a good night's sleep too.' With that, he rushed to his car and drove down the steep hill on his way to his surgery in Cloverdale.

CHAPTER 64

Megan

2008

Megan Lawson was alone with her son, Jack, in the white-walled autopsy room. She had no control over her tears. Today, it was time to confide in him about things she'd never shared with another Soul. She knew her secrets would stay in the sterile room forever. She whispered them to her only boy, the one who loved her and Gracie more than life itself.

'I'm sorry son. I should have left your father years ago to give you a better life, but I'd made a vow in my marriage and stood by it. Whether that was right or wrong, I believed in it.'

When she touched Jack's face, he was cold. When she kissed his lips, he was cold. She put her hand on his heart. 'I'll love you forever, my baby boy.' Although it was cool in the room, heat filled her face, under her armpits, like the feeling of humidity on a summer's day. Her head was clouded, thoughts running all around the place. It felt like an out of body experience. 'Gracie said she'd come to see you this afternoon sweetheart.' Poor Gracie, she's lost half of herself. 'Goodbye my darling Jack. You are free now, no more pain.'

The air was warm in the corridor compared to the cold room. "My beautiful boy" she repeated on her way to find the lift. 'Please God, forgive me.'

***

The coroner produced the death certificate and would pass the information on to the registrar once the autopsy was performed.

It took four days to get the report and detective Andrew Symons kept his promise. He came to the house and handed it to Jack's next of kin, his mother, Megan. He read parts of it out, the parts that she would understand. 'Your son, Jack Arthur Fairchild Lawson, bled to death from a large gash to the head. The gash measured 11.43 centimetres deep.' Megan threw her hands across her mouth, closed her eyes. 'The final results of the toxicology report could take up to six weeks.' He talked slow so she could understand and take it all in. 'The report will identify and quantify potential toxins. Samples were collected by a forensic pathologist during the autopsy.'

'Oh Andrew, no, this can't be!' She rested her head in her arms on the table. Her cries echoed throughout the house. Symons waited before he spoke. 'Like I promised Megan, I wanted you to be the first to know the cause of your son's death. That's why the minute I received it I jumped in the vehicle and came to see you.'

Megan didn't want to believe the results he read out to her because she was sure, like her husband that Jack had overdosed. Right in that moment, she knew that the Lawson family's lives would change forever just from that one report.

'Shall we call Gracie in?'

CHAPTER 65

08.08.08

Mid-morning of the 8th August 2008 the police came to arrest Megan's husband, Harold Lawson. The charge was manslaughter. Megan had mixed emotions, she knew the good side of Harold and right now that part was jumping out at her. The good side was the hardworking man providing for his family, the best schools for their children, a good home. She didn't want for anything, except of course her grand piano. He never wanted her to be reminded of her successful career as a pianist in the Sydney symphony orchestra before she met him. She'd worked that out years ago.

Harold Lawson was the head of the family and he kept his wife in the background where, in his eyes, she belonged. He was brought up with that, taught by his own father. His father told him women should be seen and not heard, like the children in the family.

Gracie was beside herself. She didn't care what happened to her father but it's what he did to her twin brother that bothered her. To hear the news that Jack had bled to death from the wound in his head sent her into a spin. She wept for her brother, the pain he would have gone through, maybe too weak to go to the hospital. Today, in her mind, her father died with her brother. The courts can deal with Mr Bigshot, but from this moment on, she will block him from her heart and mind. The cruel act he did was not repairable and now, nor was her relationship with her father.

Gracie and Megan were called to the police station to give fresh statements: recorded statements. Gracie handed over the original letter her brother had written, the one he'd left in the top drawer of her writing desk in her bedroom. Symons attached it to her signed statement. She held nothing back. The animal that her father turned out to be had to pay for his actions, and she'd make sure he'd pay for the rest of his life. She was done with his behaviour and had made up her mind to walk away, make a new life for herself. The two women, if necessary come the time, would prepare a witness statement for the courts.

After the statements were signed, the two women found a quiet café by the Hastings River. It was the moment Megan was about to share her recent news with her only child.

'I have some news to share but it will come as a shock. Take a sip of your coffee and relax.' She did the same before she went on. 'Your father for a number of years has been supporting another family in Sydney. Over all these years he has kept me hidden on the property keeping things going while he's got another life. Apparently he has been keeping a woman *and* a child.' She lifted her cup, hands shaky. 'Finding this out has cruelled any feeling I have for the man. He is past history. It has left me feeling totally shattered, in shock, my mind racing. To think he has hidden this other life behind my back all these years and left me on the farm to work like a slave.' She sat her cup in the saucer. 'I've been told the child, a boy, is thirteen years old. His name is registered as Isaac Lawson and he is boarding at Brisbane Boys Grammar, like his namesake did years ago.' She wiped her mouth with the serviette. 'This is the last straw Gracie.' Her eyes welled up, tears forming. She closed her eyes, lowered her head.

Gracie shook her head, distorted face. 'What! When did you find all this out?' She'd raised her voice, heads turned. 'Oh my God, he had another Life.' *Jesus wept.* She covered her face with her hands, uncontrolled noises leaping out, as if she were in pain.

Megan came back to the present moment, moved her chair closer. 'I've had a gut feeling for a while but I ignored it.' She looked into her cup then back at Gracie. 'After he flew to Sydney a month or so ago, I had a private detective at work. I also found out that he was sending money to a woman in the UK for years. He had a six month old child when I met him and he'd said nothing. He'd gotten a girl pregnant but wanted nothing to do with her. I have a feeling it was why he was so keen to come back to Australia with me. By the time the new mother caught up with him, she was married but she sought out your father to pay maintenance for his own flesh and blood.'

Gracie waved her hands in front of her face, fanning herself. 'So I have another family, great! Geez, all this news is killing me.'

'Apparently you do have another family, but what you do about that is your business.'

CHAPTER 66

Abby

2018

Abby's father, Patrick, died and Lara attended the funeral. He had his wish and came back to Cloverdale for the last time. He wanted to see the home he built, walk around the property. It brought him peace. After a few days he went into palliative care in the little hospital in High street.

Lara had been to a couple of funerals and like most people she became overcome with sadness. It was difficult to see her friend so bereft, Abby's mother too. Abby and her children huddled together. Lara remembered the day of Abby's husband's funeral, her distraught child, Aaron. Penelope was only a baby, she was spared the grief. The way life can be taken away at a moment's notice. Brad never gave a thought to come along and support Lara then or even today. She has a strange marriage. There is love but at the same time, separation. He's not the kind to support her on days like this. He works away in the mines and when he's home he doesn't take an interest in the family, like the children's sports, her interests. He spends his time watching TV, time in his shed.

"I need to wind down" he told her when she questioned him about family time. She realised that there are some things you just have to accept. He gave her a good allowance for her and the children so this was the only contention, sharing family time.

She's glad she took time out to have fun with Alex. He made her feel special for that short time. As she walked down the church aisle she bumped into Kelvin. He wore a charcoal suit and a light grey shirt, thin dark blue tie. What a great support Abby has, and he hardly knows her. Perhaps six months, that's all. What a great guy, she thought.

'Hello Kelvin.' He nodded and took hold of her arm, said nothing. There was nothing to say really. He led her into the hall where they were serving tea, coffee and cakes. 'Thanks Kelvin. It's a hard day but I can't even begin to imagine what it's like for Abby and the children. She will miss her father, they were close.'

'They were.' They both waited in turn to hug Abby, the children. Abby and her mother held back tears while chatting away to the mourners. 'Thank you for coming Kelvin and Lara. It means a lot to me.'

'Call me when you're ready Abby' Lara whispered in her ear.

'I will.'

She embraced Kelvin, eyes closed. 'I'm going to marry you Kelvin' she whispered in his ear.

He pulled back, small smile. 'This is a surprise my darling.' He hugged her tight, tears forming.

'We'll talk later. I wanted you to know how important you

are to me. Share the news with Lara?' She let go of him and moved away to be beside her mother.

Lara put her hands over her mouth, and hugged Kelvin. 'Congratulations to you both. This is wonderful news. It makes a sad day, happy.'

'I met her father before he passed away in the hospital. He told me to shake some sense into his daughter. He wanted her to have love in her life. I told him I would pursue her forever. He patted my hand and said, "You're a good man, keep trying. It would make me a happy man." Kelvin knew Abby was the one for him and now he was happy that she felt the same. 'Lara, it was a matter of hours later that Abby phoned me to say he'd passed away.'

'At least you got to meet him. That would make Abby happy and her Dad too.' He grabbed a savoury biscuit from the lady with the tray and so did Lara.

***

Abby and Kelvin married at St Thomas Anglican church the last Saturday in October, 2018. Abby wore a mint-coloured after five gown, Kelvin a matching coloured shirt with a light grey suit. The children chose their own outfits. Abby let them as it was just as much their day too. Close family and friends gathered together to share this union. Young Penelope and Aaron walked their mother down the Aisle. The reception was held in the restaurant where they met for the first time on their blind date. The following day, Kelvin took Abby, Aaron and Penelope to Fiji for their honeymoon. They settled back into Abby's home south of Cloverdale and Kelvin adjusted to country life. He still travelled with his work and Abby kept working at the private hospital in Port Macquarie. Abby's mother had no interest in staying on in Cloverdale. She said her country life was over. She's going back to her home in Adelaide, back to her social life.

'I think your Dad is watching over us Abby' said Kelvin.
'I have that same feeling darling.'

***

Jayde kept leaving horrible messages on Gracie's phone. She sent photos of Booker and her making love too. In the beginning, Gracie blubbered, but after, she straight way deleted them, forgetting all about Booker.

Jayde and Booker made out almost every evening except when his son, James, was home. One day he questioned himself, what was he doing? He didn't even like Jayde. It was Gracie he wanted to be with. At the end of the day Jayde was just a whore. If it wasn't him bedding her, it would be some stranger or one of the easy targets from the pub. He sat at home, beer in hand, thinking about his behaviour. Why? What had gotten into him? He turned out to be just as bad as her. He would begin pursuing his love, Gracie.

Booker backed off from seeing Jayde but she kept hounding him. She started sending dreadful text messages, recordings of the two of them making love, naked. One day after school, she had let the air out of his tyres. She began stalking him, making scenes outside his house. Booker called the police and a date was set to attend the courthouse. He took out an apprehended violence order against her. She was not allowed within fifty metres of him. He found out a few weeks later that Jayde Carlson had run off to Sydney to live with a fifty nine year old businessman she'd met online. Poor bugger, Booker thought.

CHAPTER 67

Gracie

2018

In early November, 2018, Gracie came home from hospital, her mother staying on to help. It had been three months since the car accident. Gracie pushed herself to the limit every day. She planned on getting herself well, back on track. She had exercise equipment delivered and worked hard every day. She took it all seriously as she did everything in life. She knew her scars would heal in time. Others were far worse off and she knew it. Move forward was her motto. The police had called to *"Rose Cottage"* to give Gracie the news that no charges would be laid regarding the accident. The young driver was 100% at fault.

On the crack of dawn two days after Gracie arrived home, Booker spoke quietly on the front verandah to Megan. 'I want Gracie back. I want Gracie to let me into her heart again. At times like this, I can be of help. I love her.' He handed her a scrap of paper. 'This is my mobile number.' He smiled, hoping.

'I know how stubborn Gracie is Booker. You seem like a

nice man but Gracie has confided in me about what happened. I think it would take a miracle for her to come around to your way of thinking.' She patted his hand. 'I will have a word with her for you.' He thanked Megan and walked to the main road where he'd parked his car out of sight. Megan had let a good man go twice, neglecting love in her life, support and companionship. She would point these things out to Gracie.

Megan picked a quiet moment to speak to Gracie about Booker. 'Life is too short darling and if you have feelings for him, let the past go and start working on a relationship with him. He's not a bad man and people who make mistakes sometimes need a second chance.' As Gracie cried, Megan took her in her arms and rocked her back and forth. She knew her daughter had struggled over these past months while in hospital, it had been tough for her in all sorts of ways and emotionally she hadn't been equipped to handle what Booker had done. Now she was a lot stronger and could see things a little different. Booker was pursuing her at least, he wanted her. She wondered who else would want her with all these scars over her body. She knew he loved her and for her to love him in return, she'd need to let the past go.

Megan invited him over to the cottage and prepared a scrumptious morning tea. Gracie dressed in her jeans and an emerald green blouse to match her eyes. When Megan prepared the table, she went to visit her doctor, leaving them alone to talk. She waved to Booker as she passed him on the dirt road heading into Cloverdale. She hoped they could discuss things sensibly and move forward. Like she told Gracie, life is too short. Gracie used a walking stick to help with her balance. When she met him at the door she realised how drop-dead gorgeous he was. He took her in his arms, her perfume familiar. 'Oh Gracie, it's you I want. I will help you heal.'

She reached up, struggling to keep her balance and pecked him on the cheek. 'We'll begin again.'

When Megan arrived home, Gracie and Booker had come to a decision. They were both prepared to start all over again, the love hadn't left. Booker wanted to take care of Gracie. He would apply for long service leave from his principal role at the high school and would move into *"Rose Cottage"* to help Gracie heal.

CHAPTER 68

Jack

2008

The news of Jack's death was on the front page of the Gazette and tongues were wagging. Small amounts of cannabis were found in his system but that hadn't caused Jack Lawson's death. Of course in the small town of Cloverdale, that bit of news got people gossiping. Jack Lawson bled to death after hitting his head on a sharp object was the second bit of news. One of the local journalists put together an editorial about Jack Lawson's life. He grabbed every bit of information he could about the illicit drugs, the mental institution Jack frequented, school results, his father's ongoing abuse. The media were after stories and a story about a local would sell more papers.

People were coming forward about the controlling Lawyer. Innocent client's spoke of the lawyer's promises only for them to end up in prison after parting with a lot of cash. The innocent charged with something they knew nothing about. It helped the lawyer and the crooked cops spend the money which was stashed away in their homes. in their homes. Tales came forward about the young Harold Lawson, the bullying he'd done to others growing up in Cloverdale. Stories were flying everywhere. Not a good article for the Lawson family to read in the Gazette.

One day, Megan heard that Harold Jack Lawson was out on bail. She'd read in the paper that the date had been set for the case, Monday, the 3rd December, 2018. He'd been out on bail for four months. Four months of freedom. It's not right she thought. She presumed he was staying with his other family in Sydney. She'd made it quite clear to Gracie when the police took him away that she wanted nothing more to do with him. It'd be up to the courts to decide his future now. Megan worked out that some lawyers were liars.

CHAPTER 69

Jack

2008

Two weeks to the day, on the 22nd August, 2008, Megan and Gracie could bury their Jack. They held a private funeral by the gravesite on the family's property. Jack lay next to Granny Maud and Pa. The Lawson family had a small section cordoned off for the family's burials. Father Henderson from the local Catholic Church in Cloverdale performed the service.

Gracie's school friends, Lara, Fay and Abby came by the family home, offering condolences. They all met in the first year of school in Cloverdale and have kept in contact since. Teachers came by and others she didn't remember. Gracie performed her duties, making coffee handing out biscuits in a robotic state. After leaving cold coffee and biscuits on the table she'd wash and dry them ready for the next lot to arrive. There were cups of tea with teaspoons of sugar mostly untouched. She threw the contents over her indoor plants.

When people phoned, there was a short silence down the line. No one could find the right words at a time like this.

Megan gave thought to her poor dead mother-in-law, Granny Maud, who had put up with Harold's abuse most of her life. Like father, like son, she used to say often.

People had left and the house was deathly quiet. 'I'm pooped mummy. I think I'll take the phone off the hook.' Megan stared, nodded. 'I can do that' she said, and did.

***

Megan and Gracie wandered around the house in a daze. The police had given the all clear for the use of Jack's bedroom so the two of them began the process of clearing out his things. They filled four bags of clothes for one of the charity shops nearby. Megan kept a few things, and Gracie took possession of his poetry book and his artwork. They worked in silence with the occasional, 'Look at this.' Sometimes they smiled, sometimes cried. They left posters of his idols on the wall and left his pieces of art. It was bare, no trace of him at all in the wardrobes. They framed certain photos and put them out on the mantelpiece. They'd taken every last splinter from his shattered desk to the wood pile in the back yard and burnt every scrap. Good riddance to the memory of Harold Jack Lawson.

Gracie didn't want her mother to know about the private letter Jack had left her. If she knew the contents of the letter it would break her heart. It was filled with anger and sadness. It held all the proof the police needed and hopefully they'd make use of it in the courts. Jack had signed and dated it. It was his goodbye letter from "Grasstree" before he embarked on his new life in Sydney. He had plans and now they would never come to fruition. It was torturous for Gracie to re-read the copy of that letter so she sealed it and kept it in the small zipped area of her handbag. A third copy was placed in Gracie's safety deposit box at the bank.

One day, mother and daughter drove into Port Macquarie and pampered themselves with massages, pedicures and the last stop, the hairdressers. Gracie dragged her mother into one of the over-priced boutiques and splurged. On the farm Megan wore jeans, tattered shirts and simple cloths. She felt feminine once more and when she looked in the mirror she looked young again, like she did in the early days of her marriage. Except, when she looked closer, lines had appeared but it was to be expected of any woman at fifty. Gracie looked into her mother's eyes. She could see a sparkle once again. 'I love you Megan Lawson' she said aloud, laughing. 'And I love you too Gracie Lawson.'

Gracie stayed with her mother for the first two weeks after the funeral then after that she needed to work. She put on her working face and went back to teaching at the school in Sydney.

Megan got on with chores on the farm. She got along with life as well as she could, the farmhands getting on with it, the place proving productive. The nights were the worst for her but she refused the offer to live with Gracie in Sydney. "You have your own life" she'd said to her daughter. She knew she was ready to make new plans, begin again and she would announce them to her daughter when the time was right. She wasn't interested in the land now, but was she ever? She wanted a different life, a change. She made an appointment with her solicitor. She would rent the homestead, employ a manager and start a new life. She'd spoken to Gracie about it and she agreed. The property belonged to the Lawson family and was set up in a family trust. Down the track her solicitor would work on a settlement for her so she could move on.

Losing Jack changed Megan's life forever. She became a shell of herself only staying alive for Gracie. How could she even get over it, wet-eyed day after day? In November, in her new home in Sydney, close enough to Gracie her cries were quiet, as if the grief was too powerful for sound. She missed Jack every day. She went to church, something she'd never done before. It brought her peace and it's where she learnt about forgiving others. She was not ready to hear about the word forgiveness less alone work on it.

Megan was dreading the first Christmas without her only son. Christmas day would be celebrated at Granny Maud and Pa's *"Rose Cottage"* and later, they would sit on a blanket by Jack's gravesite, bringing roses and tending the weeds. 'Perhaps a piece of Christmas pudding' Megan suggested. 'You know how he loved it.'

In her rented unit in Sydney, Gracie made her mother a gift for her first Christmas without Jack. She had his artwork splayed out at the printers. They copied the chosen pieces onto the calico. When Gracie got home from work, night after night she stitched them together by hand and made her mother a tea cosy. In the corner of one of the pieces on the cosy was Jack's signature. She put it to her lips and kissed it.

CHAPTER 70

Booker & Gracie

2019

Booker took great care of his love, Gracie. He'd taken three months long service leave to help her heal. It wasn't long before she had thrown away her crutches and took baby steps, practicing first in the house, then later out and about. He cooked the meals, the household chores, took her to her appointments. He reckoned he was the happiest man alive to take care of the most beautiful woman in the world.

Gracie played the piano while Booker worked, perhaps cooking lunch or the evening meal. And he peeped at times to watch her play, maybe sneaking up behind her, kissing her head before sitting down in grannies chair to listen, eyes closed. Other times, he watched her graceful hands wander up and down the ivory keys, producing sounds he'd never heard before.

One morning, beside her coffee cup was a card Booker had made for her. Stuck on the card were two pieces of a jigsaw locked tight, as if they would never be parted. He'd printed the words, "We belong together"

***

On Saturday 5th January 2019 Booker and Gracie read out their vows to each other in the Catholic Church in Cloverdale in front of family and friends. Booker arranged an ocean view apartment in Byron Bay for their honeymoon. On their first night sitting on the balcony overlooking the ocean, Booker declared his love for her with or without her scars. 'I fell in love with your Soul.' He pointed to her face. 'This here, is only skin.' Months prior the specialist had recommended Mederma scar cream. Gracie was happy with the results but she'd also learnt to accept what is. As Booker said, it is only skin. Some scars may continue to fade, some may not. She had given second thoughts to having plastic surgery. She would wait and see.

He took her in his arms and carried her to the king size bed. He undressed her, one garment at a time. Lying on her back naked, a huge smile on her face, she waited for his touch. He searched her perky breasts, her nipples fully exposed as if waiting to be caressed.

'I love you to bits Mrs Harrington. I'm going to make love to you until you say, no more.'

'And I love you too' she said. 'I'll lie back and allow you to take control tonight, Mr Harrington.'

'Free your mind of any sexual expectations' he said, before kissing her face, neck, and swollen breasts.

'I love you licking my breasts.'

'And I love you telling me.' He moved down, kissing her tummy, her moist area between her thighs. She called out his name over and over, her body writhing as he kissed her in places she hadn't been kissed before. He changed positions, led her hand to his hardness. Her arousal turned him on and it was music to his ears when she called out, 'You've hit the spot but I've lost control, I'm about to orgasm.'

'I'm going too. Come on sweetheart, let's go together.'

He lay in her arms, breathless. 'I'm so pleased I met you Gracie. I'll always love and protect you.' She caressed his face, searching his eyes helped by the soft light from the bedside lamp.

CHAPTER 71

Gracie

2019

Late January, after their honeymoon, Gracie's face opened up with excitement as she leant against the kitchen bench while her publisher kept rattling on. She tried to act calm as he spoke over the phone. It wasn't something she was expecting to hear. "Your latest book is in demand," Morris Hanlon repeated over and over.

"I hear what you are saying, but it's hard to believe. My book, my story…I need time for it all to sink in.'

"I've organised a media release. I'm sure you know that once that's taken place things may become frantic. We'll be doing a book tour of the east coast of Australia and all capital Cities. I've ordered an extra ten thousand books to be printed. The book launch will be held on your thirty first birthday, the 3rd March. The launch will begin at 7.00 pm.'

'Hang on? I need to grab a pen.'

'I'll send you an email with the full details. And I'll inform the media. Just leave it all to me.'

'I think I need a stiff drink. It's a lot to sink in.' Gracie's mobile phone was glued to her ear as she sank into the sofa.

'The week before the launch, a press conference will be held. The media will be all ears. You'll need to hold it all together as it will be televised. Many questions will be asked. Your story will catch the attention of many others who have perhaps been through similar situations. They'll be firing lots of questions and you'll need to stay calm when giving the answers. People are curious now that the truth is out. I'll send my personal assistant, Kate, to pick you up on the night. Remember to dress smart. Go and pour that drink now and I'll contact you next week?'

'Okay.' Gracie put the phone down and rested her head in her hands. She rubbed her eyes thinking about how bazaar all this was. Her story in book form that she wanted to tell to help others has turned into media frenzy. She had mixed emotions now but it was all too late to be concerned about because the proof copy had arrived, errors corrected and the books had now been printed. 'Oh shit, what have I done? I've opened a can of worms. Geez, I hope I can handle the media.' She knew she had the support of her publishers and they'd be there to support her on the night. She poured a wine and sat out on the verandah dreaming of her up and coming book launch. She left a message for her mother in the UK. She waited for Booker to return from his golfing trip. He'd be over the moon with excitement for her. *Jack, did you help orchestrate this?*

CHAPTER 72

Gracie

3rd March 2019

On the day of the book launch when she was dressed in her new outfit, her husband took her in his arms. 'You look a million dollars, Mrs Harrington. Can I check those legs out before you go on stage?'

'Why thank you Mr Harrington. You don't look too bad yourself. Legs, you can play all you like after this is over.' She reached up and kissed him on the cheek.

Gracie wore her long blonde hair out with whispers of hair covering her forehead. Her multi-coloured silk dress, made by a fashion designer in Sydney, fitted her glove tight. The hem sat a little below the knee, showing off her long tanned legs. Booker bought her a pair of silver dangly earrings and a silver bracelet. She wore her granny's lapis lazuli around her neck, like always.

Soon she would feel her baby move.

Gracie walked up to the podium with her publisher, Morris, and looked out into the audience. The seats were all taken and in the back people were huddled together trying to get a look. *Concentrate on your speech not the crowd.* The lights in the room dimmed. Morris introduced her then stepped away. The clapping was deafening. This was the moment she'd been waiting for but her stomach churned, perspiration building. *Breathe, breathe. Stand beside me Jack?*

'Thank you all for attending today, it is lovely to see so many people come along to support me, even interested readers.' Her eyes searched faces but they were faceless in the dim light, except the front two rows where she could see Fay, Lara and Abby, her school friends. Her hands clung to the podium as if glued with araldite. She looked down at her notes, the heat of the spotlights disturbing. Gracie always believed that speaking from the heart was far easier than following ones notes. Tell her story as it happened, as she knows it. Embellish nothing just tell the truth as she did in her book. Once she began to speak, she forgot about her churned stomach, shaky voice. She took over the stage walking back and forth holding the microphone loosely in her hand.

People clapped long and hard when she finished. The lights went up for Q & A and she handled her answers calmly and confidently. People wanted to know the truth and how it affected her and Jack's life's journey. Others made comments about her past and how well she'd done in her life, moving on from the pain. Some folk shared their private stories.

'It's all about focus' Gracie said. 'I was always interested in music and it is where I kept my focus. In my life story…and Jack's, I want to help and inspire people who may be suffering similar situations. Don't let others take your power away. Yes,

I could well be sitting in a straightjacket, a zombie, but with the proper help from professional people I made a decision. I decided to get the help I needed. Changes didn't happen overnight, but with the right medication and professional help, they did happen.' She smiled at all the happy faces. The crowd clapped and cheered.

She held her book in her hand proudly, Gracie and Jack's silhouette on the black & white cover, an image of shattered tears separating the two. Morris took hold of the microphone and when the clapping ceased he pointed out that book signing would be held in the foyer. 'It's all set up but be patient' he said, happy face.

A distant crack of thunder could be heard in the background, as if to announce the imminent arrival of a storm or perhaps the arrival of Gracie's start to her new life, the birth of her first book and the birth of her first baby.

In the foyer, Gracie took a deep breath as she eyed all of her books displayed on the long table, two young helpers from the publishing company on hand. A vase filled with roses from *"Rose Cottage"* placed beside her from her husband, Booker. She welled up when she read the card from the UK sitting next to a huge bunch of flowers. "I'm so proud of you for speaking up my beautiful daughter. Congratulations! Have a wonderful evening, from your loving mother and William. Remember, we'll be there in Spirit." And so she would too with her brother Jack, Gracie thought.

Gracie had bookmarks printed from one of Jack's pieces of art and she held the gold pen which was hidden at the back of her Granny's mahogany desk in the music room. A nostalgic moment as she remembered her family on this celebratory day, like her mother's flowers sitting in a crystal vase on the table. Inwardly, she couldn't have been happier. *My Soul is happy now Jack. Stand beside me?*

The queue was long but people were patient, some quietly waiting, others chatting. There was a lull in the crowd as she appeared. She sat poised, ready to sign. She looked up at the face before her. He held out his hand to shake hers, clutching her book in the other.

She froze.

CHAPTER 73

2019

He had grey whispers of hair, robust, dressed in a light-green shirt, tan slacks. Gracie noticed his cold cloudy eyes where once they were clear. He seemed smaller in height but guessed that was unlikely. Around his belly, buttons were ready to pop, thick arms and a bull-dog face. She withdrew her hand.

'Hello Gracie' he said, voice low. She held her breath and took the book he was holding, opened it to the page where the title stood out. SHATTERED LIVES *by Gracie Rose Lawson.*

Gracie could feel the panic build and squashed it down again…*deep breaths.* Without lifting her head, she asked, 'How would you like me to sign it?' It was like she was talking to someone in the supermarket she'd never met before.

'To your father would be appropriate. How about adding something nice Gracie?' She rested her right hand hard on the page hoping it would stop her shaking hand. She signed her name and handed the book back to him. She felt a lump in her throat and willed it away.

'What! No nice message for your father?' he threw it down. 'Write?' He stood, feet apart, eyes wild.

'I have nothing to say.' She held her head high eyeballing him.

'I'm speaking to you.' His voice rose to a high-pitch. Gracie could see the hatred in his eyes taste the poison in his voice. 'I…said… write.' He pointed to the book with his fat fingers. She went to open the page but they were stuck together. She struggled to get her next breath. She wet her finger and the pages came apart. She steadied her hand and put pen to paper, the page soggy with perspiration.

"To my father, may you enjoy the read?" What she wanted to say was, "To my father, the cause of mine and Jack's pain." She needed to stay composed as he was prone to outbursts if someone rubbed him up the wrong way. She put on a closed mouth smile, handed the book back.

He stepped forward pointing his finger close to her face. 'Now that wasn't hard, was it Gracie?' He stood eyeballing her, red-faced, before waving his arm, striding off, as if he was rushing for a train. As soon as he disappeared and out of sight, the tension dropped from her shoulders, but panic took over, her body trembling her chest heaving.

She beckoned her publisher, Morris. 'Please, I need five minutes.'

'Of course…you've gone all pale, what's wrong Gracie?' Morris could see that something had upset her. Words wouldn't come. She ran to the lifts and pressed the button to floor seven needing time in her room. She closed her eyes, her head splitting in two. She needed a bit of time to calm herself. How dare he? In all these years she'd had no contact with him although he'd tried. She ignored his plea for reconciliation in the early days. After he'd left "Grasstree" she'd read in the paper that he had a younger family in Sydney although her mother had filled her in on those details after she'd hired a private detective. Someone he'd shacked up with years before in her apartment close to the court house in Sydney. Just days after her husband was taken away and charged with manslaughter, her mother filed for a divorce.

Snippets of wonderful childhood memories popped up occasionally since he left, but there were too many sad moments overtaking the good. Her mother and brother Jack both put up with his abuse. His rage had surfaced out of the blue. She sat in the silence, slowly controlling her breathing. She'd been told by one of the policemen in Cloverdale that her father had been released the week prior. She wasn't concerned because she'd let him go from her mind and heart ten years ago. He was the last person she thought would ever turn up at her book launch.

Memories flooded back about the shouting, screaming, the red face, frothing at his mouth. What makes a person change in an instant? She was interrupted by the ring on her mobile.

'Yes, I'm coming down now.' How could she let all those readers down? *Rot in hell you pathetic creature. In my eyes, you are not worthy to be called my father.* A few more deep breaths and she'd be on her way to meet her excited readers. *Stay with me Jack?*

Booker stood, guiding people in the queue. Many locals from Cloverdale were there. Some he had taught others eager to read the true lives about the Lawson twins. The Lawson family had a long lineage that had lived on the outskirts of Cloverdale since the late 1890s. Many worked on the property over time, some started up businesses in the area, butchers, café's, hoteliers. The name was prominent in the area. Some had moved to Port Macquarie and others to Sydney.

Gracie looked up and saw Booker watching her, smiling his big smile, showing his white teeth. She knew he was proud of what she'd achieved since the accident but she'd worked hard at it. She learnt to lean on him and not be so stubborn. He looked dashing in his dark suit, steel-grey tie and soft grey silk shirt. She returned a huge smile.

The following day, Abby and Kelvin invited the girls and their partners to lunch. It was an exciting time all round. Gracie's book launch turned out to be a great success and the up and coming Australian tours were starting in one week. This was her week to unwind.

Lara had to beg Brad to come along. 'It's not all about you' she said. 'We need to do more family stuff. I have done everything to keep this family together. I work too Brad and I look after the family while you are away *and* when you are home. When was the last time you helped around the house, took the kids to sports?' Hands on her hips, she took a deep breath. 'I'm getting a little tired of living a single life.' Without a word, he started packing the esky with his brand of beer. Lara's baking and the children's goodies found room beside them.

'Kelvin has lit the BBQ and I think the children are ready to jump into the pool' Abby said. 'Let's all go and watch them?' It was like old times - Abby, Lara and Gracie. Before we do that, I have something to show you girls. She took them inside, down the hallway to the study. She opened the door and there in the centre of the room sat a cradle. On the walls were Aaron's colourful framed pieces of art.

'It's a nursery. Oh Abby I'm so pleased for you' screamed Lara. The girls all huddled together, congratulations all round. 'What does Aaron and Penelope think?'

'They were so excited. They wanted to run around telling all their friends. I told them to wait a bit longer. Now it's time for them to spill the beans.'

Gracie took the floor. 'I don't want to steal your thunder…' she showed a huge smile. 'Booker and I are having a baby also.'

More screams, hugs. 'They can grow up together like we have' said Lara. 'Little baby Lightfoot and little baby Harrington. I wonder what sex they will be.'

'I think my baby is a honeymoon baby, conceived in Fiji.' They all laughed. 'Good for you Abby' said Lara. 'This causes for a celebration. Let's pop the cork and talk baby talk.'

'Girls, when I told Kelvin after I got the news from the doctor, he said to me, "My Soul is flooded with satisfaction." Abby is glad she looked past his looks she realised there is more to a person than looks alone. They all had a group hug.

'Two babies on the way, how wonderful' said Lara. 'Don't look at me for the third?'

CHAPTER 74

Ricardo Ganza

March 27th 2019

Ricardo Ganza drove to a public phone box in a shopping centre and set up a meeting place. He'd been out of prison for just over a month. He would hand over half the cash, five thousand dollars to the guy who said his name was John Brown. Brown told Ricardo to meet at an all-night service station on the highway at 9.30 pm on the twenty ninth of March.

True to his word John Brown had executed his plan. They both laughed when they agreed that April fool's day was a fitting day.

In the 1990's, the lawyer, Harold Lawson, had a small private office he worked from in Sydney as well as his business address in Port Macquarie. In early 2008, he'd guaranteed his client, Ricardo Ganza, a win after Ganza had stuffed a huge sum of money into the lawyer's briefcase. He had been charged with an offence he knew nothing about.

Ricardo Ganza had information that could open up a can of worms about the corruption in the police force in Redfern in Sydney, Australia, in the eighties and nineties. In 1992, the police had the address of an informant in the suburb of Crow's Nest, Sydney. With a warrant, two policemen went to the house and blew the guy's head off, shot him dead.

In the police report, the cops said the guy, Paddy Maclean, got into a struggle, took the gun and aimed it towards his neck and fired. One of the problems here was that the warrant was issued to the wrong house, the wrong guy. They shot the wrong bloke and made it look like he'd shot himself. The whole scenario was covered up. Case closed, except there was a woman, the guy's girlfriend who'd only been out of prison for three weeks. She caused them no end of trouble, ready to mouth off to the media. The cops gave her thirty thousand dollars to shut her mouth. She was guaranteed of closing it for that sort of money. And this is where Ricardo got the news from, because the guy's girlfriend was his sister, Maria Ganza. She was charged with possession with the intent to distribute. On her day in court she stood and told the Magistrate, "Your honour, I am guilty of the charge." She was sentenced to twelve months and was out in eight.

So, in late 2007, when Ricardo Ganza was charged with something he knew nothing about, the lawyer, Harold Lawson, told Ricardo not to worry, he'd get him off. In some cases he could often pay the police to get certain crims off and this was one of those times, he was 98% certain of it. There weren't many cops that couldn't be bought in the 80s and 90's but since then the force had cleaned up a bit.

Ricardo Ganza was on remand and was refused bail. He had a great Barrister to begin with, but when needed, he couldn't be found. He found a new Lawyer who used to work for the DPP, the Department of Public Prosecution. He turned out to be useless, no help at all for Ganza. Without much ado, he got fifteen years for conspiracy to import narcotics and the involvement in a murder. He was framed by the cops. A detective sergeant and two sergeant's with links to former bikie boss, Bull face Mancini, had organised the drug smuggling plot.

The cops had sent three guys overseas and the shipment of narcotics had arrived safely on Australian soil. The importation had a street value of $15 million and was being distributed on the streets and the money being pocketed to those that put him in prison. Ganza knew nothing about all this. In his mind, Lawson was in cahoots with the crooked cops and his new lawyer. He was a greedy, slimy bastard, was Harold Lawson. Ricardo was given a sentence of fifteen years for something he knew nothing about. And he'd never heard of the guy he was supposed to have murdered. He'd be behind bars for a long time.

Ricardo hadn't forgotten his first experience at Darlinghurst prison. They gave him two planks to lie on. He had trouble getting off to sleep. Out of the blue one of the blokes in another cell started playing up, screaming out and the officers came in and bashed him to death. It's something he won't forget in his lifetime. He'd stay close-mouthed while doing his time.

They moved him around, like they did with all prisoners. The Long Bay riots started and he, with everyone else, was locked up. At Parklea maximum prison, he slept on the floor for six weeks without a shower. He was stripped off, his body searched by the guards. They ripped the room to pieces and left it as it was. That's what he put up with because the flash lawyer didn't do his part. He often witnessed the drugs being snuck in by the guards and the prisoner's digging deep, handing over the little money they had. He minded his own business but kept his eyes open. Most of the heroin was brought in by the Asians.

He got out in ten but his wife in the first year of his sentence had fled to another country with his young children. He summed it up that the little money he had left was best spent on chasing the grubby lawyer rather than chasing his family. He knew that all lawyers were liars.

His early days in prison, Ganza followed Harold Lawson's court case on the TV. It didn't turn out great for the big-shot Lawyer. The barrister with the Office of the NSW Director of Prosecutions did a lot of digging into the history of violence which made a great case for homicide. He first presented a partial brief and then he waited for further information which would help with the conviction. Young Jack's hospital records came forward, the family's witness statements, client witnesses, shoddy deals, and massive tax evasion. It all went pear shaped for the big fat lawyer. Mr Harold Lawson didn't get off lightly he got fifteen years, perhaps out in ten.

They had both spent ten years in separate prisons but Ganza dreamed of this day. They were both free men now but not for long for Mr Big Shot Lawyer. These days, John Brown told Ganza that Harold Lawson spent a few hours a week working for an accountant in Port Macquarie, so the big shot lawyer no more. He lived alone on a small property. Megan, years ago was well and truly rid of him and his Sydney female partner and child not to be found.

Ganza borrowed money from his long-time mate to do the job. He would settle the score at a later date. It was too risky to touch his bank account as that would be traced and he would be a likely suspect. Ricardo and John Brown chuckled thinking about April fool's day. 'Why not get out of town. Go visit a relative?' John Brown suggested to him. So he did, he went to visit a friend in Bateman's Bay, NSW.

At 7.30am on Monday 1st April 2019, John Brown staged a fake breakdown on the dirt track to the entrance of Harold Lawson's property two kilometres west of "Grasstree." Beechwood road was a good kilometre away. He lifted the bonnet peering over the engine when Harold's silver Toyota came towards him. Brown waved his arm indicating he needed help. Harold kept the car running, walked towards him. 'What's the problem? I need to get on the road. Haven't you got roadside assist?'

'G'day mate. Sorry to block your driveway. I figured I was lost so did a U-turn then it conked out right in front of your driveway. I think I might have run out of petrol.'

'This is a private road, how'd you get here.'

He chuckled. 'I took a wrong turn I think, way back.'

'Well, if petrol's the problem, I can siphon some from my car. I have a bowser at the house but I can give you enough to see you into town.'

'Thanks. Rob Carry is the name, yours?'

'Harold Lawson.' He clasped his hand loosely in Rob's outstretched hand.

'I've got a can in the boot, be right back.'

John Brown fetched the pistol from the driver's seat and

followed him. As Harold opened the boot, John asked, 'Do you happen to know the name, Ricardo Ganza?'

Harold shot back. 'Who wants to know?'

'Well this is a present from him.' He stepped back, aimed, and pulled the Glock 22 pistol hitting the lawyer in the left side just below the jaw and another in his forehead. The fat lawyer in the dark grey well-worn Armani suit fell to the ground. John Brown walked back to his old blue Mazda sedan, slammed the bonnet down, started the engine and headed toward Beechwood road which would eventually take him to the highway. He had a meeting with a friend of Ganza's, Stretch. The job now completed he could relax, collect the money and tomorrow he'd be in his beachside hut on the Mid North Coast throwing the line in hoping to catch a fish or two.

CHAPTER 75

2019

Booker sat beside Gracie while she face-timed her mother in the UK giving her the news. 'The police said investigations were under way but I'm not holding my breath Mummy, but do I care?' She sniggered. 'The story goes around Cloverdale that he deserved all he got in the end. He was shot in the forehead once and another just under the jaw. Apparently, he was on his way to work and there was a staged breakdown by the killer. When he was found he had a slight pulse, which means he may have been lying there for some time, suffering. After being transported to the hospital in the early afternoon, within an hour, he was pronounced dead.'

'What date did the shooting happen Gracie?'

'April fool's day, isn't that ironic?' She laughed down the line but it was forced. Some parts she still loved about her father but she'd pushed those memories down into the dark places of her mind.

'Oh Gracie, you're free from the monster now.'

'And so are you Mummy.'

'We'd like the two of you to come and visit before too many weeks have passed. I won't see you for a while now that you are pregnant. We have something to discuss with you. We will organise the tickets from this end. We just need to know dates.'

'Okay, hang on a moment?' She turned to Booker all smiles. 'What do you think?'

'Let's make it as soon as you can get the tickets because shortly your daughter won't be able to fly.'

'Okay Mummy, any day now. As you heard, Booker tells me my time is limited for flying.'

CHAPTER 76

2019

William and Megan were at the airport to meet Gracie and Booker. Everyone hugged. They dragged their bags and headed to their home in Berkshire. It had been raining but cleared up close to home. Gracie and Megan were full of chatter in the back seat talking about the baby she was carrying. 'You are glowing darling' she said. 'Pregnancy suits you. Now what date has the doctor given you?'

'I flipped when he told me. The 8th August but I'm thinking of being induced either before or after.'

'Best before, like the 7th' Booker called out from the front seat.

'Definitely not the 8th of the month, no not the 8th' said Megan, her body shaking.

'What do you both want to be called, have you discussed it.'

'We have and we reckon whatever comes out his or her little mouth first.' They all laughed and thought that was a great idea.

'I've got dinner organised and I want the two of you to rest up and have an early night. Especially you Gracie, you need to look after our little one.'

'Didn't you want to discuss something? Isn't that why the urgency to visit?'

'Yes, but I want both of you to be fresh when we discuss things tomorrow.'

'It seems intriguing.'

'Firstly, I have a small gift for you Gracie' said William. Gracie opened the neatly wrapped gift. 'Oh goodness, it is beautiful. How on earth did you get that done?'

'I have ways' William said. It was a leather bound copy of her book, gold-tipped leaves. 'This is so special. What a wonderful surprise. I will treasure it.' She hugged William. 'A thoughtful gift' she said.

'I think the first thing you should be doing is signing it.'

'Booker, isn't it beautiful?'

'It is sweetheart. There won't be too many people that would have a leather bound book. It's a treasure.'

In bed later, Booker had a feeling they wanted to discuss their wills. Neither had any family to leave their possessions to, accept Gracie. 'It's something we need to think about too love' said Booker.

'I want to think about you making love to me on the first night across the other side of the world.'

'Don't have to ask me twice.' They snuggled under the covers, skin to skin on the chilly evening.

***

In the morning, breakfast was laid out in the conservatory, the sun peeping through. 'Oh Mummy this is a beautiful room. Do you spend much time in here?'

'Oh yes, this is our favourite room and it is so cosy. We have the fireplace lit all of winter, it's ongoing. Just look at the blossoms through the glass windows. Of course, it is so spectacular in the spring and summer.' Gracie stood by the fireplace warming her back.

'You're right, but hey, I'm famished, let's eat?' said Booker.

After breakfast when coffee was served, Megan set out a folder in the centre of the table. 'We have things to discuss with you both about our respective wills. I hope you have both thought about getting a current will in place. Now that you are a couple, and having a child, it is important.'

Gracie looked across at Booker. He raised his eyebrows, shook his head.

'Before we get onto that, there is something we both want to talk to you about Gracie.' When Gracie went to speak, Megan put up her hand. 'This is not an easy thing for me to talk about but now that you are pregnant, it is important for you both to know.'

'Oh' said Booker, surprised.

'I'll start at the beginning so you will follow.' She took a sip of her hot coffee. 'When I met your father, Harold, I fell in love but within no time your father lost interest in me. He wanted a child badly but over the years I had a few miscarriages. He wasn't home at the right time for me to fall pregnant and, as I said, he seemed to have lost interest. By this time, I wanted a child badly and so did he.'

'Do you want me to leave the room' said Booker.

'No' said Megan. 'You are family.'

Megan's hand was unsteady as she picked up her coffee. 'Anyway, he came home one day and had purchased a plane ticket to the UK. No mention of me going, he was travelling on his own. Away for two weeks. I had a lot of abuse over those years but over time I learnt to shut my mouth. I was disappointed that he could go off like that alone without even considering me. I was free to go, no children.'

With downcast eyes, Gracie fiddled with her hands in her lap. Megan put her hand on hers. 'Gracie, when your father left, I contacted William. Years before, we had been seeing each other, like girlfriend, boyfriend. We had a lovers tiff before I went to the UK so I broke off the relationship and then I met your father.'

'Where's this going, I'm afraid, confused.' Gracie fiddled with the hem of her cardigan.

'William put his arm around Megan and Booker put his around Gracie. 'While your father was away William flew from Sydney to Port Macquarie to spend some time over lunch. We clicked straight away as if we had never been apart. We spent three days together. When your father arrived home he was all keen once again to start a family. He came to me every minute he could, he said he was hell-bent on getting me pregnant. He said he spoke to the boys while away and they said "Have sex every day in the month and one of those days it'll happen." I became pregnant quick smart. He was over the moon skiting to everyone. Then later, he told anyone who would listen about The twins I was carrying. He seemed to think it was all his doing. Having twins I mean.'

'There are certain things a mother knows. Gracie the

father you grew up with was not your biological father. This wonderful man here, William, is your biological father.'

Gracie sat quiet as a mouse, eyes as big as saucers.

William spoke. 'I had no idea over all these years Gracie until your father was sent to prison and your mother made contact with me again. I would have loved to have been part of your lives. Back in 1987 after the three days we spent together, your mother decided to carry on with her marriage vows, even though we both declared our love for each other. It was your mother's choice, hoping to keep the marriage together and eventually have his baby.'

With tear filled eyes, Gracie spoke. 'When did you know?'

'I had an idea early on, little things. As you both got older I realised the two of you had traits of William, like the arts. Like darling Jack, he loved his art, his music, his acting. I realised it all came from William not Harold.'

Gracie looked up. 'Why didn't you tell William once you realised, he deserved to know?'

'There are some things that happen during our lives that don't go to plan. At times, we don't tell the real truth. I was afraid of your father. What would he do? Can you imagine Gracie?' Megan took her handkerchief from her hand and blotted Gracie's tears before they reached her cheeks. 'As we grow, we wonder why we didn't do this or didn't do that. Years later we look back and say 'Why didn't I have the guts? Granny Maud was forever saying that both of you were nothing like her son.'

'Did she know?'

'Granny wasn't a fool, but of course, I never disclosed anything. She knew I went away to Port Macquarie for three days. She was not a silly woman. If truth be known, she would have been happy if I went and had an affair. She loathed her son's behaviour.'

'I'm confused, upset but happy all at the same time. I can't explain it?' She fell into Booker's arms and wept.

'We will give you some space' her mother said. William and Megan took their coffee cups and left the room.

After, Gracie stood to claim her father, the soft gentle man who later in life married his only love. 'I'm happy but it'll take a while to sink in.'

The grown-up daughter turned to face her mother, the mother who'd been with her and Jack through thick and thin all their lives. She suffered a lot to keep the family together. 'I know this would have been difficult, so thank you Mummy. How about I give you a big hug?'

'I had to tell you darling. You are pregnant and you deserve to know the truth, it's time.'

'And you deserve happiness mummy. William is the perfect person for you.'

'I've been thinking of mentioning this for some time. Do you think this is a coincidence Gracie? Remember the morning we found Jack on the ground in the dew, lifeless? The date was the 3rd August. Ten years later, the day of your car accident you were brought into the hospital. It too was the 3rd August. Is this date significant? Or is it just another date? I think of these things, they must mean something. Ten years apart and exactly the same date, isn't that weird?'

'I hadn't thought about that, but then again I was out to

it for some days in the hospital. I think a lot of things happen in life like that. It's no use searching for the whys. It is what it is.' She hugged her mother.

'I think we have something wonderful to share with you both too' said Booker. He stepped beside his wife, Gracie, and took hold of her. 'Tell them Gracie?' She looked up at him before facing her parents.

'We are having twins, a boy and a girl.'

'Gracie, Booker, oh that's wonderful news' said Megan rushing to hug them both.

'We're over the moon too.'

'Cigars all round' said William.

'I don't think so' said Gracie. 'Booker gave up smoking and I hate the smell.'

'I did a bit of searching on ancestry.com into my past and apparently my Grandmother was a twin. I had no idea because the twin boy had an accident when he was a five year old and died. Apparently a car hit him while he was riding his tricycle near his home' said William.

'Oh, how terribly sad' said Gracie.

'Well that was a long time ago. So now you can all point your finger at me.' He laughed and they joined in too.

Megan put her hand up to speak. 'Now the next thing we need to discuss at length is our Will.'

CHAPTER 77

The girls

2019

As promised, Lara and Abby had planned to take Gracie overseas when the time felt right for her to leave the twins with Booker. He figured around March 2020 would be a good time, before the twins started to walk. He'd take special leave from his job and invite William and Megan to visit at the same time. He wanted Gracie to have the holiday she'd always dreamt of with her two best friends from her school days. She deserved this trip after all she'd been through.

On the scheduled date for the birth, 7th August, Lacy Rose and Raymond Jack Harrington came into the world. First born was the girl. She was covered in what looked like white lace, so Gracie named her Lacy and Rose after her own second name. Raymond after Bookers second name and Jack of course was named after Gracie's beloved brother.

The new family of five settled into *"Rose Cottage."* Booker rented his home to a young family and continued working as principal at Rockland High. He rushed home each day to nurse his babies and hear all about their day. Booker's son, James, enjoyed having a little brother and sister and often helped rock them off to sleep. 'I can't wait for them to talk and walk' he said to his father. 'They will keep you on your toes once that happens' said Booker, ruffling his teenage sons full head of blonde curls. 'In a couple of years you'll be as tall as me' he said.

Booker held Gracie in his arms in absolute awe of what they had made together. 'I wonder what these little ones future will be?'

'I will make sure it will be their choice and their choice alone.'

Gracie walked into the music room, sat down at the grand piano and played to her babies while they slept in their cradles in the next room. She fell into the role of motherhood, like a duck to water.

CPSIA information can be obtained
at www.ICGtesting.com
Printed in the USA
BVHW081127180319
542952BV00002B/213/P